BLOOD BE DAMNED

MAGIC WARS: DEMONS OF NEW CHICAGO
BOOK THREE

KEL CARPENTER

Blood Be Damned

Kel Carpenter

Published by Kel Carpenter

Copyright © 2021, Kel Carpenter LLC

Edited by Analisa Denny

Proofread by Dominique Laura

Cover Art by Covers by Juan

All rights reserved under the International and Pan-American Copyright Conventions. No part of this book may be reproduced or transmitted in any form or by any means, electronic or mechanical, including photocopying, recording, or by any information storage and retrieval system, without permission in writing from the publisher. This is a work of fiction. Names, places, characters and incidents are either the product of the author's imagination or are used fictitiously, and any resemblance to any actual persons, living or dead, organizations, events or locales is entirely coincidental. Warning: the unauthorized reproduction or distribution of this copyrighted work is illegal. Criminal copyright infringement, including infringement without monetary gain, is investigated by the FBI and is punishable by up to 5 years in prison and a fine of $250,000.

❀ Created with Vellum

Acknowledgments

As I write this, my stepfather, the man I looked at as a father is laying in a hospice bed at home dying from esophageal cancer. He might have days. It may only be hours. We don't know. By the time you read this, his fight will be over. This may be an odd way to start acknowledgements, but this horrible disease is what has taken up so much of my mind these past months while writing and then editing this book.

Over the three months it took me to write it, we went through ups and downs with his treatments. Mostly downs, if I'm being honest. I didn't want to see them that way. I tried to believe they were just a setback. Sometimes small, sometimes large, but always something he could bounce back from. Something he could overcome.

The toll this has taken on me and my family has really impacted me in a way few things have across my life. It made me take a hard look at what really matters, and what's truly important. It's that change—that reflection—that helped me through this book.

I empathize with Piper so much on many levels. Some of that may be easy for you to see, knowing what my family and I have been going through these past several months. Some, but maybe not all. Her guilt, anger, resentment—these are all things that I've experienced. Things I've felt so deeply sometimes it was all-consuming, and the way I handled it was putting it down on paper. Making Piper's journey as raw and real—albeit with a better ending than my own.

There are a lot of people I have to thank for helping me through this one, both from an emotional standpoint and directly with this manuscript. The first and largest is my amazing, kind, and frankly better than I deserve editor and best friend, Analisa. No one ever realizes how much she does to make these books amazing, but I can promise you they would not be the same without her. My wonderful husband, Matt has always been my rock and support when I needed it, especially now. My lovely assistant, Maegan, has been such a help during this trying time, always keeping things moving in the background. My friends: Courtney Lummus, Amanda Pillar, Heather Renee, Amber McLelland, Graceley Knox, and Coralee June—you all have made such a difference in my life these past months.

And lastly, you, my dear readers, I have to thank you for following me and Piper this far. Because of you all, I've been able to be with my family during this difficult time, and I've received so much love and support. Thank you for reading.

Until the next time we're in New Chicago together,
Kel

About the Author

Kel Carpenter is a master of werdz. When she's not reading or writing, she's traveling the world, lovingly pestering her co-author, and spending time with her family. She is always on the search for good tacos and the best pizza. She resides in Maryland and desperately tries to avoid the traffic.

- instagram.com/authorkelcarpenter
- goodreads.com/kelcarpenter
- facebook.com/authorkelcarpenter

*To my parents, Shilo and Jody.
You fought a good fight.*

Nobody talks about the other loss, the loss that happens within us. We lose people and things, but we also lose parts of ourselves. We grieve those missing parts too. We grieve them, and we grieve us. But I think losing those parts creates space. For newness. For understanding others' hurts and welcoming them into our free spaces.

Caroline George, *Dearest Josephine*

1
PIPER

Someone once told me that whiskey was the devil's poison.

I was inclined to disagree. It wouldn't taste like shit if it were.

Still, I tipped the shot glass back and swallowed without a grimace. It was easier now, thirty drinks in and counting.

I slammed the glass down on the table and gave the alpha wolf across from me an expectant look. His eyes narrowed, taking in the lack of a flush in my cheeks. My pulse hadn't spiked or slowed. My eyes weren't dilated.

I couldn't see them for myself, of course, but I knew.

Because I was a full-fledged demon, as Nathalie would say.

Whatever damage the alcohol did was healed before I could take the next shot. It was a slight miracle I had a low buzz, helping soothe the taste of the cheap liquor.

As a human, alcohol wasn't something I could afford.

I still couldn't now, but my drinking opponent didn't know that.

"Come on," I goaded. "What kinda alpha are you to let

me beat you at this?" My words did the trick, rousing him. He took the bottle and poured himself another glass.

The people gathered around us cheered him on, half of them pissed because I drank them under the table too.

His muscles twitched. A sheen of sweat coated his forehead. Despite his supernatural blood, his system was struggling to process the poison as fast as mine.

I was counting on it.

He downed his shot, and I poured myself another, tossing it back before he was even finished swallowing.

"You can do better than that," I said, my voice taking on a sour quality and my bitterness peeking out. He didn't know why. My reasons for being in this rundown, piece of shit bar were my own.

Given it was the last supernatural establishment in the city I hadn't been banned from, I wasn't leaving until I got what I came for.

Punishment.

Release.

Absolution.

. . . or something like it.

When his eyes turned a shade of blue, I knew that wolf of his was rising. Of all the supe species, they were often the easiest to provoke. Their magic and baser instincts were closer to my own. I understood them, in a way. The arrogance. The territorialism. The need to control.

If I hadn't been made a demon, I could have been a wolf.

Unfortunately for him, I wasn't. But I understood all too well how they worked.

"Are you going to take another shot? Or are you late for your circle jerk? If you're in over your head, by all means, leave."

My words were brash. Bold. They did the trick.

The sound of wood scraping against wood echoed in the air as he scooted back. His chair knocked over backwards with how quickly he stood up. Easily a solid foot taller and a hundred pounds heavier, the beast of a man glowered down at me from across the table.

"For a human, you're awfully disrespectful," he drawled. His faint southern accent was tainted with darkness, and it told me he was dancing on the precipice of losing it.

I blinked once lazily, unimpressed. I stared straight at him as I reached for the bottle and brought it to my lips.

Drinking this shit was a punishment in itself. Still, I downed the half a handle in a few large gulps.

My head spun a little. The effects finally taking hold. Warmth spread throughout my chest, turning to a burn.

I liked the burn. I loved it.

I lived for it.

Too bad I'd only have a little while in this delirious state before my body healed itself again. Fucking magic. Couldn't even let me be a proper drunk and wallow in self-loathing.

I slammed the bottle down a fraction too hard. It shattered, cutting me open, its crystal shards skittering across the table.

I could say I lost control of my strength. That it slipped for a second and the shattered glass was the result.

If I were a liar . . .

"Oops," I said, knowing full well the broken bottle blew my cover. I got to my feet, a little wobbly, as the alcohol coursed through my blood faster than normal. As my magic worked, my eyes steadily darkened.

He'd know there was more to me than I had let on, but

he wouldn't know what I was. Not when my brands were covered by a turtleneck.

Once upon a time, I'd worn them so I could pretend I was human. Like a child, I'd believed if I didn't see it, it wasn't real.

Now I wore them because no one would dare challenge me if I didn't.

But I needed them to challenge me. To think me an easy opponent. To give me the only thing that helped me handle this dark, festering emotion in my chest every time I thought back to that night.

As if he could hear my thoughts, the wolf lunged across the table, his nails turning to claws. Dark hairs sprung up on his neck and face; brown eyes turning blue.

I let out a loose breath. My pulse finally quickening with something almost like anticipation.

The tips of his claws barely grazed me, adding a sizzle of pain to the fire within.

But they never went more than skin deep.

The air grew chilly as a dark shadow formed. Outside, the winds howled like a ghoul on the hunt. Power gathered, and it smelled of ozone and coming storms. It felt like lightning singeing through my veins, burning every shred of emotion away. It tasted of chaos.

The supernaturals in the bar only had a split second to take notice and run, or choose to stand their ground. Ronan stepped out of the void, his eyes blazing with dark fury. He grabbed the alpha as if he weighed nothing. His hand locked around the lesser monster's neck, holding him in place.

"Give me a reason to let you live," Ronan said. He didn't raise his voice. Scream. Shout. He spoke quietly, like the night, vast in unpredictability.

The remaining supes in the bar scattered like roaches in the light. The bartender lingered, watching the situation with wary eyes. A small part of me felt bad. He was just trying to make a living and survive. He didn't ask for me and my problems to knock on his door and wreck his bar. No, I did that all on my own.

My self-loathing rose, feeding that raging beast inside.

The alpha trembled.

"Harvester," he uttered. Reverence, respect, and more than a little fear.

He wasn't as dumb as he seemed. Ronan would let him off. He always did when they didn't hurt me, and he read the sincerity in their mind. I didn't have that ability, but his tone was true. I didn't need magic to tell that.

"Give. Me. A. Reason," Ronan replied, voice still hard. Anger still riding him. I cocked my head and narrowed my eyes.

"She's a hustler, then she disrespected me," the wolf said, scrambling for words.

"So you thought to hurt her? To teach her a lesson?" Ronan asked, an inhuman purr entering his tone. Uneasiness slid along my spine.

The wolf swallowed, then nodded. "Yes."

"Is that how you handle women who *disrespect* you?"

The wolf faltered. "I didn't know she was yours—"

Wrong answer.

I realized I'd misread my victim in the time it took Ronan to summon black fire. The alpha didn't even have time to scream when the flames consumed him—flesh and blood and bone.

A moment later, all that remained was a charred spot and tense silence. Ronan shifted his gaze to me.

The demon didn't look away as he told the bartender,

"I'll have the money my atma cost you in merchandise wired to your account on the condition that you never serve her again."

Out of the corner of my eye, the barkeep nodded quickly.

"Yes. Thank yo—" He didn't even finish speaking before Ronan grabbed my arm and the void closed in.

Fuck.

Not again.

2
PIPER

I SWUNG WILDLY AT THE DARKNESS SURROUNDING ME, SPITTING mad. Of course, my fists never made purchase, but when the void cleared, Ronan was right before me. His large hand gripped my arm tightly, fingers white from how hard he was squeezing. If not for my magic, my arm would have bruised, if not broken.

As it was, I barely registered the pain.

The whiskey was still clouding my mind. Making me sloppy. Messy. I liked it that way when the supes I picked fights with beat the shit out of me. I didn't want that feeling so much when it was Ronan I had to face. His dark eyes saw too much. I felt their judgement in every passing second. Their pity.

I hated it.

"Fuck you," I spat at him. My fist went flying again, but he grabbed it mid-air, his long fingers wrapping around mine with crushing strength.

"Gladly," he retorted. Anger and regret and something that felt like betrayal brewed between us. His lips came down on mine—hot, and hard, and demanding.

The burning in me reached a crescendo.

I groaned, biting him. Blood welled, and I licked it from his skin. My tongue curved into his mouth, swiping over his bottom lip—then the fucker bit me back.

I yelped at the flash of pain in my tongue—followed by the most blinding heat that swept through me as he sucked on it.

Fire sparked in my hands and Ronan pulled away.

His heated gaze shot to the white flames. Even if they could destroy everything else, they couldn't hurt him. I yanked my hands away, and he allowed it. With that thought came the bitterness. I closed my hand into a fist and the fire snuffed out instantly, only smoke remaining.

I didn't need to look around to know we were outside Nathalie's building. It's where he brought me every time—and there had been a lot of them.

That was my last bar in New Chicago.

Supe bar, at least.

Even in the throes of self-destruction, I couldn't bring myself to enter a human establishment. Not with the wrath that followed in my wake.

"This needs to stop," he said. "The going out, drinking. Do you really think this is going to change things? Make her want to see you?"

My hand shot out faster than he could have predicted; a response to the instant rage I felt that he would *dare* mention her.

My fist hit him square in the jaw.

A crack echoed through the empty street.

Ronan cursed, spitting a wad of blood onto the concrete. Two white teeth gleamed in the moonlight.

Regret touched me. Guilt crept up. I wanted to dig my

nails into my skin so deeply I clawed it out—because I didn't want to feel. To even think about it.

"Leave her out of this," I said, my voice icy cold and lethal despite the raging inferno inside me. The whiskey was already fading. The buzz draining away, leaving me cold and sober to my choices.

"No."

His blatant disregard only served to piss me off more. Instead of taking another swing, I turned to walk inside. He grabbed me again, pulling me up short.

I rounded on him, fangs extending in my fury. Lightning crackled across my skin. A hot wind blew through New Chicago, carrying dark clouds.

Ronan lifted his head, observing the change.

"This has gone on too long. It's been over a month, Piper. While I can wait for you to figure this out, I don't know if *you* can—let alone your world."

I calmed the magic inside me, killing the lightning with a thought—but kept the fangs. I needed him to know I was serious, even if his words did stir something deep down. They riled the part of me that saw something there, between him and I. They pulled on the last shreds of humanity I carried.

But I didn't want it.

Feeling anything was too much. I couldn't stop there because the guilt wouldn't let me. If I gave an inch, it took a thousand miles—so I couldn't.

It was better to feel nothing at all.

"Go home, Ronan," I said quietly, a hundred percent sober.

"Not without a promise."

Oh no, I wasn't falling for that. Promise was just

another word for bargain when dealing with demons—and I was one now, tied by the laws of magic, the same as him.

"Not happening."

"You don't even know what I want." The purr in his voice was a challenge. It called to my anger, and it didn't help that I was fucking tired of him trying to have this conversation with me.

My sister hated me. She said as much before demanding I send her back to Hell. When I refused, she walked out, and I hadn't seen her since. There was nothing to talk about.

Nothing I had to say.

"It doesn't matter. The answer is no. I'm not in the business of making promises anymore." I pulled again on my arm, but he didn't budge.

"Bullshit," he uttered. "That's it? You did all this—became a demon, summoned me, called your sister back—just to give up? Where's the Piper that summoned a demon and won? Where's the woman that put her life on the line to save her friend? Where are *you*?"

His incredulity wasn't lost on me. I tried to hide my flinch.

"Sometimes life doesn't go the way we want. Sometimes it doesn't matter how hard we try. Sometimes we don't get a happy ending." I shrugged. "You'll learn soon enough."

"No, I won't. You pulled me out of Hell, and I'll do the same if I have to." His surety might have roused a different Piper, but not this one. Not me.

"Pretty words won't work this time, Ronan. I don't want your help. I don't need it—"

"What happened to no more lying?"

I bit my tongue and tasted a familiar copper tang.

Fucker.

He sounded like Nat. Both of them were an itch I couldn't scratch—constantly grating me.

"It's not a lie," I bit out. Silver eyes dropped to the smudge of blood that touched my lips. He smirked, cold and cruel. It roused something in me. Something bestial. Monstrous. I knew I was going to regret my next words before I said them, but for the life of me—I couldn't stop. "You got what you wanted. We fucked. We bonded. There's nothing more you need from me. We're done. Don't you know when to walk away?"

My back hit the wall.

I blinked, feeling his magic but not realizing we'd phased through the void until a dimly lit ceiling appeared in my periphery. I fell back onto something soft. My hands dropped to catch myself on instinct, and I took a fistful of black satin sheets instead.

His bed. We were in his bed.

Ronan's hand came to wrap around my throat in a territorial hold. His eyes blazed so bright it was like starlight shining through.

I glowered as my body heated in response. Even angry, I wanted him. Hating myself, I wanted him.

It made it easier to stomach the way my heart stuttered at his touch.

Still, I grabbed a fistful of his shirt to make me feel in control.

"If you think for a second that we're done—I haven't been speaking plainly enough." He rumbled a low growl. His nose dipped, and I turned my face away. Unbothered, he skimmed the length of my throat instead. My skin prickled at our proximity. His cool breath making the hairs lift as a trail of goosebumps skittered across my flesh.

I took a shallow breath.

"On the contrary, you've been very forthcoming," I said, trying to sound unaffected.

"We bonded," he said, like I never spoke to begin with. His free hand came up to cup my breast. "We fucked," he continued, his fingers squeezing. He rolled his thumb over my nipple through the fabric of my shirt. My hips jerked. "But this isn't over," he said, running his hand down my rib cage, across my stomach, all the way to the apex of my thighs. "It's just getting started."

My grip tightened too much, my control too little. Claws extended, shredding the handful of his shirt to pieces.

Ronan saw my slip in restraint for what it was, and his own fractured.

He grabbed the front of my jeans and tugged. They ripped down the middle.

I gasped, trying to sit up—but the hand around my throat kept me pinned.

"God dammit—" My words turned to a guttural moan when he sank his fangs into my neck, and his fingers dipped beneath my underwear. Two warm fingers pushed the thin fabric aside and roughly thrust into me without warning. My body bowed.

His fangs released me with a pop. He licked the wound and then sucked my skin as it closed instantly. "There's no god here. Just you and me—and those filthy fucking lies I'm tired of hearing. You're mine, Piper." He pulled his fingers out, then thrust them back in, punctuating his statement. He lifted his head, and I turned my cheek to look him in the eyes. "*Mine.* Not just for a night. A day. A few months—this is forever. Until the magic drains from my body and my soul ceases to exist—you will be mine."

I wanted to refute him just for the hell of it.

To tell him that he was wrong.

That I'm no one's. Not even my own, it seemed.

But of all the lies I could tell, that one didn't make its way past my lips.

The truth was, I was tired. Tired of drowning. Tired of trying. I committed my life to protecting my family and then failed in the worst way. My sister hated me. My parents were dead. I deserved it all.

But it wasn't kindness that I wanted. It wasn't gentle or sweet that I craved.

Ronan's possession of me ran deeper than skin. His feelings for me were dark and twisted—matching the monster that slumbered in me.

"Fuck me," I said. Ordered. Demanded. Begged. It was a fine line to straddle. "Fuck me and make it *hurt*."

His pupils dilated. I could tell he wanted to do just that. To give me what we both wanted. Needed.

I could practically feel the lust wafting off him.

He leaned in close.

"No."

The illusion shattered, but even as he said it, he thrust his fingers into me—giving me just a fraction of what I wanted. "You don't get to use *this* to hate yourself. I need more than just your body intact. I need your mind. Your sanity. Find Bree, talk to her, and get your shit together. If I find you in a bar again getting wasted and trying to pick a fight—you won't like the consequences."

I surged upward. My hands going to grab him—hurt him—pin him; I wasn't truly sure.

I never got to find out. He disappeared—leaving me alone with his warning.

Only then did I realize he'd taken me to my bedroom at Nat's. Fire coursed through my veins. I let out a mix between a growl and a scream and launched a ball of white fire at the wide-open door.

Nathalie ducked. The flames hit the wall behind her and exploded. A hole the size of her head appeared, and I vanquished my power once more.

She let out an exaggerated sigh. "So, it's going to be one of *those* mornings."

3
RONAN

Piper was spiraling.

After the night we brought Bree back, I knew she would have a difficult time facing her sister's reactions. I didn't realize just how bad it would get. But as the weeks dragged on and the drinking, fighting, and isolating continued . . . something had to be done.

It was clear that my atma wasn't in a place to handle it. She couldn't even handle herself.

I stepped through the void, crossing the city in a fraction of a second.

The light of a new day was just surfacing over New Chicago. The edge of the bitter cold finally lifting. I appeared outside an apartment door, more a courtesy than anything else.

Lifting my hand, I knocked twice.

Footsteps sounded on the other side. A heavy sigh.

I waited for him to unlock the six bolts that reinforced his door. The handle turned, and he opened it wide.

On the surface, he appeared to be a middle-aged man with thinning brown hair and watery blue eyes. An ordinary and everyday disguise that made humans and supernaturals not look twice.

But beneath it, he was something more. Something rare.

A demon-fae hybrid.

He had auburn hair so dark, it looked a shade of the darkest brown. His skin was pale and glowed with an inner light of immortality. His blue eyes were piercing, almost as much as Piper's. Pointed ears and dark blue brands that snaked up his neck and down to his fingers like vines completed his supernatural image.

Aengus was his given name.

Anders, his chosen.

"It's early," he said gruffly.

"Blame my atma," I replied, stepping past him and into his apartment. It was humble in belongings. Minimal. He had everything he needed, but not a thing more.

Anders sighed. "How's she doing?"

"The same," I answered, keeping it short where Piper was concerned. They had a history together. He'd straddled a fine line between attempting to be there for her while remaining loyal to his prior master. Had I not been able to read his mind and see his memories, anything more than that would have landed him in the nether for eternity. He cared for Piper in a platonic way and nothing more.

"She's lived a hard life. One in service to someone else who doesn't want her. It won't be easy for her to adjust."

"I'm aware."

Ignoring my tone, he stepped around his counter and pulled a bottle of amber-colored liquor down from the cabinet with two glasses. "None for me," I said, smelling the alcohol from across the room.

Anders lifted an eyebrow. "You give up drinking? It's one of the few pleasures in this life."

Before Piper turned to the bottle, I might have agreed. Now the smell of it soured my stomach. "Watch the person you care for most drink their guilt away and you might feel the same."

Anders hummed under his breath. "That bad?"

He kept his expression guarded, despite knowing I could read him well. He may be a thousand years old, but that was just a moment in the ten thousand I'd lived. Few things got past me when it came to emotion. Humans and supernaturals weren't complicated in that. They all had pains, vices and virtues, hopes and dreams . . . and nightmares.

Anders was no different, and it was only the lack of a blood connection between us that kept me from fully reading him like an open book.

"I'm not here to discuss Piper. Tell me about Bree."

He licked his bottom lip and took a sip of his drink.

"In some ways, she and Piper are the same. She spirals, but her hate drives her to move forward. She wants to go back to Hell. She's been making friends, bad friends if you ask me. Trying to find a demon that can give her what she wants. Someone with answers."

That didn't surprise me. After her initial tantrum out of Nathalie's apartment, she returned to the streets and began plotting. I knew she wanted back into Hell.

Finding someone that could tear a hole through time and space was not the easiest of tasks, however.

"Has she had any luck finding someone?"

"Not that I know of. To this point I've made sure every search runs dry. She's getting more frantic, though. Desperate. I'm concerned . . ."

"About?" I prompted.

Anders sighed and set the glass down, half empty.

"What did Piper do when she lost Bree?"

It irked me that he continued to bring up my atma, but I went along with it for the moment.

"She hunted down every witch she could, looking for answers."

He nodded. "She chased them for a decade. Hundreds of witches were killed or imprisoned because of her. She was a dog on the hunt, and she refused to give up. Bree is the same. So what do you think will happen when she doesn't find them?"

He lifted both brows, silently conveying his assessment.

"You think she'll escalate until she finds a way," I murmured.

"I believe it's only a matter of time until she realizes if she can't get someone else, she'll need you and Piper to do it. Once that happens, I pity you both."

I detected something in his voice. A hint of admiration, perhaps.

"Are you growing fond of Bree Fallon?" I asked him, speaking directly. I stood in the center of the small studio apartment, assessing him carefully.

"Fond is a stretch. I'm not fond of many. I do find her interesting, though. She cares very much for someone on the other side. I dare say she loves them with enough passion to destroy a world, or New Chicago at the very least."

I released a tight breath. He was interested, perhaps fascinated. I could deal with that. A woman sent to Hell and turned into a rage demon, then brought back . . . it was fascinating, in a sense.

So long as he kept it at that.

"How do you think she would handle Piper approaching her now?" I asked slowly. It was the real reason I came. The twist of his lips downward was not a good sign.

"I think . . . she's calmed down enough to speak to her. But she'll demand the same as before—to be sent back. That will frustrate Piper, and being who she is, she'll say no. It'll leave them in a stalemate, the same as now."

I looked away, toward the popcorn ceiling. That wasn't what I'd wanted to hear, but it was what I'd expected.

After a few moments, I dropped my head and nodded once. "Thank you for the information. Continue watching her until I say otherwise."

I began to step into the void when he spoke again.

"Would it be so bad if she were sent back? It's what she wants."

I pressed my lips together. The image of Piper's face as Bree demanded to send her back, the shattered look, the emptiness . . .

Until either Bree forgave her and accepted this new normal, or Piper came to a point she could let her sister go, her sister's loss would only destroy her.

"Yes," I said quietly. "It would."

4
PIPER

Something soft and squishy hit me in the face. Not to mention hot.

I blinked, then looked down at the muffin. The top had broken off, scattering crumbs across the wood floor.

"Did you just hit me with a muffin?"

"Well, it wasn't a ghost," Nat quipped. She picked up another off the plate and took a giant bite, blueberry juice staining her lips.

"Why?"

"You're doing it again."

I scrunched my nose. "Doing what? Eating breakfast?"

"Withdrawing into yourself. I was talking for a solid minute and you didn't even notice." She took another bite, looking unperturbed and yet assessing at the same time.

I set my half-eaten muffin down. No longer feeling hungry.

"Sorry—"

"No you're not," Nat replied. "You're annoyed I pointed it out."

My teeth clanked as my jaw snapped shut. I leaned

back, my expression blanking out. "All right, I'm annoyed." I crossed my arms over my chest.

"We need to talk about what happened."

"For fuck's sake," I cursed under my breath. "Not you too. Look, if this is about the wall. I'll pay for it—"

Nathalie chuckled. "No, you won't. You don't have the money to. But this isn't about the wall. Not really. It's about the *reason* incidents like the wall are happening."

I let out a tired breath. "If you have something to say to me, just say it. I had a rough night."

"Every night is a rough night these days," she said, giving me a thoughtful look. "You don't want to talk about you and Bree or what happened. Whatever. It's not my job to push you—but if you're not going to talk about it, or find a way to change your situation, then you need to adapt."

I glowered. "What do you call the last month or so?"

"Existing," she said softly. "It's not the same, Piper. You're going through the motions. Eat. Sleep. Get up. Get drunk. Start a brawl. Fight with Ronan. Repeat."

My hackles rose. "It's not that simple. I'm trying to figure things out, but Ronan just won't stop."

"The problem isn't Ronan. It's you. You're drowning," she corrected. She placed the muffin in her hand on the plate and brushed the crumbs off over the sink. "Not physically, of course, but drowning all the same. In your state of just existing, you're not living. You're stagnant. Ronan is trying to help you the only way he knows how. I've been trying to give you time, but I see now that time isn't going to change this. It's only getting worse. *You're* only getting worse."

"Well, I'm sorry that killing five thousand people, becoming a full demon, and losing my only family in what felt like the span of a few days means I'm having trouble coping right now." My words were angry and stiff. Cold, yet impassioned.

"That's what I'm saying." She sighed and leaned forward. Her brown eyes were large and wide and all too seeing. "You're *not* coping. At least not in a healthy way—"

"You don't get to decide what's healthy or not, let alone how—"

"I do when you're blowing holes in my wall and nearly killing me once a week," she snapped.

I froze, my eyebrows lifting slightly. Her hand touched her lips, as if she couldn't believe she said that. I got to my feet to put physical distance between us as I felt the rage magic in me rise with my anger.

"I thought this wasn't about the wall," I said snidely.

She let out a heavily exasperated sigh. "It's not about the fucking wall, Piper. It's about the fact that I'm tired of seeing my best friend destroy herself because she's so ridden with guilt over things she can't change." Her chest heaved as she panted, breathing heavily as her own frustration rose alongside mine. "Your sister is pissed you brought her back, it sucks—but you can't make her feel differently. All you can do is control yourself and how you react—but right now, the way you're reacting is to shut down everyone in your life that cares about you."

"I told you I didn't want to talk about this."

"Too damn bad. If you don't want to talk about Bree, then we're going to talk about you."

I started for the door, having heard enough to know I was at my end. Nathalie darted toward it, blocking my way. "Don't you think I get it?" Her question surprised me enough to make me stop in my tracks. "I convinced you to go to my parents' house, where they captured me and then used their magic to control me. My body wasn't my own, but my mind was present the whole time when Lucifer died. Millions and millions of people are dead or blind or crippled because of my magic. It might not be my fault entirely, but it doesn't change that I feel responsible."

Some of the tension in my shoulders drained away because I understood that. And I knew she understood me.

"I can't sleep," she said after a moment. "I cook and bake and clean for hours a day because I can't focus. If I could lie in bed in a ball, and just shrivel away to nothing—I would. But I can't. I'm restless. I'm hearing things . . ." She looked away, the last admission making her cheeks heat with shame.

"I didn't realize you were struggling," I said after a moment, my anger having evaporated with her confession. Nat let out a bitter laugh.

"We all have problems, Piper. Human or supe. Rich or poor. Good and bad. No one has a perfect life. We've all got issues. I just refuse to let mine rule me. I can't change the things I did or the people that have died. But I can keep moving forward, keep trying."

My gaze dropped to the floor, and I let out the tight breath currently constricting my chest. "It feels wrong to keep moving forward when they can't, and wrong to enjoy anything when I know Bree hates it here. Hates me. I brought her back. I made her return to this shithole because I thought she was alone in the dark, when in reality she'd moved on. And now she's trapped in a place she doesn't want to be because of me . . ."

"Then send her back," Nat said.

My chest constricted at the thought.

"I . . . I can't," I said quietly, swallowing hard. "Without her, I have nothing. I am nothing. I know it makes me a horrible person that I can't let her go—but I just *can't*."

As the truth left my lips, it hurt but also felt a little like release.

I was acknowledging the real reason for the guilt. The drinking. The fighting.

It wasn't just a guilt from the past, but from the choices I was making now.

Nat put her skinny arms around me and squeezed tighter than I thought a person of her size would be able to.

"It doesn't make you a horrible person that you're holding out for things to change. It makes you human, or well, a human-kind-of-demon. I don't know what to do about Bree. It's a hard situation when sending her back means the end of any possibility for you two. But I do know that you can't keep going like this. Neither of us can."

I hugged her back, holding tight.

Deep down, I knew she was right. Just like I knew Ronan was.

I knew I walked the path of self-destruction and embraced it.

What I didn't know was how to find another path.

"What are we going to do?" I asked her.

Nat leaned back, and I eased up on my grip to give her the space. "Well, we're both fucked, but now that we're not dancing around it we can work on it. It's not going to be instant in either case. You're going to get pissed at me sometimes for pushing you, but you need it—and I need you. You're not the only one who's lost family in all this. Barry was all I really had for years . . ."

A sliver of guilt added itself to the pile because I'd been a shit roommate and friend. While I'd been moping over everything gone wrong in my life, Nat was suffering in silence too. God, we were quite the pair.

A drunk rage demon with guilt issues and a chaos witch

hearing voices.

I knew I'd probably remember this moment as long as I lived, whether it was a year or ten thousand. Ronan once said that people want to be understood, and despite our vastly different backgrounds—I found that in Nat.

Different from Ronan, but equally profound; somehow this witch had become my person.

"Fuck Barry. You may not want him dead, but that piece of shit is more to blame than either of us. He's lucky you traded your favor with Ronan for his life."

She said nothing, but the twist of her lips told me she didn't think I was wrong.

"He's made bad choices. Either he'll change and try to fix them, or karma will catch up with him before any of us could."

I hoped she was right about karma because I really didn't see the former happening.

"Speaking of bad choices . . ." I was going to tell her that I'd said some regrettable things to Ronan when I was angry and wasn't sure what to do about it just yet.

Unfortunately, the universe had other plans.

Several rapid thumps on our door made us both pause.

I frowned.

Nat walked over and looked through the peephole. Her entire expression changed as she scrambled to undo the door locks, then thrust it open.

Standing outside the apartment was Señora Rosara and the succubus-shifter twins, Sasha and Sienna.

Only for the life of me I couldn't tell which was which. They were both bloodied and bruised. One of them was standing and carrying the other—who was unconscious.

"These two showed up downstairs, asked to see you," Señora said, thrusting her chin in my direction.

My lips parted. The question of why was on my tongue, though it was fairly obvious in a sense.

The twin still standing stumbled forward. Her gaze was wild, and yet somehow subdued; desperate but hard. "We need your help."

"I can see that," I answered. Judging by the harshness in her tone, I was fairly certain Sasha was speaking. "How did you know where to find me?"

"The little witch. We heard a rumor she was living with the crazy cat witch." Her answer was true enough, though I sensed there was more. Señora Rosara tsked under her breath, unmoved by the gruesome twins. She rolled her eyes and then turned on her heel and went back to her apartment, muttering something about blood on the floor. Her door slammed shut, and when I didn't immediately speak, Sasha continued. "Please. I know you have no reason to trust me, but we were attacked. There was a rally for the humans. It turned into a riot. We were walking back to the shelter when someone threw a bomb. Sienna jumped in front of me." She swallowed hard. "I can't lose her." The glassy sheen of her eyes told me she was close to crying, but the proud Sasha I knew didn't let the tears fall.

"Why here? Why me? A white witch would have better odds healing her."

The bitterness in her voice was expected. But not the answer.

"I've tried that. It didn't work. She's not healing . . ." she began but didn't need to finish. I knew what she wanted then. It was the one thing that I could truly do but didn't want to.

"You want my blood."

"You're a demon. If your blood can't save her, no one can."

5
PIPER

Her heartbeat was shallow. Magic fading.

Whatever bomb had hit her, it wasn't the ordinary kind. The wounds inflicted . . . if someone couldn't get them to close, it spelled death.

You can, a small voice whispered through my mind. It was the same part of me that chose to be used as the sacrifice to Aeshma, that jumped in that summoning circle that brought Ronan here, and that begged Ronan to save Nat.

Over the years I'd tried to quell it. Never successful for long. She'd been awfully silent in the month since Bree returned.

But here she was now, once more persuading me.

The gaping wound on Sienna's chest was dripping blood onto Nat's couch. Her skin was ashen. Pale. She'd betrayed me once . . . but she also tried to save me. Much like myself, she operated in between good and bad—and would die for those she loved.

My gaze slid sideways to Sasha. Her black cat tail swished side to side in a jarred, uneasy pattern. Her skin was damp and sweaty. Her pupils narrowed into thin slits.

Next to them, Nat kneeled, using a washcloth to clean Sienna's wounds. She'd told Sasha we needed to see how bad they were.

In truth, she was giving me time to form an answer.

Sasha wouldn't accept no, but I wouldn't be pushed into saying yes.

"Every time I manage to staunch the bleeding, it starts again. The magic is festering like an infection," Sasha uttered. "She doesn't have much time."

"I'm aware," Nat said, not lifting her eyes from the wound she was dabbing. "This solution is meant to slow whatever magic is preventing her from healing. While it won't be enough to save her, it'll give her a better shot if Piper decides to give blood."

Sasha's eye's narrowed further. She picked up on that single word.

If.

"She'll die if you don't," Sasha said, her voice scathing. "Do you really want that on your—"

"If she dies, it's not on me—and guilting me won't make me help you." My voice was steady, but there was also a lie in it. It wouldn't be my fault. But I could change it if the magic took. "I have to consider the repercussions for me, and for her," I added.

Sasha's lips twisted in a frown. "If she lives, it's worth being indebted."

"That's easy for you to say," I told her. "You aren't the one who would be indebted to me. And while I don't want it—that doesn't mean the implication isn't there. Taking a demon's blood gives them power over you. She won't be able to escape that."

Sasha went quiet for a moment. She stared at her sister's limp hand, locked in between her own.

"Then take me too."

My eyebrows lifted. "No," I said after a second. "You don't need my blood. You'll live."

Sasha lifted her head, and if the shifter succubus could have set fire to the world with just a look—she would have. I believed that.

"She has to live. I can't do this without her." She didn't say what 'this' was, but I knew. I understood. "So if she has to be indebted to you for that, I will too, for asking. I'll share the burden. Pay the price. Just please, *please* don't make me say goodbye to her."

Her voice broke, though she kept the tears in.

I turned away, swallowing the lump in my throat. My hands clenched into fists.

It was too much. What she asked for . . .

Soft fingers touched my shoulder. The scent of jasmine, raspberries, and juniper made me keep myself in check.

"Sasha, I'm going to have a word with Piper in the other room."

"But—"

"I wasn't asking," she replied, steel coating her tone. "Sienna isn't going to die in the next couple of minutes," she added in a softer tone. The lack of rebuttal from Sasha told me she would deal with it. Nathalie grabbed my arm and pulled me aside, into the room off the living area. A small cot, armchair, and antique bookshelf filled with trashy romance novels were the only things in there. She closed the double French doors firmly behind her.

"She won't hear us. I have the bedrooms and this room spelled for silence."

"I don't know if I can do it," I said. "I don't know if I can tie another person to me. To have that kind of power over them . . ."

"You worry it makes you no better than Lucifer," she said. I nodded, then ran a hand through my wild, unkempt hair, pulling harder in the places it snagged.

"Demons took over my world with their blood. They turned humans into supes in return for their souls. I don't want that, Nat. I don't want to control people." I sighed harshly, the uneasy restlessness in me straining. "Maybe I should reach out to Ronan—"

"That's a pussy move," Nat said, making my jaw snap shut. I turned around, eyeing her. "If you want to save her, then save her and accept the responsibility that comes with it. But don't push it onto Ronan so that you can tell yourself it's different. That abuses what you have with him and it makes you weak. You're not weak—you're fucked in the head, as we established—but you can do this. The question is whether or not you'll do it."

I pressed my lips together, wanting to refute her. But she had a point.

"We don't even know if my blood will take. Not every supe can get blood from multiple demons. The power . . . it could kill her."

"It could," Nathalie agreed. Her arms were crossed over her chest, but she inclined her head. "But she'll die either way then, and that truly will not be on you."

While that was a possibility, it wasn't what scared me most.

No, that worry was if she *didn't* die.

Because if she lived . . .

"If your reason for not doing it is because you're scared of having anyone indebted to you, I'm going to point out I've taken your blood. You weren't half as torn up about that. So what's the difference, Piper?"

I leaned back and let my legs buckle, taking a seat on the cot. My arms braced against my knees.

"You're you—"

"Yes, me," she said sarcastically. "The pain in the ass witch you've kidnapped, tied to a chair for thirty-six hours, threatened to shoot more times than I can count—"

"Okay, smartass. You know that's not what I mean. You're you. The person I live with, and the dumbass that faced down a demon for me. You were helping me bring Bree back and tied to Ronan at the same time. We didn't have to worry about my magic killing you because you'd already taken from him. It was different. This is . . . more complicated for me."

Nathalie nodded a few times. "It's different, I see that. But what you aren't grasping is that you've already done this. Being tied to someone doesn't mean you have to use them how Lucifer did. You can set the terms. You don't have to abuse it—that part is a choice."

"And if Sienna doesn't see it that way?" I prompted.

"I doubt she'll lose sleep over it at night given she'll be alive. She's spent her whole life indebted to some demon, anyway."

I lowered my head and sighed, then let out a curse.

"Sometimes it would be easier if you didn't make sense," I said. Nathalie snorted.

"Easier doesn't mean right, and in this case—I know you. It's going to bother you if she dies, and you didn't try to save her. Just like it will bother you if Ronan saves her, and she's indebted to him. Like it or not, guilt is kind of your calling card."

And didn't I fucking know it.

I took a deep breath and pushed up off my knees. Nat grabbed my shoulders before I could reach for the door. Her face was completely serious as she said, "You're not Lucifer. You're not like the demons that took this world. You choose to be different, and that's what matters."

I pushed my lips together and nodded. "Let's hope Sienna sees it that way."

"She will," Nathalie said with all the certainty to convince me. I knew she could lie through her teeth. That this may be a brave face for my sake, but I needed it.

She opened the doors and we stepped back into the living room. Sasha's head snapped up, and she looked between us expectantly.

"Well?" Apprehension filled her voice.

"Don't make me regret this," was my answer.

Her immediate sigh of relief filled me with just the tiniest kernel of warmth. Hope.

It would really suck if they both died now.

6
PIPER

Blood slicked the edge of the kitchen knife.

I carefully lifted it over Sienna's chest. Her heartbeat was faint and continuing to slow. Her skin turned a deathly pallor in the few minutes Nathalie and I spoke. Her lips were parted and colorless. Dirt and tiny bits of gravel coated her skin where Nat hadn't cleaned. The wound on her chest was a dark fleshy pink that seemed to fester because of the magic infecting it.

I licked my chapped lips and took a slow steady breath, then flicked my wrist once. Two drops descended from the gleaming edge into the exposed part of her chest.

Sasha's golden-brown fingers wrapped tightly around her sister's.

My blood touched hers and we waited.

Sasha had wanted to go first in case it didn't take, but I refused. Sienna was already dying. If she didn't make it, I wasn't going to send Sasha to death's door. If it didn't work for one, the odds were it wouldn't for the other. Will had little to do with it when magic was at play. The truth lies somewhere in the blood for why some supes could take magic from multiple demons when it killed others.

And I wasn't gambling with Sasha's life so that she could die with her sister.

Though part me suspected that was the intention.

Seconds passed. Time ticked by. As it slowly crawled toward the minute mark, the wound in her chest began to close. Flesh knit itself back together. Every nick and scrape and bruise or bump turned to pale, but flawless skin.

She didn't gasp awake, but her heartbeat picked up and a subtle warmth flushed over her skin. She seemed to glow with an inner radiance that wasn't there before.

I let go of the breath I didn't know I had been holding. It took.

"She's going to make it," Nat said quietly. Sasha nodded her head, relief stark in her features. A single tear spilled from the edge of her eye and she swept it away quickly.

"Thank you," she said, turning fully to me. "*Thank you.*"

I pressed my lips together awkwardly and nodded once, not sure how to respond. Praise wasn't something I was accustomed to. Not after everything I'd done.

I backed away, looking for something to do and deciding I would go clean the blade.

"Wait," Sasha said. "I'm next."

I paused mid-step and looked over my shoulder.

"You don't have to. I'm not asking for it," I told her.

She swallowed once and still shook her head. "But I am. I'm the one that brought her to you, and you're right that I chose for her to be indebted because it was that or die. I want to share that with her, so she knows she's not alone."

I took a breath and nodded. "All right then, we'll do it on the floor. I'm not flicking blood into your wounds." My nose scrunched and Nat snorted.

Sasha slid to the ground, her jeans pressing into the thick cream carpet.

I took a seat across from her.

"Don't get blood on that carpet," Nathalie said when I lifted the blade. I cast her an annoyed glance, which she returned.

The blade pricked my skin. A single droplet of blood welled before the tiny wound healed itself. I ran the tip of the knife over it, gathering my very essence.

"I ask for honesty to me in all things, and that you would never knowingly act, organize, or aid someone else in harming me and those that share my blood." My wording was specific to encompass not only Nat, but Ronan and Bree as well. "I give you my blood so that you may share the burden with your sister. Sasha Loren, do you accept the terms of this bargain?" I uttered the words in Nathalie's apartment for the second time.

Because Sienna was unconscious, she couldn't set terms. I'd truly saved her life which meant she owed me it. There were no restrictions. No limitations. I could demand anything, and she'd be forced to do it—but I didn't like to hold that power over anyone and refused to set the bar there when I had a choice.

That must have surprised Sasha. Her emerald-green eyes widened for a second as her sculpted eyebrows lifted.

"I do," she said instantly and without fear.

I suppose it wasn't as scary when the blood was almost guaranteed to not kill her.

"Then take it," I whispered, extending the knife.

She took the blade in hand and licked along the edge.

The moment my undiluted magic came into contact with her, her eyes began to glow. Claws extended from her fingers. A low growl built in her throat and she clenched her hands into fists, claws tearing at the flesh of her palms.

The reaction was sudden and unbidden.

"That's not supposed to happen," I said, grabbing her shoulders to hold her up as she sagged forward. "Sienna barely responded to my magic."

"Sienna was on the verge of death. Sasha isn't," Nathalie murmured from the couch. She sat on the edge, watching us.

Sasha's body bowed as the growl turned to a scream.

The air around her seemed to stir.

The hairs on the back of my neck lifted as I sensed the shift.

Everything went dark.

The void consumed us.

Pitch black, I tightened my hold on her shoulders, to be certain she was still there. It was only when her scream broke that I realized she'd never stopped.

Heavy pants told me she was still alive, but the darkness remained.

"Um," Nathalie started. "What just happened?"

"I'm not sure . . ." I turned my head, looking in all directions, but no matter how hard I squinted, I couldn't see a thing. "Sasha?"

"I'm—" She broke off, taking another heaved breath. "I'm alive."

Well, that was good.

The void, not so much.

"Any idea how you summoned the void?" I asked. "Or how to pull us out of it?"

"The what?"

"The void," I lifted one hand to motion, but then rolled my eyes. Odds were if I couldn't see shit, neither could they.

"This. The darkness around us. It's the void. A place that exists in between one shadow and the next."

"Are you certain—"

"Yes, try to feel the ground beneath you." I was trying to keep the frustration out of my voice. I was fairly certain neither me nor Nat were the cause, which left Sasha—who apparently now had powers she didn't possess before.

"It's cold. Like ice cold—"

"Because it's the void. Everything is cold."

"You're not," Sasha pointed out, as if that fact contradicted the truth of my words.

"I'm a rage demon that channels fire when I'm pissed off. Probably why," I said tersely. Nat chuckled a few feet away.

"As funny as it is listening to you two, are we going to figure out a way out of here or . . ." Nat trailed off in silent question. I sighed.

"I can't control the void. That power doesn't lie with me."

"But you're a demon," Sasha said, some of the bitchiness entering her tone again now that the danger had passed.

"Demons aren't infallible. Lucifer wouldn't have died if we were," I threw back at her, knowing that mention of her former lover would cut the bullshit.

"Ronan!" Nathalie started yelling. "Ronan, Piper needs you! Come quick—"

Before she could finish the sentence, the light returned. We were back in Nat's apartment and she was grinning from ear to ear.

"What the shit, Nat? Seriously?" I demanded, not looking at the demon I knew was standing just a few feet away.

She shrugged, unapologetically. "I knew you wouldn't call him, and I was getting cold. Someone has to do the hard things."

"You mean screaming for help like a little—"

"Why were you in the void?" Ronan asked, his voice alone sending delicious trails of heat over my skin—chasing the cold away. Sasha let out a disgusted sound, clearly sensing that with her succubus mojo. She pushed my hands away and stood, returning to her sister's side. "Well?" Ronan asked.

"Aren't you going to just run your mouth to him, Nat? That's what you seem to do best," I sniped.

Unperturbed, she rolled her eyes. "And save you from getting into trouble? Never. I might have sworn unyielding loyalty, but let it be known I'm not a cock block."

For fuck's sake. I wanted to bang my head against the wall sometimes. How someone could go from so sensible to so annoying was baffling to me.

"I'm waiting," Ronan continued.

I wanted to snap at him in reply, but after the morning we'd already had . . . I wasn't exactly in the mood for another hate-make-out session where we exchanged savage words.

"Sasha and Sienna showed up like this. I gave them my blood to save Sienna's life. When I gave it to Sasha, she somehow summoned the void. Which is how you found us—thanks to a certain someone."

Nathalie didn't do a good enough job hiding the slight grin on her face as she tipped her head.

"Why didn't you take her to a witch?" Ronan asked, echoing the same question I had asked earlier.

"We did. It didn't work," Sasha answered, still sounding annoyed, but curbing it slightly more when she spoke to him. Probably because he was over six and a half feet tall, a true born demon, and a scary motherfucker to everyone else except me.

"There was magic laced in her wounds. Rage magic, I believe. It was preventing them from healing," Nat added. "It's strange, though. I don't believe I've encountered rage magic before Piper. I thought it was rare . . ."

Ronan froze. It was quick, almost imperceptible, then he recovered. Were I not bonded with him and able to sense the shift in emotion, I wouldn't have caught it. There was an alertness that wasn't there before. I narrowed my eyes.

He knew something.

Sure enough, he took several steps toward the unconscious shifter succubus and sniffed the air, then cursed.

"What is it?"

He opened his mouth, then paused. "I recognize the magic on them. It's faint now, but unmistakable."

"Whose magic is it, Ronan?"

Silence spanned between us as I waited for an answer. There was an apology in his eyes. Trepidation in his mind. I knew I wouldn't like the answer, but nothing prepared for the truth of it.

"Bree's."

7
PIPER

I paced restlessly like there was an itch under my skin. The scent of Ronan's magic didn't soothe me or excite me as it usually did. It pissed me off.

"Why didn't you tell me my sister was a demon?"

He sighed, taking a seat on the edge of my bed.

"I didn't know how you would handle it."

I planted my hands on my hips and stared at him. "So you chose to guard that information?"

He looked away, and for the first time I noticed circles lined his eyes. There was a strain there that hadn't been before. I'd been so deep in my own shit and hellbent on not even trying, I truly missed everything.

"You weren't doing well. She left, and you didn't go after her. I figured when you eventually decided to, you'd find out for yourself."

"That's bullshit," I snapped.

"Why?" he replied, clenching his jaw. "You can't change it. It doesn't impact your relationship with her. Why does it matter if I didn't say anything?" His words were as hard and demanding as my own.

I crossed my arms. "It matters because you lied by omission. You knew information about my sister that you held back from me. You had no right to do that, regardless of how I'd take it or that I can't change it or that maybe I would have found out eventually. *You knew*."

He looked away, and I could tell he wasn't backing down this time. Neither was I.

"You don't get to pick and choose when to be present in this. Just this morning you told me we were done and to stay out of your business."

"You don't listen."

"It doesn't matter. Not in this. You don't get to have your cake and eat it too, as the humans say," he said apathetically. Aloof. Not cruel, per se, but certainly not kind. I don't believe he possessed it in him to be that. But I didn't fault him for it either.

"I . . . I'm trying to figure things out. I realize I've been all over the place and said a lot of—" I paused, grasping for words I didn't know how to say. "Stuff. Bad things . . . while I've been in this dark place. I can't promise you something I don't know how to give. You want me, but I'm fucking broken, Ronan. I don't know what I want or who I am. All I know is that I've spent my life trying to get Bree back—and she wants to go back to Hell. I can't do that. I can't—" I gasped, inhaling a tight breath and holding it so that my voice didn't break. I hated this. Vulnerability was not my strong suit. "I just can't."

I looked away, toward the tiny window beside my nightstand that showed the grimy street below. I didn't see him move. But I felt the heat coming from him as he stood before me and brought a hand up to grasp my jaw.

"I don't care that you're broken. I can grab those jagged pieces and hold them together while you sort it out. But I need more from you than drunken brawls and dismissals." The hand on my jaw tightened, and the silver of his eyes burned. "That shit can't keep happening. I'm patient and determined, and one day you will be mine in every sense of the word—but if you want to be treated as my equal in everything *right now,* then you have to try."

My breath stuttered. "And if I fail? If something pushes me over the edge?"

He pressed his lips together, and I knew his answer.

Ronan would be there for me. He'd always be there, but that didn't mean that I'd be privy to all. We'd be back here, with a void between us he couldn't cross alone, and I couldn't see through.

"If something pushes you, then stick your hand out for me to catch you. Don't jump headfirst and expect me to be okay with it. You can struggle, but that doesn't mean you self-destruct. There's better ways to handle it, if you truly need the outlet."

I tilted my chin, lips parted. "Like?"

"Me."

I couldn't hide the shudder that went through me if I'd tried. "You mean fucking?" I asked, eyebrow cocked.

"Fucking. Fighting. Atma, you love to hate—and I can take it." He leaned close, his lips brushing mine. "But I'm the only one for you that can. Give that to anyone else, and I'll make sure it's the last thing they're ever gifted."

I swallowed hard, torn between the way his words ignited me and wanting to slap him for the alpha male bullshit.

"Your possessiveness might concern me if I was in the market for a fuck buddy," I said.

"It should," he said in utter seriousness. "By human

standards, I'm a monster. But you're not human anymore—and I'm beginning to think that you never were."

I frowned. "My parents were, and I never showed any magic until Aeshma."

"I know," he murmured. "But two human sisters are now rage demons. I thought that a demon couldn't be made except by conception. You're both the *exception*. Once? I could believe it to be a blip in the universe, but twice?" He shook his head slightly. "Something is different about both of you. I plan to find out what."

"I was human," I said, pulling away from his hold. He let me, sensing I needed space. "But I can't deny that twice from the same family can't be coincidence. Maybe something happened to her while she was in Hell?"

"Oh, I'm certain of it," he said. "The question is what."

"Even if we were different somehow, it doesn't change things. What does, is that her magic was in the bomb that almost killed Sienna and probably did kill others. Do you know why?"

"I have suspicions," he said. "How it ended up there, I can only assume she evaded my contact following her, or somehow convinced him to lie. I suspect the former."

"You're tailing her?"

He cocked his head and failed to hide the grin peeking through. "Don't act so shocked. I made Nat enter a blood promise to keep tabs on you. Did you truly believe I'd let a rage demon loose on the city, your sister for that matter, and not keep an eye on her?"

I could argue with him till I was blue in the face about how omission is still lying, but it wouldn't get me anywhere. As he loved to remind me, he was a demon, not a man—and some truths I had to earn.

Or in this case, pull my head out of my ass long enough to use my brain.

"Why do you think her magic was in a bomb, hmm? Since you clearly know more than I do." He narrowed his eyes at the sharp tone I gave him.

"She's been pursuing a way back to Hell since she returned. It's probably safe to assume this has something to do with that."

That's what I was afraid of.

"I need to talk to her," I said quietly.

"You do," he agreed. "But not today. Let me talk to my contact and see what he knows. Take the day and try to get some sleep—"

"I can't sleep if she's out there blowing people up because *I* brought her back," I interrupted. "This is my fault—"

"Are you willing to send her back right now?"

Silence.

I closed my eyes. I wasn't.

People were dying, and I wasn't even willing to consider it.

Perhaps he was right, and I was a monster all along. Either way, the glaring truth worked in his favor.

"You're exhausted, Piper, and your sister isn't the little thirteen-year-old girl you remember. She's a full-grown demon in her own right; one that's pissed off and not going to yield. Talking to her right now, at this moment, won't give you the resolution you're looking for. Give it a day and let me see what I can find out."

I pressed my lips together, reluctant to be a sitting duck and agree.

"What am I supposed to do in the meantime?" I demanded.

"Stay out of trouble?" he offered unhelpfully.

Ronan should know that even if I could stay away from trouble, it wasn't capable of keeping away from me.

8

RONAN

I BYPASSED ANDERS AND WENT STRAIGHT TO THE SOURCE OF MAGIC itself.

Bree Fallon.

One step through the void was all it took to track her. The witch was right in that rage magic was not common on this plane. While death, desire, and even spirit magic were common and fairly easy to spot—rage and chaos stood apart. Before the summoning, Piper was the only source in New Chicago.

Unlike Piper's wild, untamed fire, Bree's magic felt cold.

A wrath that ran as deep as the frigid ocean.

It was that wrath that greeted me when I entered the human realm once more.

"I wondered how long you would be." Her voice was softer than Piper's. Less raspy. Devoid of all emotion.

She sat in an armchair with one leg draped over the edge. Her hair was plaited back in a fashion straight out of the high court in Hell. She wore tight clothing that left little to the imagination, and yet kept her demonic powers a secret.

I took a sparing look of the surrounding space, not sensing anyone nearby.

It was an apartment; small, but higher end for New Chicago. The wooden floors gleamed and the counters in the kitchen were made of stone.

The only thing that struck the situation as odd was that there was no other furniture. Nothing hanging on the walls. Only a single armchair in the middle of the room sat before a wide-open window that overlooked several blocks of the city.

The apartment was empty of life, and yet Bree's magic had settled in the pores of this place. It imprinted on the wood and swirled in every inch. She'd been here a long time.

"Your magic was in a bomb. Care to tell me why?" I asked, letting a hint of my power shine through and nothing more.

Bree grinned, but it was ruthless. Vicious.

I recognized the darkness in her.

"I was human once, as you know. I'm sympathetic to their plight. They didn't ask for this world. These beings. You. Me. Piper." Her tone darkened further on her sister's name.

"They may not have asked, but enough of them have become supernaturals now that they don't have another choice but to coexist. Humans and supernaturals need to find a way to live with each other. It's the only way."

She kept grinning. Completely unaffected by my words.

"That's where you're wrong. See, I know the truth—there's a way back to Hell. You and my darling sister proved it." Her vivid blue eyes glowed with a cold, glacial kind of light. I could understand Anders' fascination with her. Where Piper was a beast that trained herself because of compassion, Bree was a monster that reveled in the unbridled savageness.

"Even if another portal could be opened. Sending demons back does nothing. Leaving just plummets this world into chaos further because there will be no one to keep them in check."

Bree tsked.

She pushed one long leg off the edge, letting her heeled boot hit the floor with a thud that echoed. The other followed.

"You think too small, Harvester." She stood, rising to her full height, shorter than Piper by six inches, but closing the gap with the height of her shoes. "Although, I can't say I'm surprised. You were a complacent ruler and didn't consider the possibilities . . ."

I narrowed my eyes.

What she spoke of—

"Oh yes," she said and smirked. "I know the truth of Hell. Who you were. Are. You made quite a name for punishing demons that acted out, but it was all a front for your own complacency. You were content to let the high court act as they did and only stepped outside your black castle walls to execute those that broke the rules. You were more of a dog on a leash than anything."

She shrugged her delicate shoulder and let out a snide chuckle.

"Being born the Harvester doesn't mean you're fit to make rules. I left the tediousness to those that were better suited."

She laughed, a peal of wind chimes.

"You and Piper are well met. You're both adept at making excuses for your choices." I grit my teeth, not liking the way this was going one bit.

If Bree knew about my past as the Harvester, that meant she was there during my rule. There in Hell, watching. But how? I'd never sensed her magic—not once—before the summoning.

"Send me back, Ronan. Or I will take the supernaturals, and perhaps the humans with me."

I froze, finally seeing where she was going. What her move was.

Her endgame.

"You plan to open a corridor both ways," I uttered, hardly able to believe it. "While the supernaturals have power here, they would be decimated in Hell. Surely, if you know this much, you can see that—"

"Hell is under new leadership. I have a feeling it might find a place for them in society . . . and if not, well—it's been survival of the fittest for so long. Maybe it's time they learned they are not very big fish when thrown into the ocean." She tilted her head, almost mockingly.

"And the humans you claim to understand?"

"Hell has the source of magic. They could enter it at their own peril. Some might change. Others . . ." She shrugged. "In a world where magic exists, the only true way for them to be free of it is to evolve or die."

She said it without remorse or care.

"You would completely destroy what is left of humanity just so you can return?" I asked, not condemning, per se, but concerned all the same. Piper would never forgive Bree if she did this. No matter the guilt she harbored, she wouldn't stand to see the people of this world led like lambs to the slaughter.

"For *him*, anything. I want to return, and if you help me, perhaps I'll never come back. But if you don't . . ." She left the threat clear as day. The stakes were set.

I pushed on the barriers of her mind, wanting to dive deep and learn every tiny detail she had hidden away. But there was a problem.

Spikes surrounded it. A mental shield that would shred me to break through.

Bree grinned further.

"While uncommon for rage demons, I have one of the strongest mental shields in Hell. I wouldn't advise trying to break through it. Even for you, that wouldn't end well." She winked and then passed me by, heading toward the door.

"There's still one problem with this plan of yours," I said. She paused. "You don't have a way to open a corridor. As much as this threat carries weight *if you did*—the fact remains, you don't. Where it stands currently, you're working with the humans in a way to kill supes and start a war—but that doesn't get you back to Hell."

Bree stared at the door ahead of her for a moment, as if considering her words.

"If Piper found a way after ten years, I will find one—but if supes and humans die along the way . . . so be it. You know where to find me when my sister has had enough and finally changes her mind."

And with that, Bree Fallon walked out of the apartment and did not look back.

9
PIPER

I cleaned my guns twice before Sasha spoke.

"Is that all she does?" Her voice grated my ears.

"Mostly." Nat shrugged and went back to dabbing at the blood on her couch with a solution meant to pull it out. Sienna helped her now that she was awake—and well, it was her blood.

"You need a hobby," Sasha said.

"Don't you have a corner you should be standing on somewhere? A dick to suck?" It was a little unfair given my background. My mother serviced vampires because that's all she could do. I hunted supes because that's all I could do. In this world, we didn't always have the luxury of choosing our profession or what we were.

But she was pissing me off.

"I don't know; if you don't stop being such a pain in the ass, that demon of yours might look my way. I have experience with pleasing your atmans, after all."

I paused, my hand jerking to the side and sending the metal pieces of the gun crashing to the floor.

"Get out," I snapped in frustration, sliding off the stool to pick up the pieces.

"It's not your apartment," she retorted.

"Sasha," Sienna groaned.

"What? Just because I'm indebted to her doesn't mean I'm going to let her jerk me around."

Me? Jerk her around? For fuck's sake, I wasn't even the one to start this.

Lifting my head, I eyed Nat, who was purposely ignoring all of us.

As if she had eyes in the back of her horns, she looked up—lips pursed and clearly annoyed.

"Make her leave," I said.

Nat groaned. "Why you gotta drag me into this?"

"Because she's being a cunt."

Sasha choked on indignation while Nat sighed. "So were you."

"She started it. I live here."

"Ugh," Nat groaned. "Fine. Sasha, can you go to your room for a bit and chill? I need her to calm the fuck down and I can't referee you two and clean this couch."

I spluttered. "What did you just say?"

Nat pressed her lips together. "Erm ... I told her to go to her room?"

"Her room? What room? They don't have a room—" I started.

"Oh, did we forget to mention that Nat invited us to stay?" Sasha said with saccharine sweetness.

Fire ignited at my fingertips. "Oh no you don't," Nat snapped. "Cut that shit out. I've already got a hole to plaster because of you."

Sasha snickered under her breath. Meanwhile Sienna gave me a sympathetic look.

I snuffed out the flames and reined in the frustration.

"So we're just going to take in every stray we come across?" I demanded.

"Look who's talking," Sasha sniped. My hands clenched into fists. The urge to hurl her through a wall was strong.

"Come on, Sasha," Sienna started, getting up to lead her away.

I waited for them to enter the side room and close the doors before releasing a breath. "What the shit? I know I don't own this place, but I live here too."

"I know," Nat sighed, setting the washcloth down. "But they don't have anywhere to go. Lucifer is dead. The Underworld burned down. They've been staying at a homeless shelter, Piper."

I leaned against the counter and ran my hand through my hair.

"Where will they even stay? That side room doesn't have a bed big enough for the two of them," I pointed out. If she was going to say I had to share my room, there would be an issue. Not because I needed my space, but because I needed space from Sasha—and I had the little habit of setting shit on fire. The twins weren't immune.

"I ordered a new bed that should be here by the weekend. Until then, one of them will sleep in the room and the other on the couch," she explained.

"And Señora Rosara? She's okay by this?" There was no way in hell she'd already ran this by her.

"Señora trusts my judgement. Besides, they're half cat. I have a feeling it'll be fine, and if it's not, we'll figure it out."

I blew out a tight breath. "I can't tell you what to do with your place, but next time please say something to me first. I get why you don't want to leave them out in the cold, but I'm also bonded to them now—a bond I wasn't exactly thrilled about—and I wouldn't have minded some space."

Guilt flashed through her features, but she nodded. "That's fair, and I'm sorry for not talking to you first. Can you try to make it work with Sasha, though? I know she's rough around the edges, but you two have a lot in common."

I gave her a flat look, and she groaned.

"I'm not asking you to be best friends. Just don't light shit on fire or get blood on my stuff, okay?"

Well, I suppose given I was still a 'guest', that was reasonable enough.

"I'll try."

She narrowed her eyes. "You better. That brings me to something we need to talk about."

"What?"

Nat flicked her wrist and an errant wind hit the handle just right, blowing the double French doors open.

"You two can come back out," Nat said, as if opening the doors wasn't a clear sign. The twins stepped into the room, Sasha looking more irritated than before—like Nat and I weren't the only ones having this conversation. "Now that we're all on the same page about sleeping arrangements, let's talk jobs. I don't mind you guys staying here, but you need to start contributing to the household. I still have bills to pay and a business to run."

I blanched. Of all the things I thought she'd want to talk about, this wasn't even remotely on the list.

"I'm still dealing with Bree," I started. Nat squinted in my direction.

"Where's Bree right now?"

"Ronan—"

"My point. Dealing with Bree *is* important," she added

gently. "And I support you in figuring that out—but you haven't dealt with her for a month, and that's not a full-time thing. At least not right now."

I sighed. "Okay, that's fair. I don't know how much I'll be able to contribute when most places won't hire a human or a demon . . ."

Nathalie squinted again. "I'm sure I'll find something for you."

I blinked, then realized that I'd missed the end part of her original statement.

A business to run.

"I can balance your books. I'm good with numbers and very detail-oriented," Sienna said. She took a seat on the plush rug and sprawled her long, lean legs out.

"Really?" Nat asked, clearly excited by this development.

"Mhmm," she affirmed and nodded. "Lucifer might have been the face of the Underworld, but Sasha and I ran most of the business side behind the scenes. Because of the supernatural tax, I'm already familiar with your business."

I knew the tax she was referring to. It was one of the few things about the devil I hadn't hated. He imposed a tax on all supernatural kind; a percentage they paid him for existing in his city. Humans were exempt from the tax, however. For a long time I'd assumed it had to do with the idea that we weren't worth taxing because we made so little by comparison. Sad, but true. I figured their prejudice against us was the reason. Not kindness.

"Good, we'll sit down and get you started this evening. I'm behind on some orders from the last few months." Nat set the washcloth aside, taking an appraising look over her couch. While damp from the solution she had been using, the blood stains were gone. "What about you, Sasha?"

"Logistics was my focus. What comes in and what goes out. The when, where, and how. Sienna ran the numbers, but I made sure things happened when they were supposed to. I can also handle clients and acquisitions, coercion, clandestine assignments to gather intel . . ." She continued on with a laundry list of skills she had and jobs she felt confident handling.

By the end, Nat let out a low whistle. "Color me impressed. I knew you handled most of," she paused, her voice catching for a fraction of a second, "Lucifer's acquisitions. But I wasn't aware of the rest of it. Most of his businesses were hidden from the public, apart from the ones he wanted us to see."

"I know how to do that too," Sasha said, her expression somber. She and Sienna had been in love with him when he'd died. I wondered if they still blamed me for it, or if Nat now shared that blame too.

"Good. With recent events, I'm pursuing other avenues of trade I'd avoided previously."

I frowned. "Such as?"

Instead of a straight answer, she gave me a mischievous grin. "Let's talk about your skills."

I tried not to grimace. The sad reality was there were only a few things I was good at.

"I can track and kill supes," I started. Nat's lips pressed together, and Sasha pointedly looked away.

"I'm aware. Dig deeper."

A tight breath unfurled in my chest. "I've spent two decades learning everything I can about supes. I know about almost all forms of magic, spells, species—you name it. I know their weaknesses and how to use them to get what I want."

"There's something you forgot," Nat said.

I lifted an eyebrow.

"You were human. You understand them in a way none of us can"—she motioned to her and the twins—"Some of my dealings are with humans, and I'll need that."

"You still haven't said what exactly this business you run is all about. I know you sell tea, but I'm getting the impression there's a lot more."

She picked up her cleaning supplies and walked around the edge of the counter, dumping a few herbs into the bowl to cancel out the magical properties before emptying it in the sink. "Tea is just the tip of the iceberg. It's where I got my start, but my business operates on a larger scale now. The short answer is I specialize in finding what makes people happy. What makes their meaningless existence in this world worthwhile—and I sell it to them. You'd be surprised at what people find sentimental or what they value."

"Unless you need some busted kneecaps, I'm not sure what I can do to help with that."

Nat lifted her head, looking me straight in the eye. "New Chicago is a dangerous place, more so now than it has ever been. Thugs rule the streets. Humans are finding ways to harness magic and rise up." She cast a glance at the twins. "Making people happy is great, but people need to be alive for that . . . which is why I'm branching out."

She looked at the three of us, and I was equal parts intrigued and concerned for what she would say.

"Into?" Sasha prompted. She sounded curious yet annoyed for the same reasons as me.

"Magical arms dealing."

My jaw slipped a little before I caught myself.

"Weapons? You want to—"

"Purchase them. Not sell. These weapons cause mass

chaos or slaughter whole groups of people. The fewer there are on the streets, the better off this city will be."

I crossed my arms over my chest. "What exactly do you plan to do with them?"

"Track where they came from and then disable them."

My brow furrowed. "That's a good idea, but your magic isn't exactly predictable."

She nodded slowly, and a creeping feeling worked its way up my spine as I sensed where all this was going. "Mine isn't," she agreed. "Thankfully, one of my new employees is an immortal demon with more magic in her pinky finger than most supernaturals can ever possess."

I looked away. "You've got this all planned out, don't you?" She shrugged in response. "I'm half surprised you're not telling me you've already bought—" I broke off mid-sentence when her nose twitched.

Oh no she didn't.

"You have, haven't you?" I asked in disbelief.

"Technically, I haven't bought it yet," she said defensively.

"'Technically' we were just talking about jobs in the broad sense—not something you had planned for who knows how long—"

"Ten weeks and two days," she inserted quietly.

I pressed my lips together and appraised her. That tracked to about three days after I burned the Underworld to the ground. Three days after Lucifer died. Three days after hell on earth.

"I had to get things together. For one, I couldn't do it alone. I needed you—but once you woke back up, you weren't ready yet. I used the time to research. It was only last week I finally got a bite. A renegade group of humans got their hands on a pistol that has the ability to temporarily steal magic and grant it to the person wielding it. After what's already happened, that's a horrible thing to let loose in New Chicago. You've got to see that."

I sighed. God damn her and her sensibility.

Damn my conscience too because it agreed.

"I'm only agreeing to this on a trial-by-trial basis, and on the condition that you tell me *everything*. No holding out on shit like this."

She nodded once then reached into the junk drawer next to the sink and pulled out a file.

"Our first deal is tomorrow night. This file has everything I know. All communications between us."

I cursed under my breath. Of course it was. I haphazardly flipped through the folder, pausing when I noticed something out of place.

"Why does this say my name?"

Nat looked at the ceiling. "Because you're the witch hunter and humans won't work with me. You will be the one making the deal tomorrow. Might want to dress warm."

Sometimes I regretted not shooting her when I had the chance.

I may be immortal, but she would be the death of me.

10

RONAN

"You didn't tell me she could shield her mind."

"Isn't it early for another visit?"

Anders didn't pause in pouring his coffee. It was an uncanny thing for someone to not react to my presence. Perhaps being half-demon himself gave him unfounded confidence.

While I could see magic, that didn't tell me what powers another might possess, though I could gauge their strength. He was a rare breed that I could not interpret, courtesy of his ability to glamour better than any other in Hell.

"I can't read her, and the situation has now escalated."

Anders sighed. "I haven't tried to influence her. There's no way for me to know these things if I haven't been within a hundred feet of the woman."

"I need something other than excuses. I can't return to Piper with this."

"You've yet to tell me what 'this' is," Anders pointed out. He took a sip of his coffee and hummed under his breath.

"That her sister is a bloodthirsty wraith whose intent is to kill everyone in her path until she can find a way to open a corridor—at which point she intends to let both humans and supernaturals into Hell."

Anders choked.

Finally. A reaction. I was beginning to question if I were right to leave his autonomy and not enter his mind.

"How do you know this?" he asked, setting the mug aside and reaching for a pack of cigarettes instead.

"Her magic was in a bomb that went off by the navy pier this morning. I approached her about it. She was . . . unnerving."

Anders nodded. "She has that effect on people. I need a smoke. Join me on the balcony."

I followed him outside into the cool afternoon sun. He snapped his fingers and the tip of his thumb flickered with an orange flame. His control over the elements was minimal, but that wasn't uncommon with spirit magic. He lit the tip of his cigarette and inhaled deeply.

"I didn't know about the bomb," he said. "Which either means she knows about me, or she suspects she's being followed and has taken precautions to evade."

"Hard to say, but I know she's working with the humans. For now. I suspect her allegiance could switch at the drop of a dime, depending on who she thinks will get her what she wants faster."

He blew out a stream of smoke that was pulled away in the wind. "She's been instigating at rallies. Spurring them on. Things are in disarray since Lucifer's death, and you haven't publicly taken control of it. She's using that to incite them into believing there's a chance," he said.

"They'll never win. The only true way humans will have a measure of control is if there are supernatural laws in place to make it so."

"And enforced," he added. "Lucifer tried, but he was too disjointed. His mind fractured by insanity thanks to Aeshma. He didn't have it in him to be compassionate toward them the way they need . . . if things are to change."

He wasn't wrong. My brother wasn't the right demon for that. His own insecurities and faults making him incapable of that sort of change.

But there was a demon that was.

A demon that cared for the humans. That understood them. That loved them.

A demon that would enforce laws if she were in charge.

"Yes, well, Bree is currently making the situation worse if the bomb this morning is anything to go by," I replied, tucking away my thoughts for a later time. When she was more prepared for the role I intended for her . . .

In Hell, she would have been my queen.

I didn't see any reason for that to not be the case on Earth.

No matter what race or species, I've found that all needed order, or they fell into chaos. Anarchy. The humans were no different in this. Society crumbled in the wake of true freedom. Unhinged by the lack of rules.

And I would be the one to fix that with Piper.

"If you can't lock her up or send her back, there's truly not much to be done about her," Anders said. "But that doesn't mean you can't work to diffuse the situation. There are other ways to take power back."

Wind whipped around us, and he cupped his cigarette, inhaling another puff. He released the streams of smoke from his nostrils. The jaded glint in his eyes and the chip on his shoulder made him look more like a true demon beneath the glamour.

I arched an eyebrow. "I'm listening."

II
PIPER

I took a long, hard look at myself in the mirror.

The turtleneck fit looser than it had before. My jeans too. I had to tighten the belt that held either holster on my hip. The gun metal glinted maliciously in the fluorescent bathroom lights. My hair was longer, almost to my waist now, but braided back in a tight French braid that pulled at my skin and made my scalp tender.

I needed that edge of pain. It helped me keep clarity. Stay in the moment.

If not for the brands on my skin, I might as well be the same woman I was four months ago.

Piper Fallon. The Witch Hunter, they called me. A human bounty hunter with too much knowledge and unparalleled skill. A woman cold as ice and on a mission.

They spoke of me still, but there was more fear than ever. More hearsay too.

If they knew the truth of what I was . . . I'd have to say they'd likely be disappointed.

I was.

For all the bullets I'd shot and fires I'd caused, inside I

was broken. Outside too. The brands proved it, in a way. My origin was Aeshma, and her marks were prominent on my skin. In there, Nat's name was woven. Ronan's too. Bree's had always been there, and creeping along my spine were the markings of guilt. Anger. Confusion. Regret.

No one could read them, except perhaps Ronan. But the truth of who and what I was lay bared on my skin, and while I could hide it beneath clothes, it wasn't going anywhere.

And I was no longer running from it.

I made an oath to myself to not be a liar, and I was holding myself to that promise—even if it killed me. Even if, sometimes, I wished it already had.

But Nat was right.

Ronan was right.

And even Bree—who I'd yet to see since bringing her back—was right.

I was a coward. I made excuses. And I couldn't change the past.

The underworld was gone. Lucifer was gone. New Chicago—hell, the entire world—had changed because of my actions.

I could crumble under that pressure, or I could do something about it.

Today, I was choosing to do something.

"Piper." Nat's fist hit the bathroom door twice. "We're leaving in five. Hurry up."

With one last look in the mirror, I headed out into the living room. The blue contacts I wore blocked out the purple tinge that darkened when I got angry; a precaution we'd agreed on to maintain the illusion I was human. There was only so long that party trick would work, but most of the people who knew I wasn't a human were dead. That was a sobering thought.

Like me, the twins dressed in black long-sleeve shirts and jeans. Since they were borrowing Nat's clothes until she had a chance to order them new ones, their midriffs peeked out, showing a hint of skin.

"Ooooo," Sienna purred, sidling toward me. Her long black ponytail swished side to side. "You look just like your old self."

Her words echoed my own thoughts and didn't make me feel any better, not that I showed it.

"Well, technically *I* negotiated a deal with this guy." I gave Nat a pointed look. "It's not like he'll buy it if I don't show and look the part."

"Don't get your panties in a twist. You only have to play along until they bring the gun out," Nat said. Something about her expression looked bothered, though I didn't think it had to do with her pretending to be me and entering a deal on the black market with a group of renegade humans.

So they claimed.

How they had a gun capable of stealing magic puzzled me. Given our own situation, I wasn't convinced they were truly human, or that there wasn't more to this so-called deal, even if she didn't know it.

"You and Sienna should go ahead to scout things out," I told her. "We don't want to risk them spooking."

Nathalie nodded. The corners of her eyes were tight and her skin a shade too pale. She appeared stressed, and while that was reasonable, I'd seen her in worse situations before. Something else was up.

"I'll try to place myself at the edge of the square so I can get out if the rally goes sideways. Sienna will be down the street on the other side of this mess. I'm giving her the keys to my car in case you two need a faster escape method."

"Nat," I said quietly. "Are you—"

"I'm fine," she said too quickly. Her voice was a touch harsh. I lifted my eyebrows, and she blew out a loose breath. "Really, I'm fine," she repeated in a softer tone. "Just a little worried about you two. I know you're powerful, but we don't know how many will be there. Stay safe, okay?"

I waited a second, watching her closely before nodding.

"We've been in tighter scrapes before," I reminded her. "It'll be fine, and if it's not, I'll figure it out." Her mouth drew up in a crooked smile. She laughed softly, the tension easing out.

"Yes, I suppose you will."

"We need to go," Sienna said, coming up beside her.

Nat clasped her hand over mine, a tiny metal earbud in it. "Keep that in. I've spelled it so they won't see it."

"Will do. Try to keep the commentary to a minimum this time."

With that, she and Sienna left the apartment.

"You're worried about her," Sasha said into the silence. "Yet it's us who are heading into the line of fire."

"I can take care of myself," I replied.

"And she can't?" I sensed her eyes on me but remained staring at the front door.

"She has a tendency of not knowing when to run. If she thinks I'm in danger, she'll dive headfirst."

It was quiet for a moment as the sound of our hearts beating, and the quiet hum of electricity settled over us. "Some things are worse than dying," Sasha said. "Losing the only family you have . . . well, you know how I feel. A life without Sienna wouldn't be worth living at all."

Her words struck me.

The truth was simple, yet incredibly profound, because I understood all too well. The part that rendered me immobile for a moment wasn't that Nat and I had found that with each other.

But that I'd lost that with someone else.

My own sister—my Sienna—she'd moved on. Someone else was the reason she carried on now. And in that time, I'd found someone else too.

It was an almost crippling realization.

For the first time, I felt more than guilt or regret or longing when I thought of her.

I felt grief.

The clock struck eight; the turning of the hand a quiet click that sounded so much louder. "It's time," Sasha said.

I packed those thoughts away, tucking it inside where I could look deeper, burying it beneath a cold, unbreakable exterior.

And then I left it there in Nat's apartment.

The woman that stepped out onto the street wasn't broken or trying to find herself.

She was the Witch Hunter, and there was a job to do.

12
RONAN

Sulphur was in the air.

A tang that was unmistakable and yet subtle enough to evade the humans' weak senses. They milled about, like sheep waiting for their shepherd to tell them where to go. What to do.

"Humans and demons are not so different," Anders said, lighting up another cigarette. "Only magic really separates the two. They're both impassioned creatures. They both have those who lead and those who follow. They both cling to power, though humans are at a distinct disadvantage there." The scent of stale tobacco smoke was fitting for the charged air and dour atmosphere. Heavy clouds hung over Palmer Square, the meeting point of the evening's rally.

"For now," I said, surveying the growing crowd from the rooftop where we stood. Shadows wrapped around us, allowing me to watch and go unnoticed until I chose otherwise. "Having ruled Hell for as long as I did, I can tell you that power is hard to acquire, but easy to lose. Magic may be what divides the two, but with Bree helping them, it's only a matter of time until they find a way to bridge that gap."

Anders took another puff of his cigarette and blew out a long stream of white smoke that was caught in a cold wind.

"You tell Piper about your little meeting with her sister yesterday?"

My jaw clenched, but I kept my eyes on the square. "No. Not yet."

The other man hummed. "And you think that wise?"

"I think that it's none of your business what I tell my atma," I replied. Unbothered, he shrugged off my animosity by dropping the cigarette butt on the roof and grinding it into the ground with the sole of his shoe.

"Not my business, no, but I am a man who has experience with women—specifically human women—and with Piper. One might think if you truly wanted to make progress with her, you'd be using every means you have available, particularly if your claim on her is more than simply what the bond demands . . ." His insinuation lit my blood on fire. I pressed my lips together in a hard line but contained the anger.

"You seem to spend a great deal of time thinking about her for someone not interested," I said quietly. There was an unspoken warning in my statement. A dangerous edge.

"I do not care for her romantically. For one, she believes I'm a forty-year-old man. For another, she's too cold for me. The way she's capable of detaching from her emotions at the drop of a hat. . . frankly, I find it terrifying." Torches and flashlights dotted the mass of people below, but I lifted my gaze to the man beside me. "Piper is the closest thing I had to a friend in the last hundred years. I simply care for her and want her to find happiness." He stared into the far-off distance, unseeing in a way that made me think he was remembering someone else. Someone that might have been his own happiness. All at once, Anders blinked, and a smooth grin appeared as he eased back into feigned nonchalance. "You're her best chance at that because you're willing to put in the work. You won't let her keep you at bay, but keeping things from her? From one man to another, honesty is always the best policy when it comes to women."

I sighed heavily. "She won't want to believe this about Bree, and she won't listen if I tell her talking to Bree won't do anything. If I can get the humans under control, then at least that makes her sister's threats empty."

"You're deciding what she can and cannot handle." Anders shook his head and chuckled. "Let me tell you, though, in case you haven't noticed—your atma handled her world being taken, her parents being killed, and then taking care of her sister since she was sixteen years old. Trying to protect her *can* and will backfire."

"I'm solving the problem before I go to her."

"You're managing her," Anders replied. "She's not a child. If it's too much and she falls, then you catch her—but don't damage whatever trust you've managed to earn. She's unlikely to give it back."

I considered his words carefully.

"Bree knows more than I originally thought. She's aware of things that Piper is not . . . pertaining to who and what I was in Hell."

He hummed again. "What I'm hearing is that you really need to talk with her. Sooner rather than later . . ." His voice trailed, catching my attention. I followed his gaze across the square to a head of honey blonde hair that glowed like the sun, even from the shadows.

My lips parted.

"I take it you weren't aware she'd be here tonight?" Anders guessed.

"No. I was not."

13
PIPER

Night settled over us. Its shadows hiding the slight glow in my eyes that not even contacts could dampen. I led Sasha, bound in faux magical handcuffs. The real ones would prevent her from using magic on me or anyone else.

These were just for show.

A pretty act.

I hoped they bought it because we were in deep shit if they didn't.

Sasha grunted. Sliding her weight back to appear like we were at odds. I rammed my shoulder into her back. She stumbled forward, planting her face into the asphalt.

Ouch. That had to hurt.

I leaned down, wrapping my bare hand around her shoulder.

"We can do this the easy way or the hard way. Choice is up to you, shifter." It was effortless to make my tone cold and cruel. A shiver ran through me, and I suppressed it for any eyes that may have been watching.

"When I get out of these handcuffs—"

"Something tells me you won't have to worry about

much when you do," I replied, wrenching her up. Her legs shook, and I wondered if she was truly that good of an actress, or if she was more scared than she let on.

"I can hear your heart racing," I muttered quietly, barely a whisper.

"Back at you, Witch Hunter," Sasha replied in a hiss.

I took her biting tone for what it was.

We were both anxious, but neither of us was backing down.

For a long time, I'd sworn that I worked alone because partners held me back. As much as Sasha and I didn't see eye to eye, she had the grit to get the job done. I respected that, begrudgingly.

Stone steps loomed closer with every second. Whispers and shouts from Palmer Square made the air charged. Strangers meeting alone in the middle of the night was a dangerous gamble, whereas meeting beside a group of several hundred, if not a thousand people, was safer in some ways. No doubt the reason they'd chosen this place.

We climbed the steps, Sasha putting on an unwilling show. At the very top, I shoved her forward and kicked the back of her knees. They gave way, and she dropped. I clamped my hand over her shoulder once more, holding her down.

"There will be others," she said acidly. "They'll come looking for me." She was careful to avoid mentions of her sister, though anyone that had known Lucifer would likely be aware of Sienna's existence.

"Let them," I said haughtily. "I've hunted witches and demons alike. Do you think a little kitty cat scares me?" Mocking. Amused. Crushing.

My mouth felt dry, but the words that spewed from my lips were perfect.

We were perfect.

A figure approached off the sidewalk, clapping slowly.

Sasha's heartrate spiked and my own slowed. My hands warmed, and I wasn't sure if it was the fire in my blood or simply sweaty palms.

"Well, wasn't that a nice show," the stranger said with a southern drawl. Our mysterious renegade tipped his hand. The wind blew, pushing his hood back to reveal a head of sandy blonde hair.

Ah hell.

"Flint?" I demanded. "You're the seller?"

His way of answering was to pull back his jacket and draw a gun.

My stomach turned. I had a bad feeling about this.

"Yeah, Pipes. Which means I know that this"—he waved the hand with the gun toward us—"this is all a little show. I doubt those are real magic-bindin' cuffs."

That sinking feeling within me grew. Beside it, the sparks of anger flared.

I dropped my hand from Sasha's shoulder and stepped forward. "What the actual fuck, Flint?"

"Was it just a show between us too?" he asked, ignoring my question and following every movement of mine with his sharp gaze. "Or was it always this way?" The latter seemed aimed at himself more than me, but still, I answered.

"Was what always this way? You being fucking insane and thinking you can stalk me—"

"What are you?" His words stopped me cold. Five feet away, he aimed the gun at my chest. "You can't be human. I didn't want to believe it, but how could a human turn on their own kind? To work with a shifter, for this—" He nodded toward the gun. "I just don't get it. But then I thought about it real hard; all the stuff I've seen you do. The tight scrapes . . . I thought you were just that good. Maybe a little lucky. But now . . ." He tilted his head, making the insinuation clear. His brown eyes weren't warm as they once were, but instead suspicious and more than a little crazed.

Despite the gun pointed at me, I didn't truly want to hurt him.

"I'm human," I said with a straight face. His nose scrunched in disgust.

"Are you?" he asked. "Are you, really? Because the Piper I knew wouldn't live with a witch or share a bed with a demon. Wouldn't be *owned* by a demon. And you know what? I find it a little suspect that the demon seems to be downright *obsessed* with you. Lucifer was too, from what they say."

It seemed he'd finally figured out what Ronan was. I wondered when that happened. Or how he hadn't also pieced together the truth about me.

"Give me the gun, Flint," I repeated.

His eyes hardened. "It's true, then. You're one of them, aren't you?"

"I said, give me the gun—"

"Tell me the truth!" he shouted. If not for the gathering in the park, his voice might have rattled the windows. But drowned out by the buzzing of the crowd, it was just another angry human.

Albeit one with a gun.

"For fuck's sake, Piper, just take it—" Sasha didn't even finish speaking. He flicked his wrist and fired. A bolt of pure dark green energy shot out, closing the gap. It struck Sasha in the chest, and she slumped to the ground, her mouth open in a silent scream. Agony etched into every feature of her face.

"Last chance, Pipes. The truth." He turned the gun on me once more, a dark light entering his eyes as his fingers sharpened into nails. Her magic—that of a shifter and a succubus—coursed through him. And she was utterly incapacitated.

Nat was right. These weapons . . . they were dangerous, and not only to supes.

My lips parted. "You want the truth?" I took a step forward, and he took one back. Magic was building in my palms, dissolving the blue-toned contacts that hid my identity. "The truth is that you're fucking insane, and I don't know how I didn't see it. Were *you* always this way? Or is this because I didn't want to get married and be your wife, pregnant and barefoot in the kitchen?" Where the mocking nature of my show with Sasha bothered me, the ice and fire that battled in my veins right then was welcome.

His lips turned down at the corners, a disappointed frown.

"I gave you the chance to come clean. Guess I should've known you wouldn't take it. Bree was right. You always were a good liar."

Shock hit me harder than any gun, shattering my concentration.

He pulled the trigger.

And I came undone.

14
RONAN

I saw the gun, but I was too late. For all the magic in this world or the next, I couldn't get there fast enough because I thought she'd stop it. I thought she'd disarm him.

I thought she had it under control.

But then she didn't.

Shock permeated her face. I felt her emotions go from red hot to blistering cold; blindingly numb. It happened in a splinter of a second, but that was all it took for the bolt of dark green magic to slam into her chest at point-blank range.

The impact echoed through the city like thunder.

Clouds thickened, and the wind blew.

A storm unlike any other New Chicago had experienced was starting, and Piper was the cause of it. On her knees, bent at the waist, I felt her magic rage in a way it hadn't before.

I stepped through the void and re-entered at her side.

Fire sparked in that step. White flames eating away at her guise.

They started at her fingers. Little sparks. Mere embers. They flickered to life and grew in her outstretched palms.

Across from her, the shooter seized. The gun fell from his hand as fire started to eat at him too.

"What's happening?" he exclaimed. Wild. Erratic. I recognized the face of Flint Daniels. Piper's former lover. The human I gave a warning to instead of killing when I had a chance. "What did you do? What is—" His voice broke off suddenly, seizing shut as my hand wrapped around his throat.

He shot her. And something was very, very wrong as a result.

I dived into his mind, tearing through the surface of it to understand what happened.

I was only partway through. Only beginning to understand what that weapon was when a pained laugh made my blood turn to ice.

"She really hates me," Piper said softly. "And you fell right for it." She coughed, then tilted her head back to take in a ragged breath. "You should have let it go. Walked away."

Her eyes turned a darker shade of violet. Flames raced up her arms, eating away at the long-sleeved turtleneck to reveal her crimson brands.

Fire started to eat away at him too. White flames licked at his skin, burning through the heavy fabric of his coats. It didn't seem to hurt him, but I knew it was coming. There was no stopping it when a human took on too much magic and their system couldn't acclimatize to it.

Brands surfaced. The marks of a demon. His were white and started appearing delicately, but slowly widened. The skin splitting everywhere they touched.

I released him, taking a step back to stare.

"What is this?" Flint demanded, staring at his flame-covered hands. "What the—"

"He's a supe!" someone declared. "He has magic!" another voice said. Footsteps sounded, drawing closer as the humans in the square finally took notice.

"You wanted to know what I am," Piper said quietly. Still on her hands and knees, completely naked, the red brands of her body glowed angrily. "You were so *desperate* to know that you made one massive mistake—you shot me and took some of my magic. Now you're going to die for it."

The words hardly left her lips when the splitting skin began to bleed. Gaping wounds formed as his blood dripped from them. The fire continued to burn, growing hotter. More malevolent.

"They're both supes! Look at em'! They're on fire—" The words cut off as flames started to spew from the injuries. It trickled down his skin, falling to the stone dais of the steps where it continued to burn. To ravage.

Holes formed in the rock. Cracks appeared, fire emitting from them too.

He began to shake. To tremble.

White light built behind his eyes as he looked down at himself and took in the severity of what he'd done.

"What are you?" he wheezed, a painful, pitiful rasp. *"What are you?"*

Piper stared. Her eyes damning and crimson red as they took him in.

Then she whispered.

"I am rage."

Lightning struck, followed by a crack of thunder so loud it seemed as if the earth itself had split.

"Run!" someone yelled at the top of their lungs. I wasn't certain who, though the voice sounded familiar. They scrambled in fear, fleeing down the streets and alleys, away from the ticking time bomb that was Flint Daniels.

The clouds opened up, releasing a torrent of rain so thick not even I could see more than several meters in front of me.

And still, both of them burned.

Both of them raged, too far gone for words. Fire burned in their eyes, on their skin, through their brands. One of them dying and the other rendered immobile by whatever power that gun possessed to steal her magic.

"He's going to blow," a weak voice rasped, barely loud enough to be heard over the storm. "The place I went to. The one you pulled us out of. It wasn't this world. Take him—"

"It won't work," I said. "The void is still of this world. It's the darkness that exists between one shadow and the next. If he releases there, the impacts will be further reaching."

"They're going to be far reaching now," the cat shifter uttered. "Last time she killed five thousand people—" A fact that hadn't escaped me and something I wasn't going to allow to happen again if there were another choice.

"We can still stop it."

"How?" she demanded.

"Piper will need to reabsorb the magic the human took."

"That's the only way?" she asked, breathing heavily.

"Yes." The only way I was willing. Only someone that could contain it had to absorb the magic. There were only two of us that could. Piper or me.

She could because it was her magic.

I could because I was the Harvester.

The stealer of magic. Of souls.

Any other being and I would do it. I would not leave the lives of so many my atma cared for to chance . . . except I wouldn't do it to her.

To take her magic—it was something I couldn't risk.

"It's the only way," I said to the shifter.

Her green cat eyes flashed between the three of us in doubt, though she didn't question it. "Then we're fucked." She sat back on her haunches, real and tangible fear in her eyes. "She can't hear us anymore. She's too far gone—"

I didn't have time for this, and neither did she.

My knees dropped onto the burning stone. Water rained down, turning to steam as soon as it touched the ground. It swirled around us, blocking out the rest of the world.

I put one hand on Piper's shoulder and used the other to guide her face up.

The being that stared back at me was her and yet not.

When stripped bare, down to her very essence, all of her humanity had fallen away.

The smooth skin beneath my fingers burned. It *burned. Me.*

Her atman.

The power she wielded for that to even be possible . . . I couldn't bring myself to think on it. Not when there was so much on the brink of being lost.

"Piper," I said her name once. A demand. A pull at the woman buried beneath the pain. But she didn't so much as blink.

Behind me, the bastard who caused this was screaming bloody murder as the fire ate him alive. We had moments. Maybe minutes at most.

"Atma," I growled, desperation leaking into my voice.

Her eyes flicked upward, still blank of emotion. Still flaming. Still the deepest red I'd ever seen them.

"You need to fight this." She blinked and my frustration grew. My hands tightened. "Pull the fire back in. Consume it. Retake it. The magic is yours—"

Her lips parted, trying to move. I couldn't make out the words.

With a growl, I crossed the bridge between our minds. But her end was walled off. Enclosed in fire. It burned to even be near it, let alone attempt to cross the blazing barrier.

But I had to try.

Mentally, I plunged one hand through the flames and a very real fire burned away at my skin. The hand touching her face blackened in the physical realm. Then charred. Pieces broke away; pieces of both my body and soul fractured as her power manifested a very real fire that burned me.

Water built in her eyes, though the blankness remained. A single tear spilled over, turning to steam when it hit the ground.

I stilled myself for what would come if I could not reach her.

If I was not enough—

A hand clasped mine back.

In the flames.

Though her mind was closed, she was fighting it. She was trying.

"He took part of me, Ronan," she said through the flickering streams of white. "I can't move. The pain—" Her voice broke, and she shuddered.

"Piper!" another voice yelled through the downpour. My atma's face turned stricken in her mind.

"Nathalie." Panic blossomed. "She can't be here. I can't stop it—"

"You can. You will," I said both aloud and in her head. "All you have to do is reach for it. Pull it in. The magic knows who its master is. That's why he cannot contain it. That's why it's raging. It needs you, Piper. You have to take it back." I squeezed her hand tight in mine. My arm healing at the same rate it was burning. The blackened skin fell away to new flesh, then died once more. A never-ending cycle of life and death.

For her, I'd endure it.

I'd endure anything.

"How?" she said softly. "I cannot calm it. It won't allow itself to be calmed. Not now."

"Then embrace it."

"And then what happens? When it needs an outlet? When it needs a way to *rage*—"

"I will be here—to take it. Just as I promised. Just as I am now."

We looked to our hands, twined in the flame.

No other in this universe or the next would be able to withstand the heart of her fire. It was too hot. Too raw. Too ... her.

Just as the void existed between one shadow and the next, there was also another place. One so brilliant and blinding and burning that the only way to find it was to create it. Where the void existed independently of me or the shifter, or any other that could access it, this place came from the soul. From power itself. From light and creation.

It was that place that she called upon as she took the fire back.

That place that answered only to her.

Just as Flint Daniels imploded, Piper took it back. She took it all back.

And the walls in her mind parted. Not to come crashing down, but to let me in.

I took a step. Just one, but that was all I needed to cross the threshold.

The doorway slammed shut behind me.

15
NATHALIE

My boots slapped the concrete, sending water splashing. My socks were soaked, squishing uncomfortably with every step, and my toes had already gone numb.

But I kept running.

I kept fighting.

Because I had to find her.

"Piper!" I screamed again. My voice had gone raw from all the coughing that came after inhaling too much rain.

Water hit my face like a cold slap, plastering my wet hair to my skin. It was only because of my memory of this city that I knew which way to go. Which way she went.

Stairs appeared before me. Only feet away.

I tried to take them two at a time, and bit it. My soles slipped, and I went tumbling forward. Falling. Flailing. My body tilted forward, and my eyes screwed shut as I waited for the cold ground to rise up and greet me.

It never did.

Hands grabbed my shoulders, claws pressing into my skin. My head canted forward and then shot back from whiplash.

I groaned, my eyes snapping open.

Tilting my head back, I looked straight into Sasha's stricken face. "Where is she?" I breathed, trying to see around her body—though the monsoon prevented it.

Stupid witch vision, I cursed internally. Piper may not like being a demon, but there were more perks than being a witch. I could control all the magic in the world, but I couldn't see more than three feet in front of me.

Some might say it was me that drew the short stick.

It was me. I was 'some'.

"I don't know," Sasha said calmly. My palms slapped against the steps, holding my weight so I could lift myself up. Her claws retracted as she dropped her arms.

"You don't know?" I repeated. "She was right there—" I pointed at the spot on the steps, where I knew it to be even if I couldn't see it. "Her and Ronan. Right there. Where did they go?"

"I don't know," Sasha repeated. "The bastard meeting with us shot her and took her magic. He started leaking fire everywhere and then the storm came . . . I think Ronan convinced her to reabsorb the magic and then took her away."

I lifted my eyebrows. "Through the void?"

"Again," Sasha growled, starting to get annoyed with my line of questioning. "I don't know. Everything went white, and when it cleared, they were gone."

My breathing steadied as I reminded myself who she was with.

Ronan would never let anything happen to her.

Come Hell or highwater, or even a monsoon—she would be safe.

Which meant we needed to get out of here.

"Where's the contact? I saw him drop, but nothing

after."

Sasha's expression was grave, but not pitying. Silently, she pointed to another spot only a few feet away. I stepped around her, taking the last two steps.

When I was directly on top of it, I turned in circles—but there was nothing there. Not a body or bones or even ashes to speak of.

I squinted at the stone dais in front of the cathedral. Fissures ran through the stone that weren't there before, leading to a set of handprints.

Burned into the ground were what I could assume were his final moments.

Now they were all that remained.

I couldn't bring myself to feel sad any more than Sasha could, given that he shot Piper.

"He knew her," the shifter said. "Somehow. They had a history. He kept going on about it and I told her to just take the damn gun to shut him up. Then he shot me."

I stared at those handprints for a few more seconds.

"Flint," I said. "They were old friends. Once. He's not a fan of our kind."

When I looked back up at Sasha, she was giving me a look that said, *no shit*.

"Where's the gun?" I asked, turning away from her to search.

"Don't know," she called back, disappearing into the wall of rain. "I tried to find it and came across you instead."

Tires squealed. A door slammed shut. I turned in the direction of the noise—only barely able to make out the outline of my car.

"You're late," I yelled through the rain.

"You try driving in this and not hitting anyone," Sienna called back. "Did you see the number of protesters?" Her question was rhetorical, but a shudder worked itself up my spine. I hadn't just seen it. I'd been in the heart of it.

While the twins' ears and tails would always give them away, I was just a witch—and a fairly unknown one at that. No one gave me a second look as I stood among them, chanting for freedom and equality. No one realized how unsettling it was to listen to speaker after speaker talk about change. How supernaturals lost their chance to give it to them by choice, and that they would take it.

What they failed to see was that in war, everyone loses. Not just us.

The number of supernaturals in New Chicago had been decimated from Lucifer's death and the subsequent death of his magic—but there were still witches out there. Still shifters and vampires and fae. There were still demons, and I knew better than almost anyone the lengths Ronan would go to if they proved to be too much of a threat to Piper.

"It's not here," Sasha groused. "It's not as if the prick could have thrown it. He dropped it and then exploded."

"Maybe it was destroyed with him?" Sienna questioned.

"Maybe," I murmured, pushing the wet strands of hair from my face. My fingers had pruned minutes ago and were now turning blue at the tips. "But we need to keep looking."

"It's raining like crazy," Sasha said. "You can't even see and I'm telling you, we've looked everywhere it could be. Either it was destroyed with him, doing our job for us, or it disappeared with Piper."

My eyes scanned the cold, watery steps, but she was right.

"If we're wrong and it falls into the wrong hands . . ." I let my voice trail, and a clap of thunder shook the city overhead, as if some angry god were looking down and chose to answer my unspoken worry.

"Let's come back when the storm lets up. We can look again," Sienna suggested.

I took a stiff inhale of the cold air and nodded. "All right, but we come back as soon as the storm lets up. Just to make sure."

As we made our way back to my car, still parked in the middle of the street—I could have sworn I saw a figure in the rain, standing at the edge of the road.

He was tall with broad shoulders. I couldn't make him out entirely, but the hint of gold that caught my eye made me freeze.

I squinted. My heart raced.

One second passed. Then two.

"Nat?" Sienna questioned, coming up to my side. "You okay?"

I jumped. "Yeah, yeah . . . I'm fine. Just thought I saw something."

She gave me a slight smile and threw an arm around my shoulders. "Come on. Let's get you home before you catch a cold."

I gave her a tight-lipped smile back and followed her, stealing one last glance over my shoulder. The figure was gone, but an arrogant chuckle followed me. Taunted me. Baited me. I knew it well.

Almost better than my own voice.

Water soaked my seats as I sidled into the passenger side, letting Sienna drive since she could see far better. The heater blasted, warming my numb hands—but nothing could lift the chill inside me.

For months, I'd been hearing him.

Whispered words. Quiet laughs.

But tonight, there was no mistaking it. No dismissing it.

He wasn't a stranger at all.

16

PIPER

I'd never experienced pain like that. Not even when Lucifer died.

Not when Bree was taken from me, or my parents were killed.

It was as if every atom of my being had been ripped apart, and only in accepting the pain, did I fuse back together. But the pieces of me . . . they writhed. Twisted.

They wanted blood for what was done.

Vengeance.

I stumbled back from Ronan, a shudder running through me. My blood heated. I screwed my eyes shut, trying to pull it taut. To confine it, though I knew it wouldn't allow me to.

"What do you need?" His voice was a lifeline in the ocean. A drop of water in the flames.

"I . . ." The words got stuck in my throat as I took in the blinding white that surrounded us. It wasn't the void. I knew that. Neither was it New Chicago.

It was something else.

"Where are we?" I whispered, eyes wide for fear that

maybe this was Hell. Or somewhere like it. Who was to say how many worlds existed? Or if I'd somehow found my way into another one.

"I believe it's the opposite of the void," Ronan said, slowly stepping closer. Watching me like I was a caged predator he didn't want to spook. "You're my opposite. My flames burn black and yours are white—pure white. This place is the opposite of darkness or cold. It feels like—"

"Burning," I said for him. "It hurts but doesn't."

He nodded. "I think that somehow you brought us here."

"Me?" I questioned, looking around. "I don't know where 'here' is. I didn't even know that another place like the void existed. I've never felt it before."

"Neither did I," Ronan said, taking another step. It didn't escape my notice he was slowly closing the distance I'd created.

"You think I brought us here, though?" I questioned, trying to ignore the fevered swelter running through me as my magic screamed for me to do something—anything—to let it back out.

"I know you did," he replied. "This place tastes of you. It feels like you. The magic that created it is yours." He loomed closer, and I took another step back. Ronan's silver eyes narrowed. "My father was the first to step through the void, passing the ability on to me and Lucifer. Perhaps you're the first to step through the light."

I turned, striding away despite the lack of a floor. The frenzied energy within me was coiling around my bones. It pressed on my organs, threatening to crush them. It wanted out. Out. Out. Out—

A cool hand grabbed my wrist, pulling my arm taut. He

snapped me back to him. My other hand landing against this chest. Our faces only inches apart.

"What do you *need*?" he repeated.

I swallowed hard.

"Out," I whispered. "I can't deal with this right now. I need—" My fingers curled into claws, my nails cutting through his shirt, pricking his skin. A single droplet of blood welled, drawing every ounce of my attention.

"Piper," Ronan said, trying to startle me. Slowly, I lifted my eyes, tongue sweeping out to lick my bottom lip. My teeth pressed down on it as I tried to stifle my own urges. "If you want out, you have to let us out."

My eyes drifted, slowly wandering back toward—

"Piper," he growled my name again. This time with heat. Hunger. "Focus." He leaned forward, lips brushing against the hollow shell of my ear. "Think of a way out. Imagine it. *See* it."

I quivered.

Legs shaking with desire, hands trembling with the need to restrain myself. My whole body shook, at odds with itself. At war.

"I need out," I repeated, swallowing hard. "But I don't know how."

"It's like opening a door," Ronan said slowly, lips trailing down the bare skin of my neck. "Reach through the light to where you want to be. Feel it." Rough hands grasped my hips, holding me steady. Grounding me. "*Believe* it."

I let my eyes fall closed and tentatively reached with my mind, still not knowing what exactly I was reaching toward, but trying all the same. I imagined myself breaking through the light, shattering it like glass, and appearing—

"Open your eyes."

My eyelids lifted, taking in the dark room, silken sheets, and a long window. The blinds were wide open, revealing a thunderous night sky. Thick clouds and heavy rain. Lightning flashed, the bolt pure and white, sending my heart racing.

A clap of thunder shook Ronan's penthouse.

I blinked, attention returning to him.

"Why are we in your apartment?" My voice came out raw. Hoarse. Full of need. Part of me wanted to kick myself for sounding like that.

The rest of me was so damn tired of fighting it.

"You tell me," he answered. "I'm not the one that brought us here."

His eyes were knowing, but his words were leading. Guiding. Seeking.

"I see," I said quietly, my eyes slowly trailing over his chest—back to that single drop of blood.

My head tilted. My body leaned. My tongue—

"I'm only going to ask you this one more time, Piper," Ronan said in a pained voice. "What do you need?"

The world could've ended. The storm could have stopped. Any number of things could have happened in that silence that passed between us—and I never would have known it.

Because from the moment we appeared in this room, I knew exactly what I wanted. Needed. My magic did too. For once, we were in agreement.

Reparations had to be paid in blood, and if I couldn't end Flint all over again, then there was only one other way I could work out the rage. One other option that I could embrace. That I could trust.

"You," I whispered.

Ronan was a demon. He didn't show emotion easily.

But there was something in his eyes at my confession. It wasn't just possessiveness or obsession. It wasn't simply victory. It went deeper than any of that. More primal than even the bond between us. More visceral than the fire pounding in my veins.

True to his word, he didn't ask again.

The hands at my waist gripped tight enough to bruise. A fucked-up part of me wanted it to. Not to simply feel pain, but because I wanted to feel needed. Not simply desired, but *needed*.

His lips came down on mine. Hard. Demanding. He took everything I gave him and then took some more. His teeth nipped, and he licked and then he sucked as I parted my lips all too willingly.

We kissed until air ran out, but we didn't stop. We inhaled; breathing—except it was each other that we were taking in. Absorbing. Our magic mingled and touched and merged. Twining tighter and tighter around us, trying to bind so thoroughly that we'd never be separated again.

At some point the back of my legs hit the bed. Instead of collapsing back, I gripped where his neck met his shoulders and pivoted—pushing him.

I wasn't sure if he let me, or if I was truly that strong. Neither of us seemed to care when he hit the mattress and I climbed on top of him. Ronan sat up, not willing to relinquish his hold on me—even as I tried to push the jacket from his shoulders.

A growl built in my throat.

Savage. Inhuman.

Then he bit me.

Without preempt or warning, his fangs pressed into the flesh of my throat. The tiny prickle of pain immediately washed out by the building desire between us.

My head fell back, but I didn't see the ceiling as stars formed in my vision.

My body convulsed and my channel clenched. Empty and hollow, I came just from him tasting me.

When the roaring in my ears settled, I heard the growls coming from him. Felt their vibrations where his lips met my skin. His hands slid down my waist to grip my ass and thighs. Pointed nails, dragging along the skin to elicit tiny slices. My blood perfumed the air around us. Heady and intoxicated to him, doubly more so because our minds were wide open to each other, and he could feel everything I did. Every pulse. Every shiver.

Every lick of flame.

My knees pressed into the soft sheets as I ground down, my slick center brushing over his slack-clad bulge.

"Stop toying with me," I rasped, pressing down harder, eliciting another growl. He drew back, releasing my skin with a pop, and then licked the smeared blood from my neck.

"It's not toying." His voice was deep and guttural. "I'm *savoring*."

I fisted my hands in his hair, twining them through the dark locks, then I pulled tight. His head tilted back. Silver eyes illuminated in the dark room, swirling with unearthly power.

"I don't want to be savored," I said softly, holding his gaze. He lifted an eyebrow in silent question. "I want to be ruined."

Still, he didn't drop his arms away so I could remove his jacket.

Still, he stared at me, expression unreadable.

I kissed him hard. Aggressive. Demanding. My teeth bit and my tongue licked. He gave in to me, but he didn't move.

Frustration built in me. I released his hair, my hands dropping to his collar. Without worry or regard, I grabbed either side and then pulled.

Buttons popped. Fabric ripped. My hands greedily moved down the planes of his chest. Tracing where I knew his brands to be. I wanted to feel them. To feel—

He pulled back.

"I've already ruined you." His words were sudden, muttered against my lips as I kissed him like my life depended on it. "You hate to hear it, but the truth of the matter is that you're mine, Piper. Your blood knows it. Your magic knows it. Even you know it. There's no one else for you anymore. The minute I stepped into this world, those options ceased to exist."

"How arrogant," I said coldly, despite the warmth I felt.

He chuckled. "Tell me, would a human male ever truly interest you?" My insides twisted violently. The wicked glint in his eye told me he knew. Somehow that bastard knew. "What about another supernatural? A werewolf? Maybe a vampire? They share our penchant for blood and biting." Still my magic writhed, and it wasn't alone.

"Are you trying to push me away? Talking about all my other options when you finally have what you want? I'm here, in your bed, willing and wanting, but—"

"Admit it," he said, utterly serious. My lips pressed together in a hard line. I wanted to tell the truth. To whisper that part of me reveled when he called me *his*. That my blood soared when he touched me.

But my stubbornness caught the words in my throat.

Hands gripped me harder, the pressure turning punishing. My core clenched.

"Why? You have what you wanted—"

"No," he said instantly. "I don't. Not yet." His words

stilled something in me. I lifted my head. "You don't want to be ruined. You already have been. You want to ruin me. To rage. To take what you want and walk away—so you can feel like we're somehow even."

I sat back, trying to put a tiny bit of space between us, but he wasn't having it. His next words took the fight out of me.

"But we're not because you already own me." My lips parted, but he kept speaking. "All I want is you. All I *need* is you. Your blood. Your wicked smile and silver tongue. Your rage. I need it all, Piper. I'm laying it out here and now—for you." My heart thundered in my ears, but his voice was all I heard. All I wanted to hear. "You're afraid because everyone else has left, but I'm never going to leave—even if you want me to." The latter confession was dark. Deep. It should have scared me away.

It should have.

But I wasn't the only one that was broken.

And maybe, just maybe, his pieces could fit in between the gaps where sections of mine went missing.

"There's this thing inside me," I said quietly. "It's wild. Vicious. I get angry and it lashes out. I feel pain and it burns the world around me. I couldn't trust it around anyone—my magic—because they can't withstand it. Then you came along, a demon in the night. Someone that saw it when no one else did; someone that wanted to feel the burn. That could withstand the fire. I didn't want to believe it, because to believe it meant I had to admit that I wasn't human anymore. That my wants and needs and desires weren't all human—and that the only person that could fill them was you."

I traced the lines of his brands with my nails—staring at that expanse of muscle and skin instead of his face.

"Look at me, Piper." I didn't. I couldn't—

Until his hand released my hip to cup my throat, his calloused thumb running over it, along my jaw, to the tip of my chin. He pushed up, and my head was forced to move.

"Admit it."

Somehow I knew he was only going to say it once, and my answer was pivotal. It was earth shattering. Life changing.

It was everything.

And I was done fighting it.

"I'm yours," I whispered. "Yours to fuck. Yours to kiss. Yours to drink." I lifted my hand to his throat in the same way he'd done to mine. My fingers wrapped around it, not able to go as far, but I gripped what I had. "But more importantly—you're *mine*."

Black fire reflected in his eyes; the only sign that his control was straining.

"The cold to my hot. The dark in my light. I called you here, and you came. I needed you tonight, and you were there." My fingers squeezed, feeling the drum of his pulse as I spoke. "I'm still broken and trying to figure it out. My head is fucked six ways from Sunday. I grew up in a war-torn world and it's shaped me. Molded me. I'm only twenty-six, a blip in your very, *very* long life. I have a lot to learn. A lot of wrongs to right. But I also have forever to do it." My chest constricted as some emotion squeezed the air from my lungs. It took everything in me to squeeze out the last two words. "With you."

His control snapped.

Ronan pulled me to him, and our lips met first. My fangs nicked his bottom lip, and I sucked it between mine.

And then everything went red.

Lust addled my brain as my magic also reached its

breaking point. But it didn't burn. There were no flames. No fire or smoke.

Because they existed within us.

With my free hand, I slipped it just an inch under his slacks and belt, then pulled. The leather snapped. The fabric ripped. His boxers tore.

Then his cock nudged at my entrance as it came free.

I reached between my legs, holding him tight as I slid down his length. My head rocked forward, lips parted in a silent moan. Ronan thrust up, filling me fully.

I nearly climaxed.

My back arched, and I brought myself up to come back down, seeking that delicious friction. Trying desperately to find a way to ease the fever in my soul.

He let go of my ass and reached up to grab my hand. I frowned, part of me still wanting to fight it, and the rest of me curious where he was taking this.

"You said you wanted to be ruined." He took my hand and brought it behind my back, then grabbed my other, and put them together, holding them in place by my locked wrists. "Let me show you," he whispered, pulling tight. My back arched as my arms bent. Tiny bits of pain shot through my shoulders, but the position was more uncomfortable than anything—and prevented me from taking him.

He took my breast in his mouth and began to suck. From below me, his cock thrust up, filling me fully and then pulling out. I gasped at the sudden movement and his grip on my throat tightened, not completely cutting off air, but creating pressure.

Somehow I doubted the lack of oxygen would kill me anyway, and it was Ronan, which took any fear away.

Ronan thrust up again while he whorled his tongue around my nipple. I tried to take in a breath, but nothing came in at first. My pulse sped up. My body tensed. He changed his grip for a fraction of a second as he pulled out, and then repeated it.

The power play turned me on, but the fire in his eyes as he did it?

That was my undoing.

Minutes turned to hours, or at least it felt like it as he brought me right to the edge and then took it away.

Just when frustration was getting too much. My body strung too tight. The rage in me riled too far. He said, "Come for me, Piper."

Breath flooded my lungs as he pumped into me, pushing me over the edge.

Light built behind my eyes. My body coiled, and then released violently.

"Atman," I choked out. He rode me through it, filling me fast and urgent as I spasmed around him. When the tremors died and my eyes fluttered open, he released my arms and dropped the hand from my throat, resting it on my thigh. He was still hard as steel inside me.

"That's what I wanted," he said. His free hand came up, and he put his finger and thumb together, holding my face only inches from his. "Now get on your back and spread your legs. I want to taste you."

"But you—"

"We have time for me. Right now your magic is fighting to stay contained. It needs to be fed. I'm going to fuck you until the red drains from your eyes."

I slid off of him and rolled onto my back.

All my life, I couldn't trust another with my body or my magic. But it wasn't either of those that worried me as he fell to his knees. No, as Ronan worshipped me for my admission—it was my very soul that I felt myself losing.

Because in matters of the heart, control didn't exist. Logic didn't matter.

Only feeling.

And for him?

I burned.

17
RONAN

"*It's been three days,*" the witch grumbled. Since taking both my and Piper's blood, she'd honed the ability to communicate with me at will—and shield her mind from all other thoughts in the process. "*How much 'rage' can she possibly have to work out?*" If not for the fact the aforementioned 'she' was currently asleep in *my* bed, her intrusion wouldn't have been nearly so amusing. As it was, the corner of my mouth curled up in a smug, satisfied grin.

"*She's asleep now,*" I answered, downing another glass of water. I stood at the bathroom door watching the slight rise and fall of her chest, unable to pull myself from her for very long. Not after her admission and what followed. "*I think it's passed. We'll see when she wakes up.*"

"*I'm beginning to think you kidnapped her for some kinky sexcapade,*" Nathalie said suspiciously. "*Normally, I'd be all for it if it means she's not blowing holes in my walls, but we've got another job—*"

"*Your last job nearly had her leveling half the city,*" I said curtly. If she were someone else, I might have stepped in and ended this little employment opportunity. Found a way to divert her attentions and then separate Piper from the problem. But Nathalie Le Fay would not be easily dissuaded from this mission of hers. She was stubborn to the bone, much like Piper in that way.

Still, I might have tried to find a way, were she not my atma's best friend and closest confidant.

"What happened in the square was a mistake. One I won't be repeating."

"Good," I replied, convinced by the gristle in her tone. *"You won't mind telling me what this job is that you need her for, then."*

I pressed on the barrier surrounding her mind, and it gave a little zap of warning. Nathalie laughed coolly. *"You should know better than to test me. Piper's magic protects me."*

"She's my atma."

"And my best friend. She also gave me an explicit order that she doesn't want me reporting to you where it concerns her. Which means I can't, even if I wanted to—which I don't."

I let out a growl that she heard through the link between our minds.

Windchimes pealed again as she laughed.

At me.

Part of me was beguiled by it. The rest of me simply irked.

Piper's breathing paused, then resumed. Her muscles were no longer languid and at ease, though she tried to appear that way, pretending she was still sleeping.

The rage had truly passed.

Now it was time to contend with the woman.

"I'll let you know when she wakes," I lied. If the witch wanted to keep secrets, two could play at that game.

"*Hmm*," came her hummed reply. It almost made me grin that she doubted it. The uneasiness I sensed from the woman in my bed dampening my smugness from before.

I cut the connection and set the empty glass aside.

The clink of it touching the counter made her stiffen.

My lips pressed together, not liking the start to this morning.

"I know you're awake."

My footsteps were silent as I padded across the polished wood floors, but she sensed me with every step as I drew near. The bed sank with my weight and I leaned over. My fingertips brushed along her bare shoulder.

"Regrets already?" I murmured, unable to keep the bitterness from my tone. "It's not even nine. I would have thought you'd want coffee first." Patience. I needed patience with her. Considering the circumstances, I couldn't expect the words she told me to be—

"No." Her words stilled me. "No regrets."

Piper rolled as she sat up. The thin sheet covering her slid to her waist. My cock hardened at the sight of her. Every bruise had long since healed. The only part of her skin still marred were the places I bit. Those would take longer.

In the time I spent appraising her body, I hadn't realized she'd been doing the same. Taking in my brands and her marks.

"You're not healed." It wasn't a question, but the frown that helped punctuate it sounded like one.

"Neither are you," I said, reaching out to run my thumb around one particularly deep bite on the side of her breast. "While we heal from all things, there's venom in our bite."

"Venom?" She brought a hand up to run down the

length of her shorter fangs, more retracted now that the magic had settled.

"Lethal to most. An aphrodisiac to our mates. It allows the bite to stay longer." Much to my enjoyment. "A few weeks at most."

She nodded slowly. I wasn't sure if it was grogginess or something deeper that made her so pensive, if it wasn't regret.

"Does that bother you?" I asked.

"No," she answered again, then pushed the sheet aside and stood up. In the early morning light, her brands still glowed a faint red. Whirling lines and twisted runes starting at the hollow of her back and climbing all the way to her neck, then branching down her shoulders. She lifted her mane of golden hair and tied it back in a high ponytail, her shoulders and back flexing the entire time. "I keep my body covered anyway."

Her second remark made me frown; something dark slithering up.

"You'd prefer to hide them."

She turned her cheek, eyeing me from the side. "Yes," she said in utter seriousness. "I would."

And that was that.

She moved around the bed, almost at ease. If not for her strange mood, I could pretend that this was normal.

But it wasn't.

"I'm going to take a shower," she said. "Do you have anything I can wear until I get back to the apartment?"

I watched her for a moment as she milled at the bathroom door. After a few seconds, her impatience showed, and she turned back, lifting a golden eyebrow in challenge. "Well?"

I motioned to the closet door. "Help yourself."

She looked from me to the door and then back. "All right."

With that, she closed the door. The shower started a few moments later.

I could tell she hadn't waited for it to heat because the glass door opened without preempt and the sound of the spray changed. Her heart shuddered in her chest, but she still doused herself.

I strode toward the door, tempted to enter. To push her.

My hand reached for the knob and then closed.

I walked away, leaving her in the bathroom, and started on breakfast. Her response when she saw the closet would be telling.

That thought gave me anticipation as I cracked eggs over a bowl and then beat them with a fork. This task was menial, and not so long ago I would have considered it beneath me. But this morning, with her in my shower, it was anything but.

I started the frying pan and drizzled oil, then turned to the fridge to see what fruit I had. She liked fruit. I recalled that from some of the memories I'd stolen. I kept a stock of it here at all times, despite the fact she hadn't visited but twice in the last six weeks. Once because I brought her here. The other, because she did.

I busied myself with cutting up a pineapple when the water turned off.

A slow smile dragged its way up my lips when she opened the bathroom door.

Water dripped onto the hardwood floors as she crossed them.

The closet lock unlatched.

Then silence.

I paused. I waited. It was only when the eggs started to burn that I focused on the task at hand. I was just plating the food when she stepped out of my bedroom. I pretended not to notice.

"Ronan."

My name on her lips was a plea not long ago. A prayer. Now it was the sultry call of a siren, but not one that was trying.

I lifted my head and took in the cream sweater and blue jeans that fit a little too loose despite their slim style.

I waited for the admonishment. The rebuke. After this morning, I had no doubt it was coming. Not that I particularly cared.

Softer eyes than when she'd entered the bathroom were not what I expected.

"Thank you."

She didn't say what for, but we both knew. Half of the closet was clothes for her. In her exact size. In styles and colors I thought she'd like.

Piper wasn't attached to clothes like some women, particularly the witch, who had assisted me with online shopping. It was both a dated and yet advanced concept. She handled navigating the websites while I picked pieces I thought Piper would feel comfortable in. Things I thought she'd pick for herself. Nathalie's disdain at the time notwithstanding.

"The witch helped," I said, not sure entirely what to say as she walked around the room to meet me in the kitchen.

Piper laughed quietly. "Of course she did."

The smile on her face was real, genuine, but still tainted.

I set the plates down on the high bar and turned to face her. "You don't regret it, but you act like you do. You don't mind the marks, but you want them hidden. You say thank you, but the sad fucking look on your face makes me think that when you walk out that door you have no intention of coming back." I couldn't contain the darkness slithering in my veins as it began to eat at me, pulsing with anger and frustration despite the way she coaxed it so easily.

Instead of pretending or lying to me, Piper sighed.

"It's not that," she said, shaking her head. I lifted an eyebrow, waiting for more. For some kind of answer. She looked away, considering her words, and then she started speaking. "I can't remember a time when I woke up so at ease. Not just content, but . . . more, somehow. But then I remembered. I was shot. My sister was a demon. The humans are rioting . . . I remembered to feel guilty."

When she looked back at me, there was a vulnerability there that she'd rarely shown me before. "I meant everything I said. I do need you, and I can't keep fighting that. I want to," she admitted. It hurt. That truth. "But that's because I want to punish myself. To drown the guilt. To feel like I'm paying my dues for the things I've done. Part of me hates it, this." She motioned to the clothes she wore and then to me. "That I'm too fucking weak to walk away anymore. But the rest of me . . ." She trailed, one hand clenched into a fist at her side, knuckles white. Blood scented the air a moment later, and I knew she cut herself. "The rest of me is beyond caring because I'm so tired of feeling guilty and unworthy and carrying this weight around when its only purpose is to hold me down."

I couldn't feel all the things she spoke of. But I wanted to crush every person and thing that made her feel that way all the same. My heart wasn't capable of breaking. But my fist knew how to smash. My mind knew how to manipulate and maneuver. My magic knew how to destroy, and that's what I wanted. To end them for what they'd done to her.

The humans and the supernaturals.

They were all to blame.

"I want to move on. To let it go. But I don't know how when I have guilt shackling me on one side and rage on the other. I don't know how to help the humans any more than I do the supes. I don't know what to do about Bree when I can't stomach the things *I know* she's doing—because of me. Because I brought her back against her will and made her stay. And then Flint—"

"He deserved his death," I said, refusing to let her blame herself for his choices. Angry that she would even consider it.

"He did," she agreed. "He chose to shoot me. But in doing so he almost killed so many people. I don't mind killing when it's called for. It's a dog-eat-dog world. But they didn't ask for it. Neither did the people in the Underworld. Or the millions that died across the states almost three months ago."

"That's not your fault, and it's not on you to hold yourself to it," I told her. "People died because Lucifer decided you were his and forced a bond that shouldn't have been made. They died because the Le Fays were a power-hungry horde that thought sacrificing a demon wouldn't have consequences."

"And after Flint shot me, the only reason no one died is because you were there to take the brunt of it." Her eyes flicked down to the hand that had burned and charred and broken. My brands were black by nature, but on that hand, Piper's magic had marked me for withstanding her fire, creating red intricate etchings in my skin.

"Your magic was ripped from you. Not all of it, but enough that there was no stopping it. Rest assured, if the roles had been switched—you're the only one that could bring me out of it—and I would level far more than New Chicago," I uttered.

The hairs on her arms rose, but her violet eyes remained steely. Her back straight.

"The fact of the matter remains that I'm drowning. Even when I kick, the waves are too high. Even when you part the waves for me, you can't do it indefinitely. Eventually they return and I drown all over again." Her eyes turned vacant as if looking far off at something I couldn't see. I took two steps forward, closing the distance between us.

"Then don't just try to stay afloat. Learn to swim and to part the waves for yourself. If you want the guilt to go away, you have to choose it. Choose to forgive yourself for the things that weigh on you. Choose to accept the parts of you that aren't perfect. You admitted that you have a lot of learning to do. Wrongs you want to right. You don't have to do it overnight."

Her eyes refocused, and she tilted her head. For a moment, I felt that thing within her look out. A hint of red touching her purple eyes. But when she blinked, it cleared.

"You're right," she said quietly. "So was Nat—but don't tell her that. She already has a big head as it is." She rolled her eyes, looking more like herself by the second. "I'm surprised she hasn't come looking for me, now that I think about it."

My face must have given me away, because the next second her eyes narrowed.

I sighed. "Nathalie has retained the ability to communicate with me mentally. She can project her thoughts and close them off. She's been badgering me on and off for three days now." Her lips parted in surprise, but then she nodded.

"I see. Well, she'll have to wait a little longer."

I lifted both eyebrows. "Oh?"

Her face was utterly serious as she said, "It's time. I'm ready to speak to Bree—and before you try to dissuade me —the answer is no. I will not wait any longer. I will not be pushed off so that you can attempt to fix things behind my back—" I grimaced, and she pressed her lips together. "Yes, just as I'm not perfect, I am more than aware of your flaws too. I run from my problems. The ones I can't shoot, anyway. And you try to fix them, however you see fit. Last time, I listened. But this time—I need to do this. Myself."

I opened my mouth and paused. Anders' words from the roof coming back to me.

And just like the witch, he was right.

Like Piper, I was not going to tell him that.

But it made me stop and consider my next words carefully.

"I'll take you to your sister, but first, there's something you should know."

"What?" she prompted.

"In Hell, the Harvester rules. We've talked about it a little bit. But we haven't talked about why he rules. Why I did." She gave me an expectant look. "To be the Harvester, you have to be born with chaos magic; something so rare it's only happened three times. I'm the third Harvester . . . because I possessed the ability to take others' magic. You asked me how you kill a demon. That's how. The only way how. To take every last drop of magic. I essentially take their souls. I harvest them."

Her jaw unhinged, falling ajar. Not out of fear though.

Her eyes squinted, the wheels turning in her head. "Why are you telling me this now? Why does it matter?"

She was astute, my atma. Clever. Cunning. And in this moment, I hoped she was feeling forgiving. I promised I'd never lie, and I hadn't. But I had withheld the truth. So much of it...

"Because your sister was there when I ruled. I don't know when or where or how, but she was in Hell. She knows who and what I was. What I am—and I'm fairly certain she hates me for it."

I expected anger. Maybe even suspicion. But what I never expected was for her to laugh and then to nod. She lifted her head and said, "Well, I guess that makes both of us. We really aren't so different, you and me. You killed demons. I killed, well, everything else. I'm glad I finally earned the truth." There was a twinkle in her eye as she said, "I expect you to tell me everything later; either after Bree and I come to a solution, or she tells me to fuck off. Again."

"There's one more thing," I said quietly.

I didn't want to tell her. Certainly not this way. Not when she was finally getting back on her feet. Finding her strength. But I couldn't take her to Bree without giving her it straight. She needed to know what she was dealing with. *Who* she was dealing with. "If you don't send her back, she plans to open a corridor between our worlds, allowing the humans and supernaturals to either be enslaved, or to find a way to rise above. She's willing to end humanity as you know it if you don't give her what she wants."

Piper went quiet. I could have sworn the wind howled louder for a second. I almost thought I saw white sparks at her fingertips.

But she pulled it all in. She embraced it.

And then she lifted her hand to mine, breakfast long forgotten.

"I'm ready," was all she said.

I hoped she was right.

There would be Hell to pay if she wasn't.

18
PIPER

My heart beat rapidly in my chest. I was thankful my magic was no longer tied to it. No longer bound to destroy me and everything I held dear because of it.

The cold of the void was brief but welcome. It soothed my frayed ends and helped me steady myself. When the dark cleared, we were standing in an empty apartment with white walls and mahogany stained floors. A window was open, letting in a chilled breeze.

A lone armchair sat facing it, away from us.

"I was wondering how long it would take." My sister's voice was higher than mine, and yet melodic. She stood, her white hair bound in braids that interlaced themselves around the back of her head. A crown of sorts. She turned, stepping around the chair where she'd been waiting. Watching. It was hard for me to see the blue in her eyes and how it glowed so obviously. Her pale skin seemed to shine. She wore a dark green long-sleeved shirt that clung to her, hiding the demon brands from view.

"Bree," I said, sounding stronger than I felt. As if she

could hear the thudding of my heart in my chest, she smiled coldly and inclined her head.

"Piper." Then her gaze shifted onto Ronan who stood tense at my side—his hand still not leaving mine though my fingers had gone numb. "Harvester." Despite using his title, she didn't nod. The term almost seemed to be mocking. "Or I should say, ex-Harvester. The Otherworld cannot run without one of you. The source will have picked someone to take your place by now—" I didn't miss the way her eyes flicked to mine, as if she couldn't help herself. She had to see what effect the words had on me. Thanks to Ronan's brief reveal, they had no impact. She tried to hide her disappointment but failed.

"We're not here to talk about him," I said, taking a bold step forward. "We're here to talk about you and me, and the solution we're going to find." I pulled my hand away from Ronan's, but he moved with me, shadowing my back. Bree noted the movement with cruel satisfaction.

"You plan to open a portal?" she asked, leaning against the back of her armchair. The chunky heel of her boots made us the same height, but somehow I still felt small under her gaze.

"No—"

"Then there's nothing to discuss," she replied. Her fingers snapped and the front door to her very empty apartment opened.

"I'm sorry," I said, but the apology sounded more like a frustrated growl than anything. Her eyebrows lifted. "I'm sorry that I couldn't stand the sight of our mother being used one more time. I'm sorry that our parents tried to hide the worst of it from you so you may not remember all the winter nights when we had no power, and it was you and I huddled together under a blanket on a single twin-sized bed trying not to freeze to death. I'm sorry that food was running out and neither mom nor dad could do anything about it. Not anything that would have mattered . . . and because of that I did what I thought I had to do. I lost big for my decisions. Both my parents and my sister gone in a single instant—"

"I'm not having this discussion with you," she said, face closing off; expression going cold. No more cruel amusement in sight.

"No, we are. Because here's the thing, Bree, I own my choices and accept the consequences of what I've done, and I am sorry, so fucking sorry that sixteen-year-old me didn't have all the answers and it cost us both. You suffered for my decisions and I can't undo that. I can't change it—"

"No," she agreed. "You can't. So why are you here? Why are you doing," she motioned to all of me, "this? It changes nothing. Your apologies are empty words. Your feelings are irrelevant. You understand you fucked up; great for you. But you're not doing the one thing I asked. You're not *fixing* it."

"Because what you want isn't fixing anything," I snapped. "You want to run the fuck away and leave me. Again."

Her eyebrows rose, and I knew I might have just pushed one step too far.

"*Leave* you? Well, that's some apology, Piper. Even while saying sorry it's still about you in the end. The victim complex gets old, you know?" She laughed once. It made the hairs on my neck rise. "You said it yourself; I didn't leave. You chose to make a bargain for power that ended with my conscience being trapped in Hell. I didn't do that. You did. I simply chose to move the fuck on. Instead of whining about how hard my life was, I made something of myself. I became someone—and not some pathetic human girl you remember. Do you understand that? Do you understand what you took from me by forcing me to come back here? To this world—" she waved her hand about. "This world where all I knew was pain, cold and hungry nights, with two dead parents and a sister that caused it."

Her words were a slap across the face because they were true. Every. Single. Word.

But I couldn't stop now. I couldn't run from them like I did last time.

"No," I said. "I don't know what your life was like. Who you were. Are." I took a deep breath, trying to gain the courage. To do what I had to do, one more time. "But I want to know."

Her eyebrows drew together, not expecting my response.

"What?"

"I want to make a bargain with you. One demon to another. A compromise."

Her expression soured. "I'm not interested in compromises with you. All I want is a portal, and if I don't get it—"

"I know," I replied, voice turning hard. "I'm aware of your threats."

"They're promises," she replied.

"They're war," I said plainly. "A war this city can't afford. Not now. I know that. You know that. Which is why I'm doing this, as much as it pains me—I can't have you destroying their lives because you're angry at me." On the surface she seemed unbothered, but I could have sworn I saw something—a faint flicker of regret. A flinch of unease.

"Then. Send. Me. Back."

"I'll open a portal on two conditions." It was hard to make those words come out. Harder still because I couldn't back out. I couldn't undo them. But there wasn't another way for us to bargain when the only thing she wanted I was unwilling to move on.

To compromise, someone's goalpost had to shift, and hers wasn't an option.

Which meant I had to yield.

At my back, Ronan tensed, clearly not expecting the words I was saying.

Bree froze. It seems she didn't either.

Her lips parted and the pure longing that entered her expression broke through the cold mask she wore. Part of me shriveled and died, feeling like the world's most horrible kind of selfish person for what I'd done. It was also the thing that gave me strength because this was the right way. The only way I might not lose my sister indefinitely.

"I'm listening," she said.

"The first is that whatever involvement you have with the humans ends. No more bombs. No more weapons. No stirring the pot or making things worse."

Her lips pressed into a thin line, but she nodded. I had a feeling she didn't care for being called out and condemned for those actions.

"The second is that you spend six months here—with me. I want to know about you. What I've missed, what and who you're so desperate to return to . . ." My words trailed as she started to shake her head.

"No. I've already been gone a month and a half. Two weeks at most."

My hands clenched into fists. *Two weeks?*

"You literally have forever laid out in front of you. Is six months really that much to ask for?"

"Yes," she said simply. "Especially when I have no desire to spend any, let alone all my time with you."

Ouch. All right, then. "Four months." She gave me a

hard look and pointed her index finger down. "Three months," I bit out.

"Three weeks," she replied, expression hardening. "Only two hours a day."

"Bree." I used her name as a curse.

"Piper," she snapped back, unafraid. Beside me, Ronan let out a low growl, not liking her tone.

I flashed him a look and then returned my attention to her. "Six weeks, half the day."

"One month, three hours—and that's the longest I'm willing to stay here."

A month. Less time than she'd already been here. I'd started this bargain with hope. A purpose. Every counter she gave me had that hope sinking. A weight in my stomach instead.

"Four hours," I breathed.

Her eyes flashed. "Fine, but only if the Harvester removes Anders from stalking me."

I jerked. My head swung around. *Anders. He was alive?*

"Not happening," Ronan said without looking at me. "You've been inciting riots and helping create weapons of mass destruction. I'm not pulling him until you can be trusted not to act like an angry child, stomping her foot because she didn't get what she wanted."

"Until I can be trusted?" She lifted her brows, as if she couldn't believe what he'd said, then turned to me. "Do you hear this?"

"I do, and he's right," I answered slowly. "You're only going to be with me four hours a day—"

"Three if you don't give me this."

My temper snapped. The fuse ignited before I had a hope of even stopping it. "I've given you *everything* you've asked. You're getting a portal in one month's time. You only have to spend a handful of hours with me a day—and then you're gone. Forever. And that ignores the fact that I don't control Ronan. This bargain is between you and me." Her jaw clenched and I sensed the rising desire in her to lash out. Before she could speak, I said, "One month. Four hours. Every day. Take it or I walk, and it will be that much longer that you have to remain here trying to find a way to open a portal. It only took me a decade to find a way to get to you . . ."

I crossed my arms over my chest and then waited. It was a tough call. Her stubbornness equaled mine, but she was impatient. Antsy. I sensed it in the desperation, and to some degree—I knew it well. I'd been the same way in trying to get her back, which is why I knew she'd take it. Like it or not, she didn't have a better option.

And neither did I.

One month was hardly enough, but now, it was all I would have.

Bree lifted her finger, the nail sharpening into a talon. She drew a line down her palm, slicing the skin open without hesitation.

I lifted my own and then stared at my nails—trying to will one of them to do the same. When nothing happened after a few seconds, Bree said, "Shall I?"

"No," Ronan said, taking my hand. There was no room for argument, and I had to bite the inside of my cheek to keep from flushing with embarrassment. While I had all the knowledge on earth and ten years' experience with turning my magic on and off—I didn't know how to manipulate it as she did.

The pain barely registered when he cut a line across my palm. The skin healed rapidly, leaving behind only a thin trail of blood.

"One month. Four hours every day. I stay away from the humans and don't assist in their rebellion—and in return, you will open the portal so I can go home."

Home. It was telling how easily she referred to Hell that way.

This gamble, it was a lost cause. I knew it in my soul.

One month wasn't long enough to convince her to stay. Even six was just a wild shot in the dark that I'd hoped she'd accept. But one . . . that was the time I had now to come to terms with the fact I'd well and truly lost her.

The time I had to accept the inevitable goodbye.

"Agreed," I murmured.

Our hands met. Blood pressed together as the magic bonded and sealed the deal. I felt a zap of power run through me, cold to the core. Bree seemed to experience the same and was more unprepared than me, given how quickly she snatched her hand away.

"It's done," she said, voice hoarse. "You got what you came for. Now get out."

"I look forward to hanging out with you tomorrow," was my reply. If she sensed the edge of a lie in my words, she didn't say it. I did look forward to it, but I also knew with every fiber of my being that she was going to make this difficult. Painful, even.

Ronan took my hand, and the void closed in. We were only there a moment before the four walls of my bedroom at Nat's appeared.

"Why would you make a deal with her?"

"You chose to take her from the cabin because it forced me to make some decisions. I'm choosing to do the same," I replied, dropping his hand. I turned and crossed my arms over my chest, lifting my chin.

"You're my atma. She's—"

"My sister."

Ronan shook his head. "You're a masochist," he said after a minute. "She's going to spend the next month poking and prodding and treating you like shit. You expect me to watch that—"

"I expect you to respect my choices because I'm a grown-ass adult—something you only seem to want to remember when you're fucking me." My head tilted and his eyes flamed with dark fire. "This goes both ways. You told me that. Now prove it. Show me what you want with your *actions*, not just your words."

His jaw clenched and the muscles in his arms bunched tight.

"It's hard to override my instincts when you were shot by a gun that had *her* magic; shot by your ex that got the idea from *her.* You were a child when you made those choices to try to help your family. She's a woman who is intent on tearing you down with her bare hands if that's what it takes—"

"She's desperate. Angry. Stubborn. We're a lot alike in that. But I'm not doing this for her, Ronan. I'm doing this for me. I've spent a decade living only for Bree. Now I'll spend a month coming to terms with the consequences. I need this. Because no matter what she feels, it doesn't matter when the guilt comes from *in* me—and if I'm ever going to move on, I *need* to let it go."

The tension drained from him and the black fire in his eyes dissipated.

"Okay," he said. "I'll respect your decision, but if she tries to hurt you—"

"Trust that I can handle myself."

"But will you?" he asked. The underlying accusation that I'd let her was clear. "I know you can. Bree isn't a weak demon, but you are one of the strongest in existence. I know you can handle yourself, but *will you* if she tries?"

"Yes," I said. "I will."

He held my gaze for a few seconds and then nodded. "Very well—"

Two knocks at my bedroom door made us pause.

"You had all weekend to fuck. I'm coming in," Nat called. The handle turned, and the door opened. Despite her nonchalant words, there was a visible tension in her that drained away when she saw me.

"What happened to the walls being soundproof?"

"They are," she said, striding forward. "But I can feel the change in the air when either of you are near."

"It's the chaos magic," Ronan said. "You have a heightened awareness of all magic around you." Nathalie shrugged, picking what I could only assume was cat hair off her sweater. Her practiced casualness made me narrow my eyes at her.

"We have work to do. This one hogged you for three days, and I don't really want to leave you two alone given your penchant for starting fires when he's around." She hooked her thumb in Ronan's direction. He appeared unamused at being referred to as 'this one'.

"Fortunately for you, 'this one' also has things that need to be taken care of," Ronan replied.

"Like checking in with Anders?" I asked, letting it be known this was not the end of *that* conversation. I hadn't forgotten.

"Yes, actually," Ronan said, unaffected by my tone. "Among other things."

I wanted to ask what other things he was referring to, but I had a feeling he'd only sidestep an answer. I took the route that would piss him off most instead. "Tell him hi for me. That I'd like to catch up. Maybe get dinner sometime."

Black filled his eyes, and I couldn't help the smirk.

Without so much as a goodbye, Ronan stepped into the void and blinked out of existence. Nathalie let out a snort, then said, "Using jealousy as foreplay. Nice, Piper. You should have just signed a death warrant."

I was fairly certain Ronan wouldn't kill a middle-aged errand boy out of jealousy, but they both kept this secret from me. Him and Anders.

So they both could deal with the consequences of it.

19
PIPER

"Let me get this straight—" I held up one hand, and she paused, leaning back, and motioning for me to continue. "You want us to 'volunteer' at a food bank you own?"

Nathalie sat back, plopping a strawberry into her mouth in a carefree gesture. The circles under her eyes had darkened heavily in the last few days. I wondered if the voices had gotten worse and what there was to be done about it. I filed that away for later when we weren't sitting in the middle of a tiny cafe. We'd just completed dropping off orders for the afternoon, the last one containing fresh produce for the restaurant where we sat. In return, they gave us lunch and three dozen chocolate swirled bagels.

Each delivery was different and unexpected. One woman paid a fortune for a cashmere blanket. Another traded hard to find herbs in return for a pack of batteries. A family with too many mouths to feed paid over four thousand dollars and a heavy, beautiful heirloom quilt in return for a cast iron pot that multiplied whatever was in it by ten. The quilt was then given to a middle-aged couple—a witch and warlock. The wife came from Lucifer's line and had developed an extreme case of arthritis after his death. She'd been the breadwinner before, and her loss of power resulted in a fall from grace—to the extent she was willing to trade her family's oldest grimoire in return for that quilt and the chance to be warm.

They were human and supe. Wealthy and poor. Nathalie did business with all of them and asked about their kids, grandkids, jobs, and struggles—all without missing a beat.

It made me wonder if the voices she'd been hearing were more than the guilt she harbored, instead it was the price she paid for an eidetic memory and sharp mind.

She chewed slowly and swallowed with exaggeration before wiping her hands on a cloth napkin and leaning forward. She placed her palms flat on the table.

"That's exactly what I want." She nodded, stood up from the table, and waved to the cafe owners who smiled broadly back as we exited the place. "Why do you sound so opposed?" She hit the clicker for her car, and it beeped once. I placed the bagels in the back seat before sliding into the passenger side.

"I'm not opposed; just confused. You made it sound urgent that we had work to do."

Nathalie shrugged. "There's always work to be done. The deliveries we dropped off today were a week overdue. I lost a lot of time trying to track down the gun this weekend while you were 'burning off rage' with Ronan."

Her side-eye was completely unnecessary.

"You try getting shot next time and see what it feels like," I replied.

"I'd rather no one get shot, but seeing as we can't find it, I have to assume you destroyed it." She pressed a button, and the engine turned on.

"I wish I could say, but honestly, I have no idea. Everything was just . . ."

"Fire?" Nat inserted with a not-so-subtle grin.

I pressed my lips together, and she laughed. "Oh come on, even you have to admit it's a little funny."

"Ronan said you were beside yourself, pestering him all weekend."

Her laugh quieted, something deeper surfacing. "I saw you fall, and I was terrified. I think the only time anything has scared me that bad was when Barry was 'taken'." Her voice turned acidic on the last word. I didn't blame her for the anger there. I would have let Ronan kill him for what he did, but she was a better person than me. "Jokes aside, never do that again. If someone holds you at gunpoint, then use all that fire to stop them. Even if it means they die. Don't try to reason with them. It's not worth it." Her eyes focused on the road ahead, brows furrowing more with every word. "It's not worth *you*."

"I don't think I was ever at risk," I said quietly. "The gun wouldn't take it all. I was more concerned what would happen to the rest of you when what he did take unleashed."

Half her mouth curved up. "Yes, well, you can't have me dying. I don't think Señora Rosara would put up with all of you if I did."

"I'm fairly certain she'd turn me into a cat."

Nathalie chuckled. "You'd make a pretty Maine Coon. All that gold hair." Then her nose twitched. "Total mess, though. Not to mention dander. My allergies wouldn't be able to take it."

"Imagine the life of a cat, though. Especially her cat. Two free meals a day. Warm bed. Cranky old witch that would kick anyone's ass for looking at you wrong. Would be just like living with an older, bitchier version of you."

Nathalie busted out laughing, the shadows clearing from her eyes.

"If that's my future, there are worse ones to have," she said, a twinkle of gold lighting her eyes.

"Please tell me you don't see yourself as a widow," I said, making a face.

"No," she shook her head, "but I could see myself alone. I like my own company more than most people. I like myself. And more importantly—I respect myself. I wouldn't be with someone just to be with someone. They'd have to be worth it, and right now I don't see myself finding that, given I live in a house with three women, run a business, and have to save New Chicago every other week. There's no time to meet someone. Let alone invest in them."

I watched her for a couple minutes, turning her words over. Eventually I settled on, "You're lucky."

She frowned. "I've noticed how things are between you and Ronan, so don't tell me you're settling—"

"No, not that." I rolled my eyes, turning to the window to hide the flush in my cheeks. "I mean the first part. You like yourself. You'd be fine being alone because it's not truly alone."

She nodded slowly. "You could learn to like yourself too," Nat said. "I'd say it's not hard, but not everyone can be as awesome as me. I can understand why it's difficult when you have me to compare to."

I cracked a smile, shaking my head at her. "You're something else."

"Something amazing," she chimed. "But me aside, I think you give yourself too hard a time. At that end of the day, if you don't like who you are—then change. Become who you want to be." She pulled into a side lot. A line of people ran around the nondescript building across the street.

"Is that why we're here? Because it's not enough to own a food bank, you have to volunteer at it too?"

The slight smile she gave me was answer enough.

I sighed, climbing out of the car. She locked it behind us, ignoring the stares as we crossed the street. I recognized the longing. The hunger. The sheer fucking hopelessness they had as they stared at the car we'd arrived in.

That desolate expression gave way to anger as we drew closer.

"Do you really think it was a good idea to roll up here and not park a few blocks away?" I muttered.

"Word is already spreading about who you are. What you are. I'm not as unknown as I once was. It's a good move to come here in the open right now."

I blinked, understanding settled over me.

"This was a calculated move."

"You were shot and lit up like a bonfire. The humans are scared of you, as are any supes that are smart. Fear isn't inherently bad—but it can lead to hate quickly. If we're going to try to ease some of the tensions, we need to show them another side of you—other than the Witch Hunter or the Rage Demon." She smiled nonchalantly as we cut ahead of the line.

A woman lifted a dirt-smudged hand and motioned to the line. She was dressed in a ripped t-shirt and mismatched long skirt with a hoodie wrapped around her waist. "Wait your turn—" The harsh grate of her voice died quickly.

Her hazel eyes widened. Her head bowed, showing me a

mop of greasy brown hair that might have once been luscious locks.

"'Pologies," she rasped. "I didn't realize."

A quiet hush fell over the line and Nat looked to me, as if it proved her point.

I grit my teeth, hating the attention.

"You didn't know," I said quietly. A faint grin lined Nat's lips when we stepped inside. It smelled like bleach. The air tasted moist from steam. The furnace was loud; a roar made more audible by the quiet surrounding it. People sat at tables, pushed together, heads down, and mouths silent. The clank of a metal ladle hitting hard plastic made me jerk.

Nat was already weaving through the long tables, her quiet footsteps the only beat of life in this place. I followed after, as if some invisible lifeline connected us, dragging me behind her. At the edge of the counter, I did as she did, slowing down as we approached. Nat waved to the girl behind it and flipped up a middle panel that connected to the wall, separating the people serving from the destitute being served.

I hid the shudder that ran through me as I followed after. While I'd never come to this particular food bank, I'd been to others. Shortly after my parents died had been the hardest time. There was no money for heat or food. Nothing but the meager scrapings I could steal for rent. It was a dark time before I became a bounty hunter. Before I became anything.

I looked away from the people in line and focused on the girl Nat was talking to.

"Piper, this is Hayley; Hayley, meet Piper."

She smiled wide, showing off pretty teeth and fangs. Despite the obvious—her being a vampire—her dark brown eyes were warm. Welcoming. She lifted the hand holding a ladle in a half wave while continuing to serve some sort of porridge that looked an awful lot like frog spawn.

"Evening," I said, dipping my chin.

"Likewise," she chimed, voice soft.

"I need to take stock in the back and then prep a menu for the next week. Hayley is going to show you around the stations." I opened my mouth when she spoke again. "Skip over Irene," Nat added. Her tone was nonchalant, but a note of warning was seeded in it. Hayley nodded dutifully, the fluorescent lights illuminating her brown skin in a way that caught my attention. While everyone else in here looked hollow beneath them, she seemed almost effervescent.

"Who's Irene?" I asked, before Nat could step away.

I wondered if she'd dance around it, but instead of avoiding it, she said, "She runs the blood donations."

Understanding filled me, followed by a sick feeling. It was probably hypocritical given I took Ronan's blood every time we fucked—but blood donations were different. These were human donors, oftentimes doing it because that's all they could offer this new society. Memories of my mother with bruises and bite marks started to surface. I shoved them down.

Hayley chuckled, the lone sound pulling me out of my own head. I frowned.

"It's okay. You're not the first that's a little squeamish around it." She read my distaste clearly, but not the reason why. I nodded once, going along with her assumptions. While Nat knew the truth, there was no need for anyone else to.

"Yell if you need me," Nat said. She waited until we locked eyes and I nodded before she turned to leave through a swinging door that led to the back.

"So, this is the serving station in case that wasn't obvious," Hayley said, ladle slapping another plastic tray as she dumped the lumpy porridge on an empty square. "It's pretty straight forward. If they put their tray in front of you, give them food. Only one serving per person, and no exceptions there. She's very strict about that."

I stepped closer to her side as someone came out of the back with another metal pan of food, placing it in the empty spot in front of me. They silently extended a pair of tongs and I took them without a word.

"What if they go through the line multiple times?" I asked, picking up a piece of overbaked bread and putting it on the tray that appeared in front of me.

Hayley smiled. "You see the guy at the end of the line stamping hands?" She thrust her chin toward that direction, and I followed it. "The stamper has a magical signature that doesn't wear off for six hours. It prevents people from re-entering the line within that time frame."

Clever. The banks I'd gone to were human only and didn't boast fancy widgets like that. It made the abuse problems worse, especially when supes came in demanding to be fed. Human-only tends to be equivalent to magicless. Also known as nearly powerless.

They were dangerous places to be. Especially after dark.

"Is this a supe-only bank?" I asked.

"No," Hayley said. "Anyone's welcome that needs it. It's been that way since Nathalie started it."

The tongs clinked against the hard plastic when I dropped another strip of bread. "When was that?"

"Little more than a year ago. We started small. Serving out of a food truck and moved up to this—" she motioned to the building around us.

"You've been volunteering that long?"

Her cheeks didn't heat as someone who had a working heart pumping blood might, but the way her lips twisted was telling all the same. "Actually, I'm an employee. Most of us are that work back here. The ones who volunteer often do it to be able to take home whatever food is left over at the end of the day to feed their families."

I nodded slowly. Employee. That made more sense. Volunteering was nice, but few had that luxury. I was now one of them. "She pay you well?" I asked, knowing she did because it was Nat, but pushing the conversation along. Past the edgings of guilt.

"Very. It's enough to take care of my husband and kids."

I blinked, and the person that stopped in front of me nudged his tray. Hastily, I dropped a piece of bread, recovering from my surprise. "You have kids?"

"Twins," she said and smiled. "Boy and girl."

I nodded slowly, wondering if they were actually hers or children she took in. It wasn't that uncommon these days, all things considered.

"I was human," Hayley said, answering my unspoken question. "My husband too. Our babies were born seven years ago. I was turned three."

"So your kids . . . they're still human?" I asked slowly. It was a delicate topic. While many condemned the turning of children, it wouldn't be the first time I'd heard it happen.

"God yes," Hayley said, letting out a little laugh. "I'd never do that to them. I didn't even want to turn Adam, but he said it would be safer that way—if he could protect them while I worked."

"Wow," I breathed. "The bloodlust is bad in the early days. How'd you both manage?"

"Nathalie," she said. It shouldn't have surprised me, given she was here. The more I learned about Nat, she seemed to have a hand in everything and then some. "She found me after it happened. Before here and this life, I sold blood to make money. One night my clients got out of hand. They were too rough. Too many bites. One of them went too far . . ." Just as she started to go distant, the edge of turmoil left her. "Nat found me on the street. We were total strangers, but she helped me. She gave me a choice to die or to live as this. I chose to live."

My eyebrows inched up in disbelief. "You *chose* to be a vampire?"

"I did, and I have never regretted it. I get to see my babies grow up now. I can provide for them and Adam. Because of what I am, they will never have to sell themselves." She smiled to herself, something I wondered if she did often. How someone could go through that and come out so happy, despite the world we lived in . . . I didn't understand it.

"You must think me crazy, being the Witch Hunter and all."

"Yes and no," I admitted. "I'm sure you've heard the rumors that I'm not exactly human either." Hayley nodded, but didn't push, instead letting me decide how much to say. "I didn't choose what I am, but I started off as human too. I searched for a way to find magic to save my family and I found it."

"Did you save them?" she asked.

"No." I pressed my lips together in a tight smile. "In that, our stories differ. Mine led me to becoming the Witch Hunter, and yours led you here." It was harder to keep the bitterness out of my voice as the conversation turned too personal . . . too deep for my liking.

"It led you here too. Maybe not as fast, but you're here all the same," she pointed out.

"You and Nathalie kept in touch after she saved you, I take it?" I asked, pivoting the conversation away once more. If Hayley noticed it, she didn't say.

"Yes. While I stayed with a local clan, she went to my home to tell Adam what happened. When the bloodlust was under control, I returned home. Six months later, I turned Adam, and he stayed with the same clan. Longer, though, because his transition was worse. Nathalie watched my kids every Sunday so I could visit him during that time."

It was really no wonder so many people bent over backwards for her knowing she did stuff like this. I spent the last decade making our world worse, but Nat spent that time fixing it. Just like she was trying to fix me.

"And when she opened this place, she offered you a job?"

"Actually, she hired me to open it. We worked out a plan together for how to build it up and find donors. We cut a deal with the clan that helped Adam and me. They funded the start-up in return for access to our blood bank."

The tongs hit the bottom of the heated pan. I hadn't noticed it was now empty. Part of me wanted to ask. Ask how she could do that given her own history. Not out of judgement, but because I wanted to know how she could possibly get past that. The rest of me wasn't sure I wanted to know.

"We treat them right," she said quietly. "Every human is handled with care. Every feeding supervised. Vampires need blood, and humans can give. I make sure the way they do protects them. It's the way I should have been protected."

"You're very open about your life," I said, not sure what else to say.

She laughed, breaking the tension. "I've been told it's unnerving, but the way I see it—I'm one of the lucky ones. If my story can help someone or I can pay it forward, I will."

"You think it will help me?" I asked, lifting an eyebrow.

"Call it a hunch, but I saw the way you reacted about the blood bank. I've heard the stories. I don't think you care much for my kind—and I understand that. Really. I was the same." She scooped more frogspawn porridge into a bowl, and I turned sideways, crossing my arms, and leaning my hip against the counter.

"True as that is, I don't think what one person feels really matters at the end of the day." Particularly me. "I was the Witch Hunter, after all, not the Vampire Hunter."

"You're also a demon," she said quietly, setting the ladle down and turning toward me. Her features were soft but serious. "In our world, demons aren't just powerful for their magic. They own it. Conquer it. Control it. And while you may not yet, you are a demon and forever is a long time. One day, when you decide you want to be in power, I want you to know not all of us are bad. Most of us were human once too, and we all want the same thing as you. A better life than the one we were given."

My lips parted. Hayley knew far more than I realized. While the fact I was a supe was becoming common knowledge, I hadn't realized how many had connected the dots.

The woman at the door's reaction to me suddenly made more sense. As did Nat bringing me here.

I didn't know what to think of it. While I wasn't ashamed of what I was anymore, I wasn't prepared for what being a demon would mean. That supes would look to me with trepidation, as Hayley did now.

I didn't know how it would make me feel, because I didn't have the words to tell her she was wasting her breath. That I might be a demon, but I wasn't Lucifer. I wasn't a conqueror. A ruler.

That I wasn't really the Witch Hunter for reasons people thought, or a demon like people expected me to be. I was just Piper.

Just another fucked-up soul like the rest of them.

Hayley smiled again, nodded once, and said, "Why don't we go look at the other stations? Danielle can teach you to make rice pudding."

She picked up her empty metal tray, and I frowned. "That's rice pudding?" I asked, following her.

"Yes, what did you think it was?" she said quizzically.

"Frog spawn."

She laughed all the way to the kitchen. But I didn't miss the look in her eye when she thought I wasn't looking.

Desperation. Not the same as the people that came here for food. But a thirst for change. For hope. A clinging desire that I might be it.

I was still thinking about it when I laid in bed alone that night.

And I wondered, if maybe it wasn't so hopeless. If maybe, just maybe, I could make a difference like Nathalie.

Not as a leader . . . but as Piper all the same.

20

PIPER

"So," Nat drawled, plopping down on the barstool next to mine. "This deal with Bree."

I chewed my bite of potato hash slowly and swallowed it down with some orange juice.

"What about it?"

"I'm surprised." She snatched a piece of toast off my plate and nibbled at it. I lifted an eyebrow, waiting for her to continue. "I didn't think you'd be willing to let her go."

I sighed. "She didn't leave me much choice."

"There's always a choice."

"If I didn't, she was going to tear this world apart and eventually find a way back, anyway. Any relationship we could have had would be lost, if it wasn't already. I'd be holding her here because I couldn't let go for anyone's sake, not even her own."

Nat nodded, chewing the toast thoughtfully. "Do you think the relationship is lost?"

I took another sip of OJ, mulling over a response. "Yes," I said eventually. "But I do hope that I can find it again, or at least make a new one."

She frowned. "Why? If she's going back in a month, isn't that harder on you?"

I nodded slowly. "Yes and no. I need to grieve that our relationship is over and know that when the time comes, she'll be okay. I have to know I tried, and she still chose Hell. I have to . . . move on."

Her nose scrunched. "And trying to get to know her while she likely treats you like shit is doing that?"

I smiled faintly. "In a way, yes."

"I don't understand that. The demon was right. You *are* a masochist."

I chuckled. "Maybe. Can you really say you wouldn't do the same?"

"For my sister?"

I nodded.

"For Carissa—no. No, I would not. Chances are I won't have to, though, given she ran from the circle and I haven't seen her since."

"And the other one?" I mused. "Your twin? Katherine?"

Her hesitation spoke volumes.

"I don't know," she said eventually. "Kat and I have a complicated relationship. As children, she surpassed me in every way and thrived off of it—but she was also my biggest defender. She kept the other witches from torturing me. Lied for me. Protected me. We were closer than sisters and yet miles apart." She set the half-eaten piece of toast back on my plate almost absentmindedly.

"What happened?"

"There was a fight. One night when we were thirteen. I don't remember what it was about anymore, but Kat was angry with me, and I her. Things were said. Then my magic . . ." She shook her head. "Kat is a powerful witch, or she was before Lucifer died. Sometimes when she got angry, bad things happened, but before that night it'd never been aimed at me. Not once." Her light brown eyes turned a shade golden. I knew what she was going to say, so I said it for her.

"She used her magic, and you used yours."

Nat nodded. "The wind blew so hard it shattered the windows. The glass was coming straight for me and I panicked. Everything turned gold. The air. The glass. My vision. And when it faded, she was a puddle on the ground, surrounded by bloodied shards." She took a slow breath. "I didn't mean to hurt her; I just didn't want her to hurt me. Kat didn't see it that way. She felt lied to. Betrayed. If I was capable of turning her own magic on her, it meant she was weaker somehow. Lesser. And while she was okay with it being the other way around, how we were raised made it impossible for her to come to terms with this. So she cut me out."

"Your parents didn't realize?" I questioned, dubious at best.

"She lied and so did I. Said she had an accident and cut herself. The fact she could harness power without words was enough to make my mother look the other way. She was so thrilled to have a magically gifted daughter. A prodigy. Witches may value beauty, and the incident left Kat scarred—but her magic was more important. It would mean she could have any match she wanted . . ."

"You could have too," I said. "A chaos witch. You're the only one I know of in existence. Clearly your parents realized even if you didn't say."

Nat nodded. "Kat was powerful, but she couldn't control other people's magic. I am not, but I can. I don't know when my parents realized, but I'm certain the reason my mother kept it from me was fear. Fear she couldn't control me. That I'd find a way to become more powerful somehow. That simply wouldn't do." She smiled, the look of pity on her face, and I'm not sure if it was for her past self or her mother or her sister. Maybe it was for all of them.

"Your family is messed up."

Nat let out a barking laugh. "Look who's talking."

I chuckled. "Yeah, well, Bree is pissed, but I'm the reason it happened to begin with. You weren't at fault in your case, not really. I was."

She pressed her lips together in a tight smile. "You were just trying to save them."

"I was," I said, pushing my plate back. "But I also failed. I can accept that I earned Bree's ire because of that."

Nat shook her head. "That's fucked up. This guilt has really done a number on you if you think you deserve it."

I slid off my seat and reached for my guns. "We're all fucked up in one way or another—even Ronan, and he's ten thousand years old."

Nat let out a low whistle. "That's old. Talk about robbing the cradle." I glowered, and she laughed again. "I mean, some say age is just a number—"

"Fuck off," I said. She only laughed harder.

It was a good moment, a happy one; where I hid my grin by looking the other way.

Then came a knock at the door.

Her laughter stopped and my grin faded. It was just after seven in the morning and the twins were still in bed. So was Señora Rosara. Could she really be—

"Your sister's early," Nat said, confirming my suspicion.

"Must want to get it out of the way," I muttered, reaching for my coat.

"What will you guys do for the next four hours?"

I grabbed a loaf of bread off the counter and said, "Feed the ducks."

Nat's eyebrows drew together. "You're going to feed ducks . . . for four hours?" She lifted both brows, and I frowned.

"We used to do it as kids," I said quietly. Nat sighed.

"Would you like a suggestion?"

I titled my head. Not long ago I would have said no and walked out. But Nat had a way with people. Maybe it wasn't a bad idea to listen.

I waved her on.

"Feeding the ducks is passive—and that loaf of bread won't last you four hours with those hungry fuckers. Not to mention it's bad for them. Take her to do something else this time. Something new. A trip down memory lane right now isn't going to make her open up. If anything it'll put her on the defensive."

I set the bread back down on the counter. "Do you have a suggestion for what we should do, then?"

Another knock at the door, this one louder and more impatient. It made me sigh. Yeah, she wanted this over with. Maybe Nat did have a point there.

"What about . . ." She looked around the room, coming back to me, before slowly lowering her gaze. "Shooting," she said. "It's something you started afterwards, right?"

I shook my head. "Our dad taught us. I was eight the first time, and Bree hated it. The way the gunshot echoed scared her."

Nat let out a deflated sigh. "I'd ask if you had hobbies, but I think we both know you have no life." She said it matter-of-factly and continued with her musing, but the words struck me. I had no life. Survival had been my way. Bring Bree back. It was the only thing I concerned myself with for a decade, and as such, all my skills were tracking, hunting, and killing—and my hobbies involved cleaning guns, and doing pull-ups and cardio to stay in shape.

Bree knocked again. Two thumps then a pause before footsteps started away from the door. I hurried over and unlatched each lock quickly before throwing it open. She was halfway down the hall and facing the door, arms crossed over her chest.

"I don't like to be kept waiting," she said.

"I didn't know you'd be here so early," I replied, equally terse. Bree rolled her eyes and sauntered back. She wore shiny black pants that looked like latex covered her legs. The same high-heeled combat boots gave her enough added inches to put us at the same height. I saw a faded AC/DC T-shirt beneath her black leather jacket. It was an older version of how she'd dressed at thirteen. I might have been able to pretend not much had changed, if not for the intricate braids that pulled her waist-long hair into a crown atop her head.

She side-stepped me through the door and took an appraising look over the inside. "So, dearest sister, what is it we're doing for the next four hours? Hm?"

I looked at Nat and she stared back, a cringey smile on her face like she also had no idea. My eyes inched toward the bread. I know she said it wasn't a great idea, but it was the only one I had...

"You're both coming with me today," she announced. I blinked and Bree's head whipped around.

"Coming with you," I repeated.

"Mhmm," Nat said, nodding twice. She slid off the stool and walked around the counter. "We talked about it last night, remember?" Nat said, chatting on. "You said you and Bree could help me run my stall at the market today."

"Right," I drawled, avoiding Bree's gaze that was flipping back and forth between us. "The market. Where you sell stuff."

"Seeds," she said absently, scrawling a note on a pad of paper and then signing it before setting the pen down and grabbing her keys. "I sell seeds and saplings, for those that need a little help getting it to grow. Today you two can help me. Let's go."

She nodded toward the door, smiling to both of us like this wasn't a half-cocked plan to find something Bree could do with me that wouldn't result in fighting.

On instinct, I reached for my jacket and paused, debating. I was only in a T-shirt and jeans this morning. Hardly anything for me, but the cat was out of the bag. There wasn't much point in hiding beneath my turtlenecks anymore to conceal my brands when spring was here and with it—warmer temperatures.

Still, my hand shook a little with indecision.

Was I ready to really embrace it? To leave behind all pretenses?

Foregoing a jacket and leaving my demon brands on display felt like just that, even if most of the population didn't realize what they were. That tattoo ink had never actually touched my skin.

"It's a little chilly out this morning, but it should warm up this afternoon," Nat said. "I'd wear it and you can put it in my car if you get hot." To punctuate her own statement, she threw on an oversized hoodie. I grabbed the jacket, shrugging it on as I walked. The door at the end of the hall closed firm and Nat said quietly, "After you."

Bree's footsteps trailed behind, almost silent. Nat's were louder. Her rhythm slower. Her Doc Martens thumped softly with every step, not that she ever noticed. Her senses weren't so heightened that she would.

I hit the button on the elevator and the twin doors slid open.

The awkward silence that ensued as we all stepped in was nothing short of painful.

There was a time when I would have told her anything. We would have stayed up until dawn talking about what we wanted, what we wished for, and the grandiose futures we'd dreamed about as children.

The elevator dinged, and the doors slid open, Señora Rosara's shop reminding me that our reality was as different as night and day.

"Gracias, Señora ," Nathalie called over the dusty stacks of leather-bound spell books.

"Don't tell me you've brought home another stray." The old woman tsked from behind the counter. She narrowed her eyes at Bree, who stared back utterly aloof. I chuckled at the insinuation, given that's what I called the twins.

"Not this time," Nat hummed. "Bree is Piper's sister. She'll be in town for a little while. We're taking her down to the market on York Street for the morning."

"Don't sell Oleander to the man with a scar," Señora replied. "He'll give you a sob story. It's a lie."

"Thanks for the heads up," Nat said.

I looked back at her from the door. She was scratching one of her cats on the chin, hip cocked against the counter. When she saw me staring, she lifted a dark brow and added, "Today is a good day to wear a jacket. The chance of rain is high." Her eyes flicked to Bree and then back to me. Her expression was pointed.

"Thanks." I dipped my chin and stepped outside. Despite her warning, it was clear skies overhead. The actual meaning didn't escape me. It was better to keep my brands hidden. Bree was likely to either cause a storm, or I would because of her. Lovely.

"You keep interesting company these days," Bree said once we were out of earshot of the shop. "Living with Nathalie Le Fay, third daughter of the infamous—and now decimated—black magic line. A short-sighted seer witch for a neighbor. The old Harvester is your atman . . . my, my, to think how much has changed in ten years."

Short-sighted seer, eh? I understood it now, though I hadn't put it together at first. Short seers saw the direct future of minutes to hours, and they were incredibly accurate. Long-sighted seers only saw possibilities, but nothing concrete.

"You've been busy," I mused. "Spying on me?" Nathalie stayed quiet, but I could tell she was listening despite her disinterest as she unlocked her car.

"I've been looking for a way home, and knowledge is power." She repeated the old adage our father would tell us again and again as children.

"I'll take that as a yes. If you wanted to know, you could have just asked. Contrary to what you might think, I didn't bring you back to imprison you here. It wasn't meant as a punishment." I tried, and partly failed, to keep the bitterness out of my tone as I opened the passenger door and slid in, closing it shut before she could respond. Bree slid into the back and didn't bother with buckling up.

"I know," she said while Nat started the engine. "You brought me back because of your need to save me." I could tell she was rolling her eyes. Not even five minutes and it was already going downhill. I sighed, leaning against the side of the door.

"I'm curious," Nat mused. "What's Hell like? I have to

assume it's not just some burning inferno or you wouldn't be so keen to return—love or not." She lifted an eyebrow at the rearview mirror.

My sister cocked her head, assessing. "Hell is . . . indescribable."

Nat made a face. "If that's all you have to describe it, it sounds riveting."

I snorted, trying to cover it up as a cough when Bree shot me a sour look. "The world is brighter. More vivid. There's colors there that don't exist here. The trees are taller. The oceans deeper. They don't have technology because they don't need it—magic exists in the very core of their world."

"The Source?"

Bree nodded. "Earth is one of the few dimensions that doesn't have magic. It's the furthest from the Otherworld. If you stacked playing cards on top of each other, the Otherworld is the top and Earth is the bottom. That's why it is so difficult to create a portal from here to there, but not the other way around."

"You call it the Otherworld," Nat said. "Is that what they call it?"

"No, but it's about as close a translation that exists. Hell is a human construct. A fable created by Lucifer to demonize the world he left."

Nat's features tightened. "His atma rejected him and condemned them both."

"Because he was unworthy—which he proved by running away like a coward instead of issuing a challenge as he should have." Bree's cool expression didn't reveal much.

"A challenge?" I asked.

"In the Otherworld, soulmates are uncommon but not

rare—so is rejection. Not every demon wants to be tied to another so permanently, especially if they consider the other to be weak. While the bond is hard to resist, it can be impossible for males. To prove themselves, they can issue a challenge—where the rejected party fights the one rejecting—to the death or to bond."

My face drained of blood. "That's barbaric."

"That's the Otherworld." She shrugged. "Demons can't have kids unless they're bonded. The magic demands it. Evolution must move forward."

"By forcing the other person?" I grimaced. "That's fucked up."

"They're not being forced," Bree said in a harder tone. "They can choose—the bond or death."

"That's hardly a choice."

"Just because you don't like it or agree with it doesn't change the facts," Bree snapped. Nat's hand darted out to squeeze my knee, a motion I'm sure my sister didn't miss.

"Well, I guess it's fortunate then that Ronan chose to go against his nature in how he pursued Piper."

Bree's face twisted at her words, something almost like jealousy crossing it.

"He would have been challenged in the Otherworld for it. Not by you, but others. It's beneath his station," she said. "The Harvester reducing himself for a demon that can't control their magic?" She shook her head, and the barb pricked at my hard exterior. It shouldn't have surprised me that she figured it out so quickly. I'm not sure which bothered me more: the way she insulted me for it, or that in her eyes, my magic equated my worth. "He would have had to have killed dozens of challengers who would have questioned his right to rule after that."

"What if the other demon—the one being rejected—is

less powerful? Is there no other way to prove themselves except by dying or winning?" Nat asked. "I would think such an advanced society would account for that somehow, unless every match is equal in every way."

"There is a third way . . . but it's not common. Sometimes a partner can be given an impossible task. Something to prove themselves worthy if the other demon doesn't want to reject them but needs to know their mate is strong enough to be tied to so irrevocably." She looked away, leaning back, and crossing her arms over her chest. "That's still beneath the Harvester, though. If anything, you should have been the one to do it."

I rolled my eyes. It might have bothered me more if she hadn't started off describing how barbaric they were. As it was, something warm touched my chest that even then, when he knew nothing about me, Ronan didn't do that.

Instead of belittling or forcing me into something, he coaxed me there—playing a game of hunter and prey. I smiled a little to myself, noticing Bree's jaw tighten in my periphery.

"For someone so concerned about getting back, you seem to have a lot of thoughts about me and Ronan."

She snorted in derision, as if it were nothing. Like I was imagining things. "Please, are we really doing this? You think I'm interested in him?" She chuckled. "I've already found my atman, Piper, and I'm trying to go home to him. Your relationship with Ronan simply confuses me, mostly on his part. After becoming a part of the Otherworld, I don't understand how one as old as him could go against everything ingrained in his being."

She'd found her atman. Her Ronan. The sudden clawing anger she had toward me was beginning to make sense. Bree wasn't simply in love. She felt the pull of magic drawing her back to him. Ronan crossed worlds for me. She was utterly prepared to do the same for her soulmate.

"You know," Nat said. "The same could be said about you." She nodded toward the mirror in reference to Bree. "You were human when you went to Hell. A decade may be a long time for us, but to demons? It's nothing. A blink. Yet, you returned more demon than human and hellbent on returning. Maybe you understand more than you think you do."

Bree's expression tightened, and I didn't understand it. Her anger? Yes. Her desire to go back? Certainly. But this—whatever it was—this I didn't understand. It bothered me more than the rage because there was something calculated in it. Something she wasn't saying.

Our eyes met in the mirror. Blue to violet. Similar in every way down to our magic, and yet worlds apart.

"Perhaps," she whispered.

21
PIPER

The York Street market was busy. More so than it had been during the last week we'd been here. Wood-paneled stalls and tents lined the block, selling wild game, medicine, herbs, and in Nathalie's case—seeds. She had them in metal cannisters. My job was to bag and label them. Well, mine and Bree's.

My sister wasn't the helping type, which left it to me.

"I need more lemongrass," Nat said, navigating conversation with three customers at once. I rifled through the jars, searching for it when she added, "Lavender too, and an Aloe Vera sapling."

I glanced up at Bree, who was playing with an orb of dark green magic. It slipped over her hand and under her palm, twisted and turning with fluid grace. She juggled it across each of her fingers, the orb weaving around them with precision. It never wavered. Never grew.

A kernel of jealousy settled in me, making my words more biting. "Are you going to help, or just continue fucking around with your magic in the middle of a human market?"

Bree's eyes slid sideways. Her silver eyebrows lifted. Her

attention was fixed on me, and the orb continued to move flawlessly around her fingers.

"You told me I had to spend four hours with you. You didn't say I had to participate."

My teeth ground together in frustration.

"It was implied."

"No, it wasn't," she scoffed. "If it had been, the magic would demand it, but here I am—and the only magic in sight is mine." I pressed my lips together, and a smirk crept up her face. "Unless this isn't about helping."

I ignored her and continued digging.

Licorice root. Lilac. "There's no lemongrass in here."

"I know I bagged some last week," Nat said. "Look again."

I growled under my breath and fire sparked in my palm. I closed my fist, extinguishing it. Anxiety shot through me, but it was too late. Bree saw.

"You know, if you learned to use your magic, your life would be easier."

I opened my mouth to tell her to shut hers, but the snap of her fingers interrupted me.

Instantly, two bags of seeds drifted up from two different boxes.

Lemongrass and lavender.

I stared at them, avoiding her taunting gaze. I took a deep breath, trying to cool the fire coursing through me. It was always there. Always smothering me.

I grabbed the seeds out of the air and rocked back on my heels. As I turned to give them to Nat, the Aloe Vera sapling she'd asked for floated in front of my face. Mocking me.

Wordlessly, I snatched that up too.

Tossing the seeds on the plywood counter and putting

the plant down with a too-hard thud, I muttered to Nat, "I'm taking ten. Can you manage?"

"Well, actually—" she started, flashing the customer in front of her a smile while talking to me.

"Thanks," I said, like she didn't just disagree. I marched out the back of the tent, ignoring Bree's stare and Cheshire smile. It was quieter in the back, but not empty entirely. A small stretch of sidewalk was all that stood between the row of shops and the brick building behind it. I turned down the empty side and started walking without a destination in mind. All I needed was to get away for a few and escape my sister's taunts before I did something I'd regret.

I made it halfway down the block before she materialized in front of me.

"Piper running away from her problems," she laughed. Vicious. Cutting. Harsh. "What's up for your next act? Saving someone? Oh, I know, avoiding that atman of yours to keep him keen. It's clever, really. I've got to applaud you for that one—"

"What do you want?" I sighed, crossing my arms.

Bree regarded me in silence, either considering her words or making me wait for the hell of it. Probably the latter.

"That's a loaded question, one you already know part of the answer to." I rolled my eyes and tried to step around her. She blocked my step, forcing me to either push her, stay, or walk away. Given how she appeared before me, something told me walking away wasn't actually an option.

"If this is about you going back to Hell—"

"It's not," she said, tongue sharper than a blade. "Not this time, anyway. This is about you."

Great, my least favorite subject.

I tilted my chin, waiting for her to go on.

"Aren't you going to ask, 'what about me?'" she said, mimicking my tone.

"No. You'll either tell me or won't, but I'm getting tired of these games with you. For the last week, all you've done is insult me or insinuate how I'm not worthy of Ronan. I won't lie, I knew some of it was coming. Nat warned me. Ronan warned me. But I really thought I could handle it for the sake of one month. Congratu-fucking-lations, Bree. I was wrong."

She yawned like she was bored. "Are you done with the pity party yet?"

Fire snapped through me and erupted out of the very ground where I stood.

I blinked, stumbling back. The surprise helped me get it under control and put it out immediately. I looked around wildly, wondering if anyone saw it. Never mind the foot-wide hole in the sidewalk and chunks of concrete surrounding it.

Bree lifted an eyebrow. "This is just getting comical now. But thank you for proving my point—"

"What are you going on about now?" I snapped, slamming my shoulder into hers to get past. I made it several feet down the walkway when she called out.

"You need to learn to use your magic."

I stopped, foot frozen midair. Slowly, I put it back on the ground and turned around.

"I'm honestly shocked Ronan hasn't taught you anything. For a while there, I thought you were hiding it. It's only the last week that I've come to realize how utterly powerless he's left you."

My lips parted, and I wasn't sure what to think, let alone say.

The word that came out wasn't what I expected, but it held anger all the same.

"Powerless?"

"Are you deaf now too?"

Smartass.

"I assumed you'd misspoken given it was *my* power that pulled you from Hell. *My* power that took you out of the Underworld. *My* power—"

"That you don't know how to use," Bree interjected. "You're strong—yes. I've no idea how strong, though, because you're a ticking time bomb with no purpose. No target. Your power is leaking out with every emotion because you don't know how to funnel it, control it, or use it in any functional way. Which makes you the weakest sort of demon—because it means your power is there for the *taking*."

"Is there a reason you insist on bringing this up again and again—"

"For fuck's sake, you're denser than I remember." She pinched the bridge of her nose and inhaled slowly. "I'm offering to help you."

I narrowed my eyes. "That's what you call an offer?"

She twisted her lips. "Saving people isn't my forte. That's yours."

I clenched my fists but kept every spark of fire in me. I had no doubt my eyes were shining red in that moment as I said, "Fuck you."

She lifted her eyebrows, but before she could respond—shouting filled the market. Smoke began to swirl in the air. I turned toward the noise, dread thickening in my stomach.

It was coming from Nat's tent.

22
PIPER

I couldn't run fast enough. My breath hissed between my teeth. My heart thundered. The shouts grew louder with every passing second.

"It's our time!" they shouted. My worry grew, blossoming into something like panic.

This was a human market, and while Nat looked human enough . . . she wasn't.

I crashed through the heavy tent material of the back and made my way forward. She stood behind her plywood counter, calm and controlled despite the angry mob.

"It's. Our. Time," they continued to shout. One particularly burly man got in Nat's face, making her flinch when his spittle flew everywhere. I stepped up next to her and the mob turned their attention on me. Every word they said grew more frenzied. Every face contorted in rage.

The relative safety that existed in between peace and war was fraying the thread that connected them, waiting to snap. It was that place where heated words turned to fists and fire.

"How did this start?" I said, speaking loudly for Nat to hear me over them.

"Someone recognized me," she murmured. A fist thumped against the table. I reached for the gun strapped to my waist when a cool voice interrupted me.

"Are you sure that's wise?"

I turned my cheek to stare at Bree, just inside the tent, leaning against the metal shelves. I glowered. "I don't have a better option."

She snorted, then waved her hand for me to continue. "If you say so."

Her response grated me but caused me to pause.

There were dozens of people gathered here. I was a good shot, but I didn't want to kill them if I didn't have to. That said, firing a warning shot would likely escalate this quickly. It was only a matter of time until one of them crossed that invisible line.

"You should call Ronan," Nat said.

Bree's sharp cackle was a knife against my skin.

"So much power . . ." my sister said. "And still utterly powerless. This couldn't have been better if I'd organized it myself."

"It's not powerless to ask for help," Nathalie said.

"It is when you have the ability to stop it. You don't *need* him. Or you wouldn't if she knew how to use her magic."

"That's well and good if I could do more than set everything on fire," I snapped.

"You would be able to do more if you'd learn."

"That doesn't help her in this moment," Nat shot back, coming to my defense. I almost told her to stop. Fighting with Bree was like arguing with a brick wall.

My hands clenched into fists. I needed to drown them out.

Both of them. Nat. Bree. The thundering voices of the mob.

I just needed it to stop.

But none of them did, and standing frozen with indecision about how to handle a group of angry humans—the choice was made for me.

Flames sparked, but they weren't mine. They started at the edge of the tent—slowly eating away at the fabric. The chant became broken with a new cry. A new purpose.

"Kill them!"

"Burn them!"

"Let's send a message!" It was that last battle cry that had humans storming us even as I scented smoke. They climbed over the table and grabbed blindly. On instinct alone, I punched the first fucker in the face. He fell back into the crowd and two others took his place.

My hand reached for the gun again, reservations quickly dwindling.

Bree sighed disappointedly in a way that only served to piss me off more, but I was a little busy knocking protesters back to address her.

Nat reached under the counter to grab a baseball bat, swinging it wildly. It worked the first few times. Until someone had the bright idea to catch it and rip it out of her hands.

"Well, fuck," she said.

The bat came down on the center of the table, cracking it in half.

The fire spread, on the verge of lighting the stalls next to us aflame. Humans stormed over the broken table and I didn't know left from right as true chaos exploded in the market.

"One time," Bree said, striding forward in her high-heeled boots. "And only because this is disgraceful to demonkind."

One of the protesters tried to tackle her.

She waved a hand, and the ground shook. I expected it to open up. To swallow us all whole.

Instead, silver and grey bits rose from it. They snapped together into bands that shot to every person in our vicinity and wrapped around their wrists. The bands guided them back down, latching back into the ground.

The shaking stopped.

The mob completely subdued.

Bree stepped in between them, not bothered by the thrashing as they fought her power.

"Metal," she said, turning to me. "It's the element I have the most control over. I can pull it out of anything and bend it to my will."

"Fucking supe," the man next to her spat. A wet glob hit her shiny boot and her brows lowered into a hard line. She stepped on his splayed hand, heel first.

Crack.

The bones shattered, echoing through the market. The humans went silent, apart from the one now yelling in pain.

"Stop that wailing," she groused, and another metal band appeared that wrapped around his mouth, muffling his screams. "You should really know who and what you're insulting before you do. I'm not a fucking supe. I'm a rage demon, asshole. And I'm tired of the ruckus." She snapped her fingers, and the metal lifted out of the ground, pulling them up to mid-waist so they could kneel. "You're pissed at the supernaturals for how you've been treated. That's understandable. Like it or not, you're also weaker. Picking a fight with them will only end in your death. For every supe you take out—they kill a dozen of you. More, even. Is that what you want? To die? For your children to die?"

A few people looked away, others rose to the challenge.

"We're already dying. They enslaved us all. We've got nothing left to lose," one man said. Bree regarded him.

"Nothing? You don't value your life? Surely you do, or you wouldn't be fighting for your imagined future."

That quieted him.

Bree sighed and looked from them to me. "Power is what you make of it. You used your guns to enforce your words. Fire is no different. I could behead them all where they sit. I could stab them. Choke them. Really anything, even poison them if I felt like it. Now they know that."

Nat began coughing as the air thickened with smoke. Bree didn't even look her way.

"Put the fire out."

I bit the inside of my cheek and focused on the flames. On extinguishing them.

They winked out of existence without a second thought.

"How did you do that?" Bree asked, without letting anyone up.

Embarrassment filled me, but I didn't let it show. "I willed it. They do what I want them to ."

"Because it's all about intention. You know how to start and stop it. Apply that to the other parts of your magic."

I lifted my hand and focused on creating a tiny ball of fire. It burst to life without any effort. Thinking back on how she'd played with her magic earlier, I wanted it to do the same.

The ball laced over and under each of my fingers, weaving through them. Surprise broke my concentration, and the ball spluttered off course. I extinguished it before anything else went up in flames.

A slow clap started.

I looked at Bree, who didn't show a single emotion on her face as she brought her hands together.

"Congratu-fucking-lations. Isn't that what you said earlier?"

I wore the same indifference she did, staring blankly like that wasn't the first minor accomplishment I'd had.

"What are you going to do with them?" I said, reframing the conversation.

"Tell them to get the fuck out of here and remember this the next time they think it's wise to attack someone for being a supe. They're on the bottom of the food chain for a reason. If they want to change that, they either need peace or power—and only one of them is feasible."

With that, she snapped her fingers and the metal bands dissolved into thin air.

The humans kneeling looked around as if they weren't able to believe she let them go.

A second passed for that information to set in before the vast majority of them ran like they were on fire, tripping over each other to get away.

Bree sauntered back to the tent and regarded it with a keen eye.

"I'd suggest using a glamour if you want to return," she said to Nat. "And our four hours are up," she added for me.

Bree started to stride away, and it irked me that she walked when I knew she didn't have to. She could have disappeared right then. But she was waiting for something. Or rather, someone.

"Will you help me?" I called out.

Bree paused, and I saw the smirk on her lips as she turned her head sideways.

"I'll pick you up at seven tomorrow. Don't wear anything you're attached to."

Then she vanished.

"She's an even bigger asshole than you," Nat said with a whistle.

"You're telling me," I grumbled, scowling at the spot she disappeared.

I could have sworn I heard a condescending laugh on the wind.

23
PIPER

I sensed him the second before he appeared. His magic thickened the air. Chaos twined around me, brushing against my skin. The hair on my arms rose to awareness. I kept my back turned while I selected another bell pepper for dinner.

"I gotta say, I'm surprised."

"About?" His voice was husky. Dark. Something had happened in the last few days we were apart. Something that made me tip my chin and narrow my eyes at the ripe orange vegetable in my hand. The snap of the stem was sharp in my ears as I pulled it.

"How long it took you." I turned to the side and kept walking, pretending to search for something else even though I had all we needed. "Given how many spies you have in the city, I assumed you'd hear about it earlier."

"I did."

My step faltered.

"I felt it when it happened. I was there, just outside the market," he said. I blinked to hide my reaction. "You're surprised." It wasn't a guess. I suppose I should have known he would know. My emotions were far from closed off to him —thanks to the bridge that always connected our minds.

"You have a habit of trying to save me," I replied, taking another step and looking over the lush green trees and plants, but not truly seeing them.

"You told me you didn't want to be saved." I paused again, hand covering over a crop labeled parsley. "I couldn't stay away. That was out of the question. When you panicked over Nathalie, I felt that through the bond, and I almost killed the humans right there..."

"But you didn't."

"You're trying. I can try too."

While Ronan was a man of few words, they were poignant. Important. Deeply so.

"I appreciate the vote of confidence," I said, finally setting the basket down and turning around. Eyes like winter skies and steel speared right through me. Burning with cold, cruel heat.

"I almost didn't," he admitted. "I was this close." He held his index finger and thumb only a sliver apart. He took a step forward.

"What stopped you?" I asked softly, a huskiness entering my own voice.

He smiled faintly, but it wasn't kind. "I don't think you want that truth."

"Do I ever want anything else?" I lifted an eyebrow in challenge.

"If they laid a hand on you, I could end them. Even from where I was. I didn't even need to lift a hand. You were never in danger. Only them."

I chuckled, but it was flat. Hollow. He'd held himself

back because he didn't need his hands if it came to that. "I suppose you did warn me."

"I never lie to you," he said, taking another step forward.

"Except about Anders?" I shot back without missing a beat.

His eyes darkened. Fire coming to life.

"I didn't lie."

"You omitted the truth as a way of lying."

"Why does it even matter?" he questioned, taking another step. "You worked together. He handed you over to Lucifer. Nothing more."

I cocked my head, a wry smile fighting its way to my lips. "And if we were?" I questioned.

He reached out to wrap his fingers around the nape of my neck, forcing my head back to look at him. "Were you?"

"Does it matter?" I purred, enjoying the way his hand was beginning to burn.

"Yes," he bit out.

"Why?" I said, egging him on.

"Because he's downstairs helping Nat and the succubi with dinner, and I need to know if I'm forcibly removing him before we go down there."

I blinked. That was not the answer I expected.

Slowly, a wicked smile curled around my lips. The fire banked just a fraction in his eyes as he realized I was messing with him. "Really? You *really* think I was fucking him?" I laughed.

Ronan's head dropped forward. He cursed darkly in a language I didn't understand, and didn't believe I'd ever heard before.

"You're going to be the death of me, woman," he growled sharply.

His lips came down on mine. He bit my bottom lip, making me gasp, and used the opportunity to kiss me deeper. His tongue brushed against mine, tasting of cinnamon and chaos. Tiny embers of fire sparked, heat curling around my core.

I reached up and fisted my hands in his sable locks, pulling him closer. Ronan groaned, pushing me back. My butt bumped into a hard edge before pressing against it. He grabbed my thigh and pulled it up, giving him better access. I curled my leg around his waist, and he shifted his hold to my ass—lifting me in a single swoop—as if I weighed nothing.

I swung my other leg around him, locking my ankles behind his back.

"If we break the table, I'll never hear the end of it," I murmured against his lips.

"I'll buy her a new one."

Well, that answered that.

Ronan pushed me back, balancing my ass on the edge of it. Too far back to stand and too far forward that I'd fall if not for his body wedging itself between my legs.

I pulled hard on his hair and he pulled hard on me.

We probably shouldn't have been doing this, on the rooftop, in the greenhouse where anyone could find us. But ...

He reached around to pop the button on my jeans.

"Grab the edge," he ordered.

"And if I don't?" I taunted.

He dropped to his knees and my body rocked forward. The only reason I didn't face plant was the hand against my abdomen.

Twisting my lips together, I did what he said. My hands curled around the table. "Up," he commanded. I lifted my weight so he could grab both my jeans and panties and peel them down the length of my body. Usually we didn't go through this step—fire and all being an issue with clothes. It seemed this time he was taking precautions.

"We have to go back downstairs," he said, answering my thoughts.

"You could just take us through the void."

"I don't have clothes here," he said. I narrowed my eyes, finding his logic odd given he could just as easily go back to his place—

The flat of his tongue pressed against my clit, drawing a guttural moan from me.

"Stop thinking," he growled.

"Keep doing that and I will," I breathed.

Ronan was happy to oblige.

Two blunt fingers entered me. My lips parted as the breath hissed between my teeth.

"Fuck."

"I plan to," he murmured against my thigh. His fingers crooked, tapping that place deep inside me that made me want to scream. Instead, I spread my legs wider. His stubbled jaw brushed against the sensitive skin. He turned his head away from my apex, nuzzling my thigh. I breathed easier for a moment.

I should have known better.

He struck like a snake, fangs burrowing into the artery there.

I rocked forward as the force of my orgasm swept through me. Sudden and unexpected. He reached up with his free hand to clap it over my mouth as a scream that could wake the dead forced itself out of my lungs. My pussy clenched over and over again.

My legs quaked, going taut then loose.

Shivers worked their way up my spine, turning to tremors as he took another pull and pinched my clit. The oversensitive nub protested his abuse. I tried to swat his hand away and he caught it.

Black eyes stared deep into mine. Despite knowing without a shadow of doubt this was the Harvester, I didn't feel fear.

Not breaking eye contact, he licked the tiny droplets of blood that dotted my thigh. His puncture wounds already healed.

"Whose pussy is this?" His voice was soft as velvet and cold as a winter's night.

"Mine," I replied, unable to resist the fight. How could I? I lived for it. Thrived on it.

His lips didn't twitch with amusement. "And who do you belong to?"

"Myself."

While our dynamic was ever-changing, evolving along with our relationship, we were still ourselves at the core. I wanted the fight. Ronan wanted me to give in.

I would. Eventually. But not before he worked for it.

He leveled me with a hard stare. When I didn't change my answer, he leaned forward and grabbed the corner of my T-shirt , lifting it. He pointed at a section of red-tinted symbols—sweeping lines edged with shadow and lined in chaos.

"What does this say?" he prompted.

I pressed my lips together and his eyes narrowed. Never in a million years did I expect what came next.

Softly, so quietly that I almost missed it—he whispered my name.

My true name.

The one no other soul, dead or alive, knew.

It was a beautiful sound, my name. The syllables didn't exist in this realm. They encompassed all that had been and all that I was. My darkness. My light. My rage. My desire. My struggle. It was all there.

So was my power.

Because to know a demon's name was to own them.

To have the ability to control them.

Ronan whispered mine for the first time, and said, "Whose name does it say right here?" He pointed to the same section of text.

I swallowed hoarsely.

"Yours."

His eyes darkened with hunger. "Say it," he commanded.

Unable to deny him, I uttered his back. The name that belonged to the true Harvester, king of demons, stealer of magic, soulmate of mine.

His eyes closed and his nostrils flared. An emotion akin to being fulfilled passed from him to me over the bridge between our minds.

"What does it mean that my name is branded on your skin?" he asked.

My nipples pebbled. The breath in my chest shook.

"That I'm yours," I said quietly.

"I'll only ask one more time, then." He leaned forward, and his cool breath hit my sensitive skin, making me flush. "Whose pussy is this to lick?" He spread my legs further, licking me from bottom to top. "To suck?" His lips locked around my clit and pulled hard, making me shudder.

I inhaled sharply. "Yours."

"To ruin?" he continued, a glimmer of amusement now surfacing.

"Yours," I repeated, a little more impatiently. He whorled his tongue around my clit, eliciting a sharp jerk from my hips that nearly sent me sprawling. A laugh rumbled deep in his chest.

"I think you need a reminder," he murmured.

"Ron—ah," I gasped as his lips sucked on me greedily.

"Not my name, but I could get used to it." I felt him smile against me as he pushed two fingers back in. Sensitive to the touch, I jerked back from him.

Ronan wouldn't have any of it.

His mouth plucked and pulled while his calloused fingers dragged along every nerve ending, sending delicious sparks of pleasure shooting through me. The climb to my next orgasm was harder. He kept me on the edge, my body tense and yet tired. Ready, yet resistant. Every time he got close, he'd ask who owned me. Who owned my heart. My body. My fucking soul.

I knew what he was doing. Collecting every piece. Hoarding them to himself, these raw words and admissions I could only find when we were intimate.

He'd once said he wanted to own me, and I never doubted that.

It was only later that I realized the only way he ever could was if I gave myself to him.

Chose him.

It wasn't a bid to control me . . . it was about choice.

Ronan said he wasn't truly a man because he never had been. He was a demon, through and through, bred from the very pits of Hell.

But for me, he chose to be different. He chose to defy his very nature.

And I chose to give in to mine.

Give in to him.

Ronan worshipped me with his mouth. His tongue. His teeth. My back arched and my legs grew stiff. Taut. I balanced on the precipice of oblivion, waiting for him to take me there—because while I loved the fight, losing had never been more delicious.

"Come for me, Piper."

I detonated. My body shook and my magic unfurled. I vaguely felt the prick of my fingers splitting as claws grew. My fangs fully descended, and promptly bit my bottom lip in an effort to not scream.

Ronan worked me through it, and when the fight left me and my body sagged, he got to his feet. "Better?" he asked.

"Aren't you—" I struggled for words and motioned to his erection to get my question across.

"Later," he said. "Nathalie almost has dinner ready, and I want to show you something first."

My brows drew together in a quizzical line. "Show me something," I repeated.

His answer was to hand me my clothes. My curiosity grew as I slipped my damp panties back on and buttoned up my jeans. I grabbed the basket, and he grabbed my hand, tugging me to his side and back toward the stairwell that led inside to the elevator.

"Is what you're showing me at Nat's place?"

"No," he answered.

The doors slid open, and we stepped inside. I twisted my lips, trying and failing to guess what he was getting at. I reached for the button to the second floor without thinking and paused when I saw another.

The lit-up number three made my insides turn.

"Press it," he said.

My mouth went dry, and my hand shook as I hit the number for the third floor. A number that hadn't existed in the months I'd lived here.

The elevator bounced and then moved, traveling too fast and yet incredibly slow. It jerked to stop, and the doors pinged before opening.

I held my breath, not sure what to expect.

"What is this?" I asked, voice hoarse for a whole new reason as I took it in.

Gray-planked floors that still smelled faintly of varnish spanned on and on. A roaring fireplace, already lit, gave the room a slight cedar and smoky scent. The flames created shadows that were absorbed by black leather couches.

I could pretend I didn't know what this was, that I didn't understand, if not for the picture sitting on the mantel.

Two little girls stood hand in hand, feeding the ducks.

It was the picture I'd had on my nightstand for over a decade. I'd left it behind when Lucifer sent assassins . . .

Emotion clogged my throat.

"I can't accept this," I said without even thinking the words through.

"It's not a gift," he replied.

I blinked. His response somehow pulling me out of the inner panic that was surfacing.

Ronan stepped into the space and the lights in the kitchen turned on instantly, illuminating distressed oak countertops and bronze fixtures. This place would cost a fortune. I knew that without a doubt, and I hadn't even seen the rest of it.

"I wanted to be closer to you. The place I was living was just one of the many residences I took from the Antares

Coven. I wanted somewhere that was my own . . ." He turned and leaned back against the countertop, crossing his arms over his chest. "With you."

"I don't know why I didn't think about this building having another floor," I said, searching for words that delayed the answer to the unspoken question I knew was coming.

"It wasn't finished. Señora was using it for storing her more ludicrous items." He shrugged.

"And she just gave it to you?" I asked, skeptical.

His lips curled around the edges, a slight smirk. "I made her a deal she couldn't resist."

Despite the tension that made my muscles bunch and kept my guard on high, I couldn't deny the snort that escaped me. "Of course you did."

Ronan stared at me. Deviously, brutally, cruelly beautiful in a way that was truly beyond this world.

He wasn't pretty in the way Lucifer was. He was darkness. A true demon from the night, brought to life with sensuous flesh wrapped in sin. His eyes were inhuman and terrifying in a way that the devil couldn't manage. His body larger than any ordinary man. Power oozed from the very pores of his skin, as if his body itself could hardly contain the beast within.

"You don't have to answer me right now. I know that change is hard for you. But make no mistake, I intend for this place to be ours." A shiver worked through me.

My tongue felt heavy in my mouth. I struggled for a snappy reply. Something to brush away the feeling edging through my chest.

"You haven't even shown me the rest of it," I settled on. The candidness didn't land when I took too long.

Ronan smiled, somehow easy yet wolfish. He extended a hand to me, striding forward. "Come."

My legs moved before my mind did. I took his fingers, and they laced between mine, the pricks of my clawed nails brushing against his skin.

"I wasn't sure what you'd like," he started as we walked down a short hallway that opened up. Three different doors. Ronan chose the one on the right first.

I knew without a doubt it was our room.

The black satin sheets and king-sized bed screamed Ronan, but they weren't what captured my attention. The entire back wall had been turned to glass.

My hand slipped from his as I started forward.

"Is it real?" I asked, pressing my fingers to the cold pane. It certainly felt real.

"It is. But the outside is glamoured to look like the side of the building."

"So you can see out . . . but they can't see in." While it wasn't the penthouse view, a few blocks of the concrete and metal jungle that was New Chicago glowed in the purple and orange tints of a sunset. Clothes lines, potted plants, painted graffiti brick walls and all—it felt like home. Imperfect and untraditionally beautiful as it was.

"I wanted to see the storms you create," he said quietly. Somehow that admission felt more intimate than anything we'd done physically.

My hand lowered away from the glass. Without looking at him, I walked through to the adjoining en suite bath and closet. It was similar to the penthouse he'd been living in for months, but wholly different. While simplistic, there was a warmth that went into this place. Consideration. Small bits of me and my life were layered throughout. Pictures he'd stolen. Furniture taken from my previous apartment that surprisingly hadn't been stolen or scavenged over the months. He combined the new with the old flawlessly. As if it were always that way.

"How long have you been working on this?" I asked, taking a passing glance at the second bathroom before starting for the third door.

"A while. The renovations took longer than I planned. Everything was put on hold when you went into stasis."

"And after that?" I prompted, twisting the handle on the third door.

"You needed time."

His words were punctuated by the sharp intake of breath. My breath. "This one's empty."

"For you to decide how you want to use it."

I mulled that over, closing the door firmly behind me. Not only had Ronan created a home, but he'd also left room to expand. That filled me with trepidation and fear. Fear of the unknown. Of the possibility—because it was a possibility. Everything was now.

Where once my life was hunting witches and scraping by to make ends meet—now it was more.

Slowly, I walked back into the living room. I put my hands in my back pockets and took a daring glance.

I was scared, and I wasn't too proud to admit it. But how many things in my life had I been scared about? How many fears tied me down? Hadn't I learned my lesson about running from my fears? Hiding from them?

I admired Nat for knowing what she wanted in life and taking it.

Could I be the same? Could I become the kind of person I actually wanted to be instead of embracing the scraps of myself that had barely survived this life?

"I don't need an answer this moment—"

"It'll need adjustments," I said, before I could talk myself out of it. "The elevator"—I nodded toward it—"there are people in this world that can repel magic, and I need to be prepared for all threats." I looked around the room, and the more I let myself consider what a life here, with him, would be—the more I could see it. "If this floor isn't soundproof already, it needs to be. Our room too—and because we have no front door, I want an alarm for when someone comes to this floor."

"Is this your way of saying yes?"

Dark. Delicious. Dangerous. His voice washed over me, closer than expected. My heart beat wildly, but for the first time in a long time, it beat for something other than fear or rage or panic.

"Yes," I breathed. "But there are conditions. Things I won't yield on—"

"Done."

I whirled around and crossed my arms. He planted his hands at my hips, grasping tightly.

"You don't even know what they are."

"It doesn't matter." He leaned forward, his thumb stroking that spot on my abdomen where his name was branded. "Whatever you want, consider it done. If you need assistance in the changes, tell Anders and he'll handle it. We can go over the rest of the details this weekend."

"I still have my visits with Bree," I reminded him. "And responsibilities to Nat. Even if I'm not living with her, I did agree to work for her—"

"And you can," Ronan said. "But at night, you're mine. Every night."

I swallowed hard, my fingers flexing and then curling as I fought the erratic urges running through me.

"Sometimes I love your intensity. It matches my own."

"But?" he asked, his lips curling with amusement.

"All my life I've been in fight-or-flight mode. Sometimes it draws that out and makes me want to run," I admitted. "Not out of fear, per se. But because that's what I do. When things get too hard, I run. I move on."

I stared hard at his chest because it was easier than looking at his face.

"I'd chase you," he said softly. "There would be no moving on. No hiding."

"I know," I replied, a slight smile edging my lips. "Why do you think I said yes?"

I tilted my head back and lifted my chin to look him in the eye. As silver as mercury and just as deadly. "This thing between us, it's literally branded in my skin—and yours. I tried running once, and you found me. I tried fighting, and you didn't let go. Maybe it's time I tried something else. Besides, we're already bonded for eternity—moving in seems like a small thing by comparison." My lips twisted into a smirk.

His mouth descended on mine. Hot and hard and demanding.

"As much as I want to fuck you right now, I'm fairly certain the witch will find a way to have her payback if we don't stop delaying her from dinner," Ronan muttered against my lips. "Make no mistake, tonight, you're mine."

My skin heated in anticipation.

Then he stepped through the void, taking me with him.

"It's about damn time," Nat said. A spicy scent filled my nostrils. "You can't have fajitas without peppers. Hand them over."

I stepped out of Ronan's grasp to plonk the basket on the counter. She snatched the peppers out and quickly went to work washing and slicing.

Sensing another presence and eyes on me, I turned around.

"Hey, Pip," a familiar, albeit younger and far deeper voice said from across the living room. I blinked, my brain trying to process what—who I was looking at, sitting between Sasha and Sienna.

Nothing about this person was remotely recognizable. The lush brown shoulder-length hair, hard body, strong jaw—none of it. Except for a pair of sad blue eyes that saw too much. The realization washed over me, and my fingers reached for my hip where there was usually a gun, just not this time.

Anders laughed softly, then patted Sienna's knee before standing up.

"Glad to see some things haven't changed—"

Crack.

My fist swung hard and fast, striking him in the jaw once. There was a time I might have hesitated knowing I had demonic strength I couldn't control.

Given the otherworldly gleam in his eyes, luscious locks, and flawless skin—I'd say he could take it because he sure as shit wasn't human.

"You're a fucking supe?"

"Ugh," he groaned, putting a hand to his jaw and working the muscle. "Really, Pip? Coming from you?" He lifted both eyebrows and a hint of shame touched me that I ignored.

"I thought you were dead," I snapped. Empathy softened his eyes. "Instead you're alive *and* working for him." I hitched my thumb over my shoulder to the demon at my back.

"I'm not the one that made the decision to not tell you," he said quietly. My jaw tightened as I glanced over to Ronan who was all too proud of himself for that second.

I hummed. "Why am I not surprised?"

"It wasn't important. " Ronan shrugged.

I turned my cheek to stare at him over my shoulder. Lifting an eyebrow, I said, "We'll be talking about that *tonight*."

"Something tells me there won't be much talking involved," one of the twins muttered. Sasha it seemed, given Sienna let out a girlish chuckle. I rolled my eyes, but otherwise ignored them.

"So am I to take that to mean she said yes?" Nat asked from the stove.

I whipped around to stare at her. "You knew?"

"Who do you think sold the stuff Señora Rosara was hoarding in there?" She chuckled. "Also who helped him with the renovations? Mind you, I was helping because I didn't know he had a henchman yet." She waved the tongs toward Anders.

"Colleague," he corrected. "Partner. You've got a plethora of options there—"

"Colleagues aren't told what they can and can't do," Nathalie said. "That implies equal ground. Have your plans for New Chicago changed, Ronan?"

The peppers sizzled when she tossed them onto a cast iron pan.

"No."

Nat smiled, enjoying being right, as always. "To answer your question, Piper, yes. I knew. And I'm glad you said yes." She stole a quick glance at me, eyes dropping a bit, then smiled. "I do hope you'll continue to help me during the week, though, around your time with Bree. I'll pay you double since you don't live here anymore—"

"There's no need," I waved her off. "You pay me well as it is. Just know I'll be here for dinner most nights and we can call it even."

She chuckled. "You got it."

We all knew among the four of us that lived here, Nat was the only one who could really cook. Growing up poor, it wasn't a skill I'd learned, though it was probably my favorite indulgence in this new life. One I wasn't so ready to give up, even if I was capable of learning—and so was Ronan for that matter.

"Dinner's ready," she announced a few seconds later, then promptly began serving people food. We sat at the bar, on the couch, and in Anders' case—on the floor.

"I haven't had fajitas in years," Anders said, speaking first. "Almost three decades. Not since El Paso." He took another bite of the spicy goodness and hummed.

"El Paso," I questioned. "Where's that?"

"Texas," he and Nat answered at the same time. "It borders Mexico," he added.

I studied him closely, taking in the more subtle aspects of his new appearance. There was a certain ageless quality about him that a witch or warlock couldn't get. It was something only the immortal had.

And crossing borders between territories wasn't what it used to be. Demons and higher-up supes ruled the world—and they didn't take kindly to passersby.

"You were here before the wars?" I mused, feeling him out for more information.

Anders chuckled. "You could say that." He nodded toward Ronan. "Not as old as that one, mind you."

Nat choked on a bite as a laugh forced its way out of her, turning to a coughing fit. She drained half a glass of water and swallowed a few times before muttering, "That's not saying much."

Ronan shrugged, unbothered by their jokes. But I pressed on. "How old?"

Anders regarded me for a moment, then set his plate aside. "Old habits die hard, Pip?"

I scoffed, brushing it off. "I don't know what you're talking about. It's just a simple question—"

"Knowledge is power," he said, quoting me. "You studied me and wrote me off when I was human. Now you want to know more. Is it the rage demon or the Witch Hunter asking?"

I placed my half-wrapped fajita taco down and wiped my hands on a towel.

"Come on, guys, it's just dinner—" Sienna started, trying to smooth over a perceived conflict. It wouldn't be—if he answered my questions.

"Both," I replied. "You know me. You studied me. Now you're working closely with Ronan. I can't help but be curious about your actual origins when I'm not certain what you are—and if I need to worry about it."

Ronan's hand rested on my knee, silently telling me it was okay. I pushed it off, judging for myself.

Anders grinned, an easy smile of amusement so similar to the man I knew before, yet wholly different. It was that difference that filled me with uneasiness.

He reached down to the edge of his sleeves and slowly pulled them up—to reveal brands. Demonic brands.

"I'm not a demon," he said when he saw the way my eyes narrowed. "But I am part-demon. My father was one and my mother was fae. I exist somewhere in the middle."

"Only mated demons can have children," I said.

Beside me, Ronan went tense, but Anders merely nodded. "My mother was turned by my father, then the bond appeared. While supernatural and demon pairings are truly rare—it can happen. I'm the proof of it." He motioned to himself. "But to answer the real question at hand, no, I'm not a threat. I took the job with Ronan because I want to see a better world than the one I've lived in the last thousand years. One where humans and supes can coexist—and I know the only way that will happen is with the right demon in charge. So in that, we're not so different."

My chin dipped in acknowledgement. "I had to ask," I said by way of apology. I was too stubborn to offer a real one. And I wasn't truly sorry.

Anders grinned as if he knew that. "I'd be disappointed if you hadn't. You've shot me for less."

Sienna choked and Nat looked between us. "He's the one from the door at your apartment?" she asked, recalling the early days when we'd first met . . . when she was my captive, newly-turned accomplice.

I nodded. "He showed up at my doorstep unannounced, making threats. You just don't do that these days unless you want a bullet in you."

Nat threw her head back and laughed. Sasha shook hers like she had thoughts about that. Ronan chuckled, his fingers finding their way to the back of my neck, threading through the loose strands there. Claws pricked my scalp, making me immediately aware of his proximity.

"I didn't think you'd actually shoot me," Anders said. "It was a bitch to lug around that boot for days, pretending I'd broken my foot. Couldn't have you asking questions, though, when and if you came for him. I knew it was only a matter of time, even when I thought you were human. Too much fire in you to go down that easily." He shook his head in amusement.

"Well, I guess you won't make that mistake again." I shrugged.

"You got a cold woman, Ronan. She always has been," Anders said with a shake of his head. He was grinning despite the exasperated sound of his voice. "Probably always will be."

The hand at my neck tightened. I flushed in response to the possessive move.

"I hope so," Ronan said, his tone even and not betraying the lust I felt rising in him. "A cold woman is strong enough to survive this city."

Anders nodded along, but I turned, distracted, as the ghost of a voice that I almost thought I'd imagined whispered through my mind.

A cold woman is strong enough to rule it too.

My lips parted. I looked sideways at Ronan in question.

The slight curve of his mouth was my answer.

24

PIPER

I haphazardly braided my hair back as I waited for the elevator doors to open. My foot tapped with impatience. Anxiousness.

They couldn't open fast enough.

I came face-to-face with my sister. Her bright eyes narrowed.

"You're late."

"I know," I breathed. "I'm sorry about that. My new . . . accommodations didn't have my alarm clock. I didn't think to move it. I'll rectify that tonight."

The harshness in her gaze sharpened as if she could see right through what I was saying. But she didn't call me on it. She simply gestured for me to get in the elevator, then hit the ground floor. It closed shut and the leaden tension grew.

Without Nat as a buffer, I was well and truly flailing.

We exited the elevator in silence. I was halfway out the door when a voice from deep in the shop called out, "Stay away from caffeine."

I paused, looking over my shoulder. I couldn't see her

buried behind the stacks and shelves of junk. "Do I want to know why?"

A thoughtful kind of silence passed.

"Not yet."

I blinked, finding her answer out of place, but the caustic voice at my front kept me from lingering. "Three hours and forty-six minutes."

She was counting off for the twelve minutes I was late. Lovely.

I stepped out of the shop and closed the door behind me. She waited; arms crossed.

"I'll teach you everything I know. Everything. But you have to promise that you won't tell Ronan any of my abilities. That you won't inadvertently tell him, or one of his people. That you won't communicate them in any way, to another living soul—or dead, if you have that power."

I narrowed my eyes. "Why the secrecy?"

She lifted a shoulder haughtily. "I'm not back to Hell yet, and on the off chance something comes between me and home—I'd rather no one have a heads-up to what I can do."

The right corner of my mouth turned down. "But you'd show me? The sister you hate?"

She stared at me for a full ten seconds before answering. "Yes."

"Why—"

"Piper, I'm not going to share every thought or detail of why I want something with you. I'm giving you what you need. I'm also fulfilling our bargain. Isn't that enough? Can you not just leave some things be?"

I took a slow breath then nodded.

It wasn't enough. Nothing short of her staying was enough.

But it would have to be because it was all she was offering.

"All right."

"Swear it."

"I swear I won't tell or communicate what you can do to anyone, dead or alive." This wasn't a bargain, but a promise. No blood had to be exchanged because it wasn't an oath. It was just me giving, and my own magic binding.

Bree extended a hand to me, and for some inexplicable reason, I didn't hesitate.

Maybe I should have after making a promise, all things considered.

But the second our fingers touched, we both disappeared.

"What the—" I flailed, releasing her hand. In an instant, I reappeared. "What the hell, Bree?"

My sister turned corporeal beside me, looking far from amused. Without offering an explanation or asking permission, she grabbed my hand again, locking tight. I disappeared once more, and so did she.

"You can make yourself... invisible."

"Not quite."

Then the street disappeared. One second we stood outside the shop, and the next we were in a wide-open field. Our bodies reappeared just in time for me to process the storm as rain pelted my clothes. Wind whipped at my poorly braided hair. Lightning streaked across the sky, casting Bree and I in harsh shadows. Her face was grim.

"What are we doing here?" I demanded, speaking louder than necessary despite the roar of thunder.

"Learning," she replied, stepping away. "You need to stretch your limits. Putting out small fires isn't enough." Bree waved a hand to the storm. "When your control starts to fray, it's not just fire you have to worry about. It's storms. Your ties to the elements . . ." She tilted her head back to look at the sky. "I haven't seen a demon with so much raw power that was so unrefined. Let's find out how deep it runs."

My lips parted and lightning struck not more than five feet from me.

Bree disappeared.

Fuck.

I turned in circles, knowing she wouldn't be there, but still needing to look. As far as the eye could see, it was grass and sky. Not a tree in sight.

Only me and the land and the storm.

I took a deep breath and planted my feet, lifting my eyes to the sky as Bree had done. A vortex circled overhead. Angry clouds and turbulent winds, going round and round and round.

Thunder clapped riotously.

I told it to stop.

To disperse.

To calm.

Mentally, I tried to command it like I would a dog, and I felt all the stupider for it.

The gust that followed nearly pushed me over. Stronger. More virulent. As if my demands had angered it further.

"Don't coax it," my sister's whip-sharp voice said. "Control it. *Own* it." I whirled around to the sound of her, but there was no one there.

I clenched my hands into fists.

"Control it," I muttered to myself. "Own it," I groused. My jaw clenched as I pressed my lips together. "How instructive."

A phantom laugh descended over me, sparking the anger inside. Despite the cold, it warmed me.

I stared at the sky defiantly and the storm stared back.

Intangible and yet completely destructive.

Lightning struck again. Closer still. Near enough the hairs on my arms singed at its proximity.

I lifted a hand, slowly extending my awareness. Letting myself *feel* the storm.

Feel its violent energy. The way the wind slapped, and the rain pelted. How the air thickened in its grips.

I'd felt energy like that before. It might not be burning, but the darkness was there all the same.

I reached for it, but I didn't try to whisper sweet nothings.

Calm wasn't in me. It never had been.

So I reached for that other thing, where my magic laid inside me, where it bloomed and prospered.

I reached for my own darkness. My rage. My fury.

Embracing it. Becoming it.

My breath slowed to a crawl. Blood roared in my ears.

The storm continued around me as I descended deep into that place.

I felt it when energy sparked between the clouds. My hand was open and waiting when that bolt looked for an outlet. A way to rid itself of that destructive heat.

Lightning struck me.

It invaded my body. My pores. And I let it.

This deep into myself I didn't feel pain. There wasn't even the heat I'd come to associate with my magic. Only power. Pure. Raw. Primal.

Nature wasn't magic, but it had a power all its own.

But in the face of mine . . . it tried to run. To flee. To escape the prison of my body and flow back to the earth.

I didn't let it.

My fist closed. I grabbed hold of the lightning as if it were a thread attached to the sky. My skin lit up like a star as it raged within me. At my defiance.

I didn't care.

The world opened up before me as I got it. I really got it.

The storm may not have started in me, but it was an extension. Because I was a demon with power over the elements. Not some half-cocked magic user, but a demon. A creator of power. Of fire and storms.

And if I wanted—destruction.

I pulled on that thread of lightning and made the storm dissipate.

Like it was just an extension of my body and as simple as moving an arm or a leg, I cast the winds away and evaporated clouds. The thunder died, and the lightning broke apart. Sparks fraying down the cord I held in my hand.

I blinked, opening my fingers, thinking I'd find nothing.

Instead, the lines of my brands extended past my wrist, sweeping over my palm in delicate, yet harsh strokes. While abstract, I knew without a shadow of doubt that my name had changed once more—because this mark was for the moment I caught lightning and conquered a storm.

"Faster than I expected," my sister said from behind me. I whipped around to see her standing with her arms crossed over her chest, clothes dry and hair fixed. As if the storm never happened. "At least you gave me a good show. Nice touch, catching the lightning. Very theatrical."

I lifted an eyebrow, unamused with her antics. "I wasn't sure what to expect with you 'teaching' me. I should have known it would look more like you throwing me into the deep end and telling me sink or swim." I chuckled.

Bree wrinkled her nose. "You need it. Ronan's too soft

with you, and no one else can teach you." She shrugged a shoulder and then added, "Besides, you always excelled in high adrenaline situations, even before you were a demon."

I cocked my head, surprised she'd mentioned our childhood, or that more thought went into her method than I'd assumed. Before I could question it further, she rolled her eyes and said, "Come on, we've got another storm to catch."

25
RONAN

"Welcome," the incubus said. He spread his arms wide in an inviting display that motioned to his club. "I've heard this is your first time to Paramour," he purred. "Could I interest you in a sampling of what we offer?"

He snapped his fingers, and two lovely succubi appeared. One was a striking beauty with hair that looked like nightfall itself. She had one icy blue eye, and one green. The other was equally stunning with warm brown skin, shiny black curls, and amber eyes that glowed like the dawn. They stepped forward in unison, as he said, "On the house, of course."

"Not interested."

Anders leaned against the bar, chuckling under his breath.

Rafael, the incubus, twisted his lips. It was a motion similar to my atma's, but hers was more amusing than this conman's.

"We do have others," he continued, "that might suit your fancy."

Another incubus came up to his side.

He wore a collar and nothing else. The leash attached to it dangled to the floor.

My annoyance grew when he didn't take the not-subtle hint the first time.

"I was under the impression that you were the new head of the incubus faction in this city," I said quietly, assessing him.

Rafael tilted his head in surprise. "Of course, that is why I offer you only the best. A toast to what I hope is a very prosperous friendship."

I took another step forward, dismissing his offerings without a glance, and lowered my voice. "For someone who is in charge, you must not be well informed—or you'd know I am bonded to another."

The incubus smiled deviously like he knew just that.

"Ah, the Witch Hunter. I'd heard rumors. But I also know that beings of such power sometimes like to enjoy other *things*." He snapped once more, and the other incubus and succubi drifted away obediently, back to the shadowy couches where other patrons waited. "You aren't the first of your kind I've entertained. My mistake."

I hummed, not amused by the games he was trying to play. "You must never have worked with a demon who was soul-bonded. While I can see pretty *things* for what they are, they hold no desire for me. Only my atma."

"She is a lucky woman," Rafael said as easy and fluid in this game, as though he'd played it a hundred times. I disliked him instantly. It brought out my cruelty.

"She's also a rage demon with enough power to level this city and more. One who doesn't take kindly to betrayals. I think it's you who is lucky that I am not that kind of demon—and that she is not here."

Rafael jerked. The bead of sweat at his temple gave me a

cold sort of enjoyment. The race of his pulse reminding us both that we were not friends. I was the ultimate predator, and if I decided, he would simply be prey.

Anders laughed, all too amused. Today he wore a glamour, albeit not a human one. With the level of animosity in the city, it wasn't safe to pretend to be human in a supernatural establishment. Instead, he opted for full fae; a role easy enough to play given it was half his lineage.

"I don't think she'd burn the city for his suggestion," he said, placing his empty glass on the bar and starting toward us. "But she is prone to shooting things that annoy her . . ." He trailed off, clearly thinking about their history.

The story eased my callousness for a moment because it was wholly Piper.

"Shall we get to business, then? I'm sure you're very busy."

The change in attitude was appreciated. Anders and I shared an amused look as Rafael led us deeper into Paramour, the incubus' whore house of lust.

I'd seen enough establishments like it in the Otherworld. Their purpose there was slightly different, however. An entire faction of demons were born with desire magic and needed it to feed off of. Like all things that might be a necessity, though, there was more than enough room for abuse.

Rafael led us into an office that smelled of tobacco and cologne. The harsh scents burned in my nostrils as he took a seat behind his desk and motioned for us to follow.

I opted to stand.

"You want me to swear an oath," the incubus said, being straightforward for the first time since I stepped on the premises.

"This city is going to tear itself apart if peace isn't found soon. The supernaturals are infighting for resources. The humans too. We're on the brink of another war," Anders said, speaking for me since he was the official go-between. "Someone has to take control before we plunge back into anarchy. The witches tried—and failed. The humans have no power. Your kind make excellent spies, but you're not fighters. Not truly. If that happens, you're as likely to be slaughtered as any other group—"

"I'm not disagreeing with you," Rafael said. "And I'm not opposed. You aren't wrong that we need someone to lead. My hesitation comes from what happened with Lucifer. His fall." The incubus tapped his fingernails on the desk softly. "To swear an oath is to take the blood. If it takes, I grow in power, yes—but if the demon I took from *falls* . . ." he trailed off, dark eyes flashing. "I need assurances."

"I'm the Harvester," I replied. "You might not know what that means here, but where I come from, there is no other who is stronger. I am not my brother—"

"Yet you were chained just the same," Rafael replied.

Ah. Now I saw. He did know far more than he let on.

"Lucifer ruled for thousands of years in the shadows, but his downfall was the woman you call yours. The Witch Hunter. We know it. Some might blame the witches, but they wouldn't have been able to sacrifice him if not for what she had done."

I tilted my chin. "Oh? And what did she do?"

Rafael looked down at his desk. "I'm not sure. All we know is that he followed her one night to an alley—the same night you killed every person in the Seventh Circle. She walked out of that alley, unharmed. Lucifer walked out, nearly dead—and the witches finished the job."

I crossed my arms behind my back. "How do you know

about that night?" I took a step forward and stared down at him. "As you said, I killed everyone."

"Everyone in the club," Rafael replied. "The twins were not, and Sasha Loren made sure it was no secret what caused the end of her lover . . . that was before she swore herself to your mate."

The pieces started coming together, and I suspected where this was going. "Lucifer made mistakes. One of many was pursuing Piper."

Rafael smiled unhappily. "He did, and the people pledged to him paid for it." He placed his hands on the desk and rose to his feet. "I won't be one of them."

"Diego Cortez ruled the incubi and succubi on the east side of New Chicago until two days ago when he turned down this offer," Anders said, inserting himself into the conversation while Rafael and I stared each other down. "His spot has since been vacated. With the Harvester's power and backing, you'd be strong enough to take it."

"I don't want your backing," Rafael said without looking at him. "I want the Witch Hunter's."

Inside, my pride swelled—alongside my annoyance.

While I knew where this was going, I also knew Piper would not take on another blood oath right now. Not when she had such issues accepting the twins.

"She's not on the table."

"Isn't she, though?" Rafael said. "You said yourself she could level the city. The only one the Morrigan could not chain was her. She destroyed the Underworld and caused Lucifer's fall. If anyone is going to be a safe bet, that's strong enough to lead and not be exploited later, it's her."

"She isn't the one—" Anders began. I lifted my hand to silence him, and he stopped.

"Is that your final answer?" I asked. "Blood oath to my atma, or no oath at all?"

Rafael's chin dipped. There was a slight tremble to it. He feared my anger, and the consequences that came with it.

"Diego died because he refused," I said.

His Adam's apple bobbed. "I'm aware. But I'm not refusing. I'm saying not you."

I waited a few seconds, giving him time to break. To yield. To see how hard his resolve was.

When a full minute passed, I nodded.

"I'll speak to Piper," I told him, turning to leave his office. "But I will warn you, she may not be an option. Piper is particular about those she goes into a blood oath with."

"I know," he said. "But I am willing to earn it."

I nodded once, not giving anything away.

"Very well."

Anders and I exited his office and then the club. I grabbed his shoulder and took us through the void to expedite the process. Back at his apartment, I released him and stepped away.

"She's made a name for herself," Anders said. "Earned, but unexpected. By bonding with the twins, she's all but declared herself a player in the game."

"She doesn't see it that way," I sighed. "She felt responsible for the twins, and guilt is what drove her to bond with them. She'll have no desire to take on others."

"Perhaps," Anders agreed. "But she might do it if she knew it would keep this city from falling apart. She didn't spend a decade tracking down a way to bring Bree home and cleaning up the trash for nothing. This is her home. She won't want another war."

I considered it, but quickly concluded I had no idea.

Piper was unexpected with these things. She resisted me when I thought she'd yield, and she gave in when I expected her to run. While I could see what Anders was talking about, he also didn't understand the immense responsibility a blood oath would be on her. To that end, neither did I. Only Piper could tell us what she was prepared to do for this city.

"Does she know your plans?" he asked, interrupting my train of thought.

"To some degree," I muttered. "She knows I have every intention of taking New Chicago. I haven't brought her in on the specifics to this point because she has enough on her plate at the moment."

Anders nodded. "You may want to loop her in sooner rather than later. I know you hoped to wait until Bree returned to the Otherworld, but that may not be an option."

"Unfortunately," I murmured. Internally, I looked to the bridge that spanned between our minds. I often did it throughout the day, just to check in. My awareness prickled as I realized that she wasn't at the apartment, the market, or anywhere else I'd expected.

I expanded my search, a growing unease quickly building.

"What's wrong?" Anders asked slowly, the furrow of my brow having given it away.

"She's not in New Chicago."

"What?" He snapped to attention. "Then where—"

At the very periphery of my reach, I felt her. The calm current of her emotions. The wash of her rage magic stretching its claws. If she'd been in the city, I wouldn't have missed it; how much power she was harnessing.

But she wasn't here. She wasn't even on the same continent.

Without answering him, I stepped into the void and reappeared in Nathalie's apartment. The witch was singing at the top of her lungs about a highway to hell while whisking something in a bowl.

With a look at the music box, the sound cut out.

She jerked to a stop, slow to register who was here.

"Where's Piper?" I demanded.

She turned around and lifted her eyebrows. A dusting of flour lined her jaw. The circles under her eyes were worse than they'd ever been, despite the way she poured herself into music and cooking. "How would I know?"

"She's always with you," I said, trying to make sense of how she'd ended up on the other side of the world.

Nat scoffed. "Hardly. She doesn't even live with me anymore—"

My breath stopped when Piper disappeared entirely.

There was no thinking. Just going through the motions as I searched the entire globe—and found nothing.

"Who's she with?" I asked quietly. Deadly. Nat sensed the shift and didn't hesitate.

"Bree."

The only thing that kept me half sane was that our bond hadn't snapped. The bridge was still there—but her presence. I couldn't find it.

I couldn't see—

All at once she appeared again. Downstairs. Right outside the wards I'd placed so that no one other than us could enter the building by magic.

"I'm sure she's fine, Ronan," Nat said. "They're off practicing magic. Better way to spend the hours with that one, if you ask me—"

"She what?"

Nat blinked, her expression smoothing. "Piper didn't tell you?"

"No," I said in a clipped tone. "She most definitely did not."

26
PIPER

We chased storms until my four hours ran out. By the end of it, my body felt languid as if finally exhausted and satisfied, the release of magic similar to a great workout. When Bree took us back to the shop, I gripped her hand more tightly. Extending the moment before I'd reappear.

"Thank you, for today."

She tensed, the muscles in her hands tightening between my fingers.

"It's nothing."

"Maybe not to you," I said, not letting her sudden coldness deter me. "But I appreciate it all the same."

She started to pull away, and instead of forcing the moment, I let her go.

My body reappeared and so did hers.

"How do you do that?" I asked.

Bree opened her mouth, but instead of answering, she paused. Her eyes focused on something over my shoulder. Her stance changed, turning from indifferent to defensive. Her spine straightened, and the look in her eyes turned cold.

"Ask me tomorrow," she said, then disappeared.

I sighed deeply while the shadow at my back quietly seethed. I didn't have to be bonded to him to know that Ronan was pissed, and I was the cause.

No, the menacing pull of his power spoke for itself.

Still, I jerked when he finally spoke.

"Care to tell me how you ended up on the other side of the world this morning?"

I crossed my arms and pivoted on my heel to face him. However, when I opened my mouth to say Bree took me, the words froze on my tongue.

I couldn't say that. It would give away, at least in a fraction, one of her abilities.

The stumbled silence fanned the flames of his anger, as he assumed—wrongfully—I was searching for a lie.

"I thought we were past this," he said quietly. And while he was right, part of me straightened at his comment.

"Past this?" I repeated.

Dark fire grew in his eyes, eclipsing every hint of mercury. "Lying," he said. "When were you going to tell me you asked Bree to train you how to use your magic?"

"Lying? Like how you failed to mention working with Anders?" I snapped back.

"That's different and you know it," Ronan said. "By your own admission he was just someone you worked with, and now he works for me. Bree actively had a hand in the gun—"

"This again?" I lifted both eyebrows. "Last I checked, I can't very well ask her to move on if I'm not willing to do the same."

"It's not the same," he growled. "Bree is more than capable of hurting you on her own. You'd be near powerless if she tried—"

"Whose fault is that?"

Ronan stared, and I stared back, unflinching.

I opened my mouth, wanting to strike out further, and then snapped it shut as I thought better of it, shuffling forward and trying to step past him. A calloused hand grabbed my arm, trying to halt me.

Annoyance bubbled up, sending a crackle of electricity down my arm.

Ronan jolted, but held firm. His nails sharpening to claws with his own riled frustrations.

"Well, she must not be training you that well if your magic is still lashing out."

I barked a harsh laugh, grating even to my own ears.

"Today was our first day, but thank you for making me feel like shit over the small bit of progress I made."

I didn't look at him, but I sensed the shift as his power banked and recoiled.

"I didn't mean—"

"You did," I snapped, this time willing a bolt of blue energy to ripple over my skin. Stronger and hotter than fire. It was enough to make him drop his hand.

Without saying anything else, I stepped into the shop and started for the elevator. Ronan followed closely behind.

"You disappeared. I couldn't find you. When I realized you were in *Africa*—"

"That's a shitty excuse for being an asshole," I replied, mashing the button for the second floor.

"*I couldn't find you,*" he repeated. Ronan's hand swept out to hit the emergency stop. The elevator jerked to a halt.

My exhale came out as a hissed breath as his arms appeared on either side of me, caging me to the wall. "I shouldn't have said what I did, but you still didn't tell me.

Not in the greenhouse yesterday, not at dinner, or in bed later that night—"

"I was a bit preoccupied," I retorted. The feel of lips grazing my neck, followed by the prick of fangs being dragged along my skin made my blood sizzle.

"Were you in the light dimension?" he asked quietly.

I opened my mouth to answer. To say no. But once again, not even a single word would come out. I realized with a frustrated growl that I couldn't say because if it wasn't my power that took us there, it was hers.

"I can't say."

He froze, his hard chest pressed to my back. "Can't or *won't*?"

"Can't," I growled, annoyed at how he still doubted me. "Bree had me make a promise to not reveal any of her abilities."

I sensed the rising anger once more, but he kept it on a tight leash. "She teleported you there."

"I can't answer that."

"If she hadn't, you'd have been able to tell me you crossed through the light dimension. I know she can't use the void. I would have sensed her. Which leaves very few options of teleportation to get you there."

Instead of repeating myself like a broken record, I stood there in silence. He already knew I couldn't say. There was nothing to add.

"That was stupid of you to agree to," he continued.

I turned my cheek to glare at him out of the side of my eye and he nipped me sharply, drawing only a tiny prick of blood. Arousal and anger battled inside me.

"Don't give me that look."

"Don't insult me," I replied. "I understood her reasons.

If for some reason her return to Hell falls through, she doesn't want another demon having an advantage over her."

He snorted. "Then why show you her hand?"

My hands clenched into fists at my side. "I don't know. At the moment I'm assuming it's because she's teaching me. If we ever came to blows, she'd have the advantage of knowing my strengths and weaknesses. I'd be powerless, at least in the immediate future, as you so nicely pointed out." I couldn't keep the acid out of my voice. That one stung given it was the same word she'd used to convince me to train with her to begin with.

I was a lot of things, but I wouldn't allow myself to be powerless.

"Which is why it was stupid," he said again. "I don't understand why you went to her. If you wanted to learn to control your magic, I would have taught you. If you'd given any indication that you wanted . . ." Ronan shook his head.

Understanding washed over me. What this was about. The anger. The sense of betrayal. Ronan was . . . hurt. That I didn't go to him. That I didn't ask.

I wondered if he realized it or if this was one of the first times in his exceptionally long life that he'd felt that.

"I didn't ask," I said after a moment. "Not at first, at least. She spent the last week taunting me. Telling me I'm powerless because I have all this magic and don't know how to use it. Then the mob happened at the market and I froze." My head dipped in shame. "If they were supes, I wouldn't have hesitated to shoot, but they weren't, and I knew I wouldn't be able to control any fire . . . I was powerless. She was right. So I took her up on it. She's a rage demon like me, and—"

"—The person who's helped make magical weapons—"

"—my sister," I finished. "She's mean and callous at times, most of them in fact, but I can't help feeling like she wants to help me. Like she still cares, somewhat."

"Piper," he breathed and something featherlight pressed against my hair.

"I know. *I know* she's going to choose Hell. She's got an atman waiting for her. But I think this might be her way of loving me—trying to give me the tools to protect myself."

Ronan sighed. "You still could have come to me. I might not be a rage demon, but I have rage magic. I've trained hundreds of demons across my life. It would be *my honor* to train you. It should be mine. I told you I want every part."

I cocked my head and lifted an eyebrow. "Is that your way of asking?" I tried to twist around but his body kept me caged. "If so you're as bad as she is."

"I'm not asking. I'm telling. The only reason I didn't sooner is I didn't want to push you on that. If you're going to accept lessons from Bree, though, you'll be getting them from me as well. I need to make sure she's actually helping you."

I rolled my eyes. Only he would make the jump from being hurt to taking control.

Typical.

"Are you done being an alphahole now?"

He chuckled, cool breath fanning that patch of skin below my ear that sent goosebumps rising along my arms.

"Making sure my atma is properly trained is hardly being an alphahole."

I hummed. "Coming at me with assumptions and insults is."

"I'm sorry," he said quietly.

I paused, tilting my head. "I couldn't hear that. Can you repeat yourself?"

"No," Ronan said, before biting my neck.

I gasped, my core tightening with delicious heat.

"Are we really doing this here?" I breathed as his length pressed into my ass. Ronan's fangs released me with a pop. He licked over the tiny incision, doing nothing to sate the budding lust inside me.

"That depends," he murmured, lips trailing my jaw, "on when you apologize."

I inhaled indignantly. "Me? Apologize? For what?"

Despite the amused curve of his lips, he was utterly serious when he said, "Trying to run back to Nathalie's place because we were having a disagreement."

I narrowed my eyes. "That wasn't a disagreement. That was you being an ass."

"Be that as it may, you tried to run. Again. Not even twenty-four hours after agreeing to move in with me. I'll chase you, Piper. Every time. But I also want you to get to the place where I don't need to chase."

I could have lied and said I was planning to visit Nat. But it would have been just that. A lie, like he accused me of from the beginning. The truth was I was fully prepared to march in and tell Nat I needed my room back.

"Old habits die hard," I said quietly. "This is still new to me. It will take time . . . but I am sorry for jumping to that. Even if you were being an ass."

Ronan pressed a kiss to my temple, chuckling under his breath.

"I can't promise I will change. As you say, old habits die hard. But we have all the time in the world—and if that's what it takes, so be it."

We didn't talk after that, but as he took us through the void, directly to our room—something more profound slid into place for me. More permanent.

It wasn't marked on my skin, but I felt it all the same.

And it scared me.

27
PIPER

WHITE FIRE WEAVED BETWEEN MY FINGERS IN THE SHAPE OF A dragon. Its long, lithe body rolled over my knuckles with hard-fought concentration. Sweat beaded my brow, but the dragon continued moving—which meant I was winning.

"You've come a long way in a short time," Bree said quietly. She stood a few feet away, leaning against the metal rail. This morning we were practicing in Paris. On the no longer functional Eiffel Tower, to be exact. Bree claimed it was because the air was thinner this high up. That it would provide a greater challenge to me. But I couldn't help noticing, our lessons were always at beautiful, faraway places that we once talked about visiting as young children. Places on a thirteen-year-old Bree's bucket list we probably never could have visited. You'd never know the girl that stood before me was the same person, but hints of her were there, her brilliant blue eyes locked on the fire in my hand. "Your control over fire is nearly there. Lightning too."

"Water and wind could use some work," I said, not as thrilled with how my progress was there. It had only been a week and a half, but I was impatient. I could separate both elements now, instead of simply summoning a storm. Wind was easier than water. Ronan said fire was less complicated because it was my first element, and the one I would probably always favor. Bree said it was because fire was my crutch.

In their own ways, they were probably both right.

"Earth too," she added. "You can make it split and quake, but that's not exactly useful the vast majority of the time." She waved her hand and slivers of iron lifted away from the tower, gathering in a tiny sphere that orbited before her. It melted and molded, the rumored shine returning once more as she played with it.

"Do you think I'll also have the affinity for metal?" I mused, watching her manipulate it without much effort.

"Possibly," she said, still watching it. "A bonded demon's magic no longer grows, but you don't know the extent of yours to begin with. To this point, all your powers have manifested as the classical elements, and metals are just chemical elements of the earth."

She wasn't completely right, but she also wasn't wrong. While I was bonded, I did have things outside that spectrum. Things like the light dimension, and the way that my nails would shift. Ronan said it meant I had the ability to shapeshift, but our progress was minimal there at best. Still, he was helping me on those, so I didn't bring them to Bree. Not when she wasn't honest or upfront with me about herself.

"Most of your powers don't lie within the elements," I said.

"That's not a question," Bree said, watching the metal flatten and grow prongs. A rose formed at the base. She spun the hair clip with a twirl of her finger, examining every detail and making small adjustments before she finally let it float back and settle into the braided crown around her head.

"How is it that we're both rage demons and our magic comes from the same place, yet it's so different?"

"Why are witches different?" Bree said. "Rage is the fuel. It's what powers us and how we use it. The shape the power takes . . ." She shrugged. "That's left to chance and personality."

"So your personality is hard as metal with a penchant for disappearing on people?" I nudged, pushing more than I would have a week ago. Time was running out. While these days were the best I'd ever had with her, with Nat, with Ronan—they were coming to an end. Soon she'd return to Hell, taking any answers to questions I didn't ask with her.

Bree chuckled. "You never were good at beating around the bush."

Instead of the coldness I'd been used to, wry amusement flitted over her features.

She settled against the railing overlooking the ruined city. Much like New Chicago, it wasn't what it once was. War and famine had ravaged here too, made worse by the vampire lord that decided to claim the territory for his own.

"I'm curious. Can you blame me?" I asked. "You came back a demon, one with very different powers than what our run-of-the-mill supes have."

"Part of that is because I'm not a supe. Part of it is me, and how I got my powers."

When she didn't say more, I turned my chin to stare pointedly. She didn't glance my way or make any movement like she noticed. "I'll make you a deal," Bree said, still without looking in my direction. "Tell me what happened when you were in the summoning circle and gained your power, and I'll tell you how it happened with mine."

I blinked. "You know what happened."

"I know you were supposed to be the sacrifice and somehow you took a demon's power. Tell me more."

I turned my cheek, staring at the wide blue sky. "I was searching for power as a way to help us. Mom was running ragged from her clients. There were so many times we didn't know if she'd come home alive. Dad was exhausted and depressed because it was getting harder to protect us. I wanted more for them. For all of us, and I thought magic was the way. It's what separates humans and supes, after all. I tried to get vampires to turn me. Wolves to bite me. It's harder than you might think. Those species had issues with turning someone my age. They told me to come back when I was older, but at the time it felt so far away. Then a man named Claude Lewis approached me with an offer I couldn't refuse. All I had to do was be in the center of a summoning when the demon was called. He said I'd be able to bargain with it."

"You fell for that?" Bree questioned.

"I was desperate," I replied. "And while we knew a lot about vampires and shifters and witches—we didn't know much of anything about demons. There was so few. What I did know was if I were going to get the power I needed—that was my best shot."

Bree snorted. "It worked."

"It shouldn't have," I said quietly. "I didn't know until after that I was meant to be the sacrifice. During it . . . I was scared, but more than anything I was angry. When my life started draining away, it didn't take a genius to figure out they'd duped me." I flexed my hands against the railing before curling them into fists. "My heart started racing. I can still remember the sound of my pulse as it drummed in my ears. After everything we'd been through and everything I'd done to change our lives, I was pissed that it was going to end that way. Then I felt her."

"Who?"

"Aeshma," I breathed her name, and it sounded almost as familiar as my own. "She felt my rage, and I felt hers. She was still coming into this world when we collided. By using my life force to power the portal, they made me the first point of contact—not them. That was their mistake. I don't know how, but I know that's the reason I absorbed her."

Bree stilled. "Absorbed her?"

"I was so angry, and she was drawn to it. When she came to me, I felt her curiosity. Her interest. Her intention. If I survived, she would have made me her first supernatural slave because she liked my fire. My anger." I laughed softly, but there was no amusement in it. "I didn't want that—to be a slave. I'd already lived sixteen years as one and I wasn't going to anymore. Then I felt her panic. My heart was still racing, but it was changing. I was changing. Her anger became my anger. Her panic, my own. The rage I felt at being lied to and used made me out of control. Then my heart stopped."

I could still see and feel it all so clearly if I let myself think.

Aeshma was long gone, but for a suspended moment in time, we were one and the same.

"You never made a bargain," Bree said. Not a question, but a realization. "Neither did I." She moved away from the railing and slowly walked along the metal cage flooring. "When the curse hit me, it felt like I was falling. I tumbled into the Otherworld, but when I landed, it didn't hurt. There was no impact. It was only after days of wandering through the forest alone that I realized I wasn't there."

I frowned. "What do you mean you weren't 'there'?"

"My consciousness was, but my body wasn't real. I didn't need to eat. I didn't feel tired. I was essentially a ghost." While she kept the conversation casual and easygoing, a note of somberness entered her tone, and I had a feeling that her time there was anything but.

"When you become invisible..."

She smiled at my insinuation. "An ability that comes from how I became a demon. I don't think I'm a ghost because I've seen ghosts, and I'm not entering a new realm. I think what I'm doing is probably best described as astral projection."

"And the teleporting?"

"Something I learned after a few months of wandering. Eventually, I came across people—demons and their creatures. It was easier then, even if they couldn't see me."

The bitterness... being alone...

"How long were you like that?"

"Years," she whispered, staring at me from across the tower. It's like her eyes willed me to not show pity. To not crumble in the face of what I'd brought down on her.

"At some point, the loneliness turned to anger. Anger I was there. Anger no one could see me. Anger that I was going to be trapped like that for the rest of my life... and then I wasn't."

I blinked. "Just like that?"

Bree nodded. "It didn't last, that first time. Or the one after. But slowly, I got the hang of it. The ability to choose when to astral project and when to exist in the physical realm."

"Just going to Hell made you a demon?" I asked.

"I... don't know. Not for sure. I have theories. I got stronger when I was around other demons, stronger still when someone made me angry. I think that somehow I was leaching power off of them. It wasn't until I found Lorcan that I made the full jump, I think."

"Bonding to him?"

She looked away. "Killing his partner."

My lips parted. I snapped my jaw shut just in time for her not to see the shock when she glanced at me. "I knew he was mine from the moment I saw him. Lorcan . . . he didn't see it. I was so angry that when she grabbed me . . ." Bree smiled, and it chilled me to my core. "I wasn't trying to absorb her or her power. But I did."

"It's not your f—"

"Don't," Bree snapped, her voice like a whip. "It is my fault, and I don't feel sorry. After all the bad shit, I earned my happily ever after. With Lorcan."

I wasn't sure what to say. It was more than I thought she would tell me, and while I clung to every small detail of her life . . . I hadn't expected it to be like that.

Then again, I wasn't sure what I expected.

She was a human that became a demon. If my own process were anything to go by, there was strife involved. Anger. In the depths of mine, I'd made some pretty horrible decisions.

"I should take you back," Bree said at once. Her boots pinged off the metal as she strode forward and grabbed my forearm. If I didn't know any better . . . I would've said she was embarrassed.

We disappeared and Paris vanished.

Bree dumped me at Señora's shop front, but before she could leave, I said, "I hope you have a long, happy life with him."

My sister paused. The loose T-shirt shifted in the light breeze. Her sharp jaw tilted.

Whatever our sessions had brought us, whatever ice had thawed inside her—something visceral surfaced.

"If you really meant that, you would let me go home instead of being selfish and forcing me to stay."

I didn't react as the words landed like a knife to the chest.

Not even when she vanished.

Because despite those cold words, I felt her—the metallic tang in the air that I'd come to know was her magic.

It followed me through the shop, up the elevator. Only when I entered my apartment did it vanish.

Only when I knew I was alone did I let a single tear fall.

Then the anger came.

28
RONAN

"That's the third time this week someone's asked to swear the blood oath to her," Anders sighed. "You need to talk to Pip." He walked over to the kitchen bar and poured himself a drink.

"I know," I sighed.

"If you know, why haven't you?" he responded, taking a sip of the pungent liquor.

"She's making progress. Getting control of her magic. The time with Bree is helping her—and I haven't wanted to interrupt it." Anders opened his mouth, likely to tell me to stop assessing what Piper could and couldn't deal with. I flashed him a warning look. "I know she could handle it. My reasons this time are more . . . selfish. She can, but I'm enjoying seeing her happy for once. I don't want to throw something in the mix that could change that."

Pity flashed across his features. The fae-demon hybrid bastard shook his head.

"I don't blame you, for the record." Anders moved away from the half-full glass of brandy, stepping around the counter and then leaning back. He crossed his arms loosely.

"She's had a hard go at it, and Bree's time is coming to an end, which is going to make it hard again. But I don't think we can afford for you to wait on this much longer. Rafael is impatient to hear from her, and he's not the only one. Like it or not, Lucifer's end has created doubt in demons, Piper notwithstanding. Earned or not, too many of them don't want to swear themselves to you for fear they're signing a delayed death warrant." Anders sighed at my lack of a response. "I know there's a chance she may still say no—"

"She won't," I interrupted. "Not with what's on the line. Not if I explain it to her. New Chicago is in a tenuous position. We're teetering on the brink of civil war. Someone has to take control, and it has to be us. Without her, I won't be able to stop it. Not unless I take the city by force. True force." I scrubbed a hand through my hair, not liking my options.

"She wouldn't forgive that," Anders said quietly.

"Maybe," I replied. "If she didn't agree, and I did what I had to, I think in time she would, but her own guilt is what would become insurmountable. Forever may be a long time to fix things. It's also a long time to live with the mistakes you've made."

"Talk to her," Anders said. "While there's still time for her to consider it. We're at three people now that won't take the oath with anyone else. There will be more, and we need to have an answer for them."

"I will," I agreed begrudgingly. He was right. I never disagreed with that, but when it came to Piper, not every decision I made was based on logic. "Soon—"

A sudden presence in my mind made me tense.

Ronan, something happened. You need to come home now.

Like a cold snap had occurred within, I went frigid.

"What is it?" Anders said, his arms dropping as he strode forward.

"Emergency. Cancel all my appointments for the day."

I stood up from the couch and entered into the void. My blood sang of violence fueled by fear. Of what I'd find.

In a single step, I was back home.

It was worse than I'd thought.

"I came to pick her up for work and found it like this," Nat said, hysteria bleeding into the witch's tone. "I haven't tried scrying for her yet. I thought you'd be faster—"

"You did the right thing calling me," I said quietly, walking through the destruction.

Glass was smashed. Couches overturned. Holes punched clean through the walls to the other side. Bricks had cracked. Crumbled. The fireplace gone out, leaving only ashes behind.

As I took in the sheer amount of rage magic still lingering in the air, my dread sank further, filling me with a cold fury.

There was a fight here. A struggle.

Except it was all Piper.

"Ronan," Nat whispered my name. She'd crossed the room to pick up something. I walked up behind her to see. Amidst a pile of glass and splintered wood was a picture.

Half of it burned with sheer precision.

"You need to find her," the witch said. "Before she does something she'll regret."

The photo that once showcased two smiling girls feeding the ducks, now had only one.

Bree was burned out, and in Piper's rage—not even ashes remained.

29
PIPER

I walked without a purpose.

Anywhere but here. Anywhere that I could drown out the rage. *The pain*.

Some anger was born of righteous fury—and then there was the rawer kind. The type that came about from despair. Hopelessness.

I'd known she wasn't happy here, but I thought things were better. I thought we'd made progress. I thought...

It didn't matter.

To her, I was just a captor. A selfish bitch holding my own happiness above hers.

I wasn't sure when I dared to hope, despite knowing this was how it would end—but I did.

And it was stupid.

I was stupid. A fool. An idiot blinded by what I wanted to see.

Flashing lights caught my attention, but it was the scent of smoke and pull of magic that lured me in. It was soft and subtle. It promised me numbness from this fire. Absolution from my pain. Oblivion.

I followed, barely registering the sign above the door.

Sin.

How ironic that sin would bring peace. I suppose that was why all saints were still sinners. No one could be that moral without something to keep them grounded. Even the best of us needed to play in the dark so we wouldn't become blinded by the light.

Tonight I would play.

Revel.

I walked in with the intention to forget. To lay down my guilt and anger and pain, and instead walk the path of . . . sin.

As if the universe heard me, 'Walk with the Devil' by Karliene played; a smooth beat and a sultry voice. The perfect thing to lure me deeper. Lucifer might be gone, but the longer I lived, the more I understood how he ended up the way he did.

The pain of Aeshma rejecting him drove him here, and he cloaked himself in sin to forget. To move on.

I couldn't forget forever, but for tonight . . . I walked up to the bar, ignoring the curious glances my way. Dressed only in a T-shirt and ripped jeans, my red-tinted brands stood stark against my warm, pale skin. While not everyone knew what those brands meant, enough of them did. And those who didn't could deduce who I was from the reactions of others.

My name was a whispered curse over the supernatural club that night.

Witch Hunter. Rage Demon. Those titles followed closely behind, quiet enough a lesser being wouldn't hear it. There was another title though. One I'd never heard before. One I never expected.

Queen of New Chicago.

I wasn't sure who said it, but I paused and surveyed the crowd with cool calculation. Bright eyes met my stare, and while I'd sworn up and down I was no one—nothing, a demon without a purpose... I liked the power it gave me.

A cruel smirk found its way to my lips, and without a word I headed to the bar.

I'd never wanted to rule . . . but I wanted power. The ability to protect what's mine. Being a hunter didn't give me that, and neither did being a demon.

Maybe being a queen might.

Maybe the title alone could keep the monsters in line, both human and magical alike.

It was something to think about.

"What'll it be for ya, beauty?" a girl that looked too young to be serving asked. She had green and purple hair, parted down the middle and pulled into pigtails. Her eyes matched the colors, opposite sides of the hair. It was a striking combination that I'd never seen before.

"Whisk—" I paused. Whiskey was what I'd turned to before.

I could tell myself I'd stop at one drink. That I wouldn't go for the bottle. Then take another. And another. Drowning myself in liquor until I'd consumed enough to get a buzz.

I wanted to. I was honest enough to know that. Something else held me back, though. This nagging feeling. The part of my conscience that gave me guilt when I made bad decisions. I wanted to be free of it, especially for tonight.

If I drank, I'd just be slipping deeper. Becoming more entwined with my horrible coping mechanisms. No, I wouldn't touch the stuff. If for no other reason than my own self-respect.

"Water," I corrected.

She tipped her chin, lifting a purple eyebrow. "Not what I expected," she said, pulling a glass and shooting cold water in with the nozzle.

"Oh?" I asked, not touching the water as she slid it across.

"Usually when someone comes here wanting to forget, they turn to the bottle." She smiled wryly.

"Who says I want to forget?" I bristled. The magic swarming the bar tugged at me, trying to soothe my frayed nerves.

"You're here."

Her eyes were knowing, amused, and somehow challenging me to refute the assertion all the same.

Instead, I chuckled under my breath.

"Fair point." I downed the water in three gulps and slapped it back on the varnished bar top with a light thud.

"There's other ways to forget. If alcohol isn't your drug of choice," the bartender mused as she started wiping down glasses, "there's sex. Smoke—"

"No," the word popped out of my mouth before I could think.

Her eyebrows inched higher.

"If you don't want alcohol, sex, or magic—what are you here for, uncrowned queen?"

I blanched. It was one thing to hear the whisper, and another to have it said to my face. But I didn't hate it.

"I . . ." The quick and easy answer sprang to my tongue, but it wasn't the truth. I came here to forget, but booze wouldn't do it. That would just drown me further; sinking me so deep it would be harder to say no the next time. Harder to turn away. Drugs were just another booze in a different form. Sex . . . I wouldn't touch anyone other than Ronan, regardless of his threats. I truly had no desire to be with anyone else, certainly not a meaningless fuck. I'd already known that life and what it had to offer, and I didn't want it. Not anymore. "I want release. Drugs won't give me that."

She regarded me with far more intelligence than I'd expect of someone her age. Despite the colors of her eyes, they were old. Older than me.

"They never do," she said. "Few realize that, though." She set the glass she was wiping aside and placed her hands on the bar. "What will bring you release?"

"Living."

I hadn't thought about it, but the moment the word left my lips, it was like a lightning strike. I'd left because I was lost. Angry and hurt. The reality was Bree's words affected me so deeply because despite knowing I needed to say goodbye—I clung to her. I clung to what she meant.

I clung to who I was because who I wanted to *be* scared me.

I didn't know what a world without Bree looked like.

But maybe I could.

The bartender smiled. "Smarter still. I knew I chose right."

"Chose right?" I murmured.

"M' names' Dahlia Le Grange. Come find me when you're ready." The saucy wink she gave me felt genuine, and yet deceiving. Like the girl before me was far more than meets the eye.

"Ready?" I questioned.

"You'll know."

She turned away to help other customers without a further glance, leaving me to ruminate over her words and my own realization.

Between the music and the spells weaving its magic, I

slowly released the pent-up anger that wasn't truly for Bree, but myself. I released the guilt that caused it.

Because I fucked up, but I also tried to fix it.

I didn't banish her from Earth because I hated her. It happened because I tried to save her. I made choices, both good and bad, and I tried to make amends for the ones that hurt her.

But if she couldn't forgive me and move on after all this time . . . it wasn't my problem anymore. We'd made a deal, and she would go home. I tried, and that's all anyone can do.

But if I could learn to love a demon and live with a witch, she could forgive if she wanted to. It was a choice.

A second strike hit me.

Love a demon.

The word sounded absurd when thinking of Ronan, who loved to mock human love. But it was there. Not instant like the spark of flame. It was a vine that grew between the cracks in the concrete, despite the lack of sun and against all odds. You might not notice it for weeks, but then one day you walk by and it's climbed up the wall and around the windows, until it's all you can see.

I could have laughed under different circumstances.

Instead, I sat there in my newfound revelations and felt peace.

Real, true peace.

Until someone had the gall to interrupt it.

"So you're the Witch Hunter they whisper about."

I half turned in my seat, lifting an eyebrow.

"What's it to you?"

His eyes were so dark red they appeared brown. His jaw was angular and his cheekbones high. He had a cruel face. It danced on the line of horrifyingly beautiful and deceptively monstrous. His pale blond hair wasn't as yellow as my own. Not like sunlight, but rather the white light of death—the one humans claimed they saw when they died and were brought back.

I didn't know who he was, but I knew without a doubt —he was powerful.

"Curiosity," he answered with a smile I didn't believe. "How one could be the Hunter, the Demon, and the Queen ... I had to see for myself."

I rolled my eyes, but it was a practiced move. Something about this guy set me on edge. Something made me take notice.

"People have given me many names, for things I've done and things I haven't. I stopped correcting them because there's not much of a point. My reputation is bigger than me. Sometimes it's annoying, and sometimes it comes in handy."

I started wishing the bartender would come back and refill my glass so I had something to sip with this stranger. I stared at him, unblinking. It wasn't the most nonchalant expression, but the energy he oozed wasn't either.

I wondered if I was the same. If my energy did things to people.

"You let people come to their own conclusions," he murmured, brushing his thumb under his bottom lip. "I can't decide whether that's clever or cowardice."

I could easily be offended, but instead I found myself leaning forward.

"You don't?" I asked. "In my experience, people will form opinions either way. I've just reached a point that I don't care."

He stared at me with such intensity his pupils dilated. "With the power you have, you could reshape it. Redefine this world . . . and yet you don't. You simply let it go on around you because you don't care."

His tone didn't sound condescending or condemning. It was confused, as if needing to understand and splicing apart my words was the only way how.

"I shape the world in my own way. Some assume demons are meant to rule; maybe we are. But maybe that's just how it's always been. I do what I choose, for better or worse, and let people draw their own conclusions."

He tilted his head, and his keenness made me wonder about this chance encounter.

"And if one day you wanted to truly be queen and not just let people draw their own conclusions, would you reshape history and tell people what to believe?"

"No," I said without hesitation. "Our history is important. It teaches us good and bad. It's a reminder of our mistakes and our triumphs. I don't believe in rewriting history..."

"But?" he prompted, softly, yet almost commanding.

"Every action we take shapes the future. It's history written in the moment. I would hope that whatever choices I made would speak for themselves, given I will live long enough to contend with whatever the people of later decide to think of me. If not . . . at the end of the day, all that matters is what I think of myself."

I knew that, and it didn't take a realization to see it. My guilt was my own. My anger too. My resentment. My prejudice. Those things all came from within. The only thing I gave a shit about regarding someone else were their actions and how they treated other people. Their opinions weren't exactly a priority worth wasting time on.

"Lucifer did that," the mysterious stranger mused. "He

let the masses govern themselves. Look what became of him."

"He half-assed his job," I replied, combing over the bar in search of its keeper and still not seeing her. "He kept supes in line to some degree, but the blatant abuse they still doled out to humans largely went unpunished."

"His treatment of the humans isn't what brought about his demise," the man said. "He didn't keep the supernaturals of this world in line. He was lax. You said so yourself. Half-assed. Isn't that the true cause?"

I cocked my head, assessing him. No, it wasn't. I knew deep in my soul it had something to do with me, something to do with his scorn of Morgan Le Fay, and perhaps a little bit of resentment from the witches. There were many factors that went into it.

"You could also make the argument that his death was caused by trying to control what they thought and did. Instead of simply enforcing good behavior, he sidestepped somewhere along the line," I mused. "The madness settling in him probably had something to do with that."

The stranger didn't say anything as he sat, considering my words and weighing them. "You're intriguing. A conundrum at the very core."

"Maybe," I shrugged. "Or maybe I'm just an asshole that hides behind the titles people give her."

His lips twisted, as if that somehow told him an answer to a question I didn't know he was asking. "Clever, it is," he murmured. "That's a pity."

I frowned, gaze sharpening.

"What did you say your name was?"

The smile he gave me was chilling to the bone. "I didn't. Until next time, Piper."

He slid off the seat and started into the crowd. I toyed

with following him, hunting him, as some baser instinct told me I should. By the time I slipped off the seat, though, he was gone.

Vanished.

Something cold filled me. A chill that burrowed under my flesh.

It preoccupied me so fully I didn't immediately feel the dark tendrils of chaos weaving through the bar. Not until Ronan appeared.

Dread filled me for a different reason as I remembered the way I'd left our apartment, and how he was now finding me.

In a club... sitting at the bar.

Shit.

30
PIPER

"What did Bree do?"

I blinked. It shouldn't have surprised me. I'd been upset, after all, and burned her out of the picture in our living room. It was such a small thing to notice among the flipped couch and broken glass...

I cringed. While I'd been upset, I might have overreacted.

Pain turned to anger quicker than I'd like to admit, and my resulting actions weren't thought out. Just reactionary.

"She did nothing," I said after a moment. The music seemed to slow around us. I sensed that the supes of the club had taken notice, but they didn't say anything. Where some had whispered my name as queen, Ronan wasn't necessarily their king. I was of this world. I was born here. Raised here. My blood soaked this ground. My pain was cultivated in this city. Ronan was apart from that. He stood out as *other*, like some dark god that wouldn't answer their prayers. Only destroy them.

"Don't lie to me."

"I'm not," I snapped. "She didn't *do* anything. I'm the

one that got my hopes up thinking things had changed . . ." I sighed, shaking my head. "I got upset when I realized that wasn't the case, and then lashed out. I'm sorry about the apartment—"

"I don't give a damn about the apartment."

Ronan strode forward and brought one branded arm up to pinch my chin between his thumb and forefinger, tilting my head back. "But this *is* what I was concerned about. Your sister has issues. If being around her upsets you this much—"

"I can handle it," I replied defensively.

"Can you?" he challenged. "Because you've always had a problem with your temper, but from where I'm standing, she brings out the worst."

I twisted my neck, pulling away. "Be that as it may, she's my sister. We talked about this—"

"And now you're in a bar."

"I haven't drank—"

"I know," he interrupted. "This conversation would be going very differently if you had."

I reeled back as if he'd slapped me.

Standing from the bar, I mustered all my will together. Ronan stepped forward, crowding my space. He placed a hand on either side of my waist, leaning forward.

"Piper," he said my name. Equal parts warning and pleading. As if he saw the look in my eye and knew what was coming.

I willed the bar and the lights and the music to disappear.

I willed Ronan to disappear, and in doing so, I summoned the light dimension—just like he'd taught me.

Brilliant, near-blinding white surrounded me. And silence. So much silence it couldn't even echo.

This was my place. My dimension. My power.

Bree had astral projection and Ronan had the void. But my place was here, in a world of white.

I sensed his concern turn hot through the bond. Even through dimensions it burned me. Scalding the defenses in my mind.

What happened to no running away, his voice whispered over the bridge? A shout turned to nothing more than a breath of air from the distance that spanned between us.

I grit my teeth.

Even here, in my own damn realm, he could reach me.

The same thing that happened to not trying to control me or make assumptions, I answered, pacing. *You may not like Bree, and I get that. I do. But she's my sister, and I'm choosing to have this relationship—even if it'll end in hurt. You may not like it, so let this be the reminder—I make my own choices. I am a demon in my own right, and more importantly—I'm a woman.*

This isn't about that and you know it, Ronan answered. *I don't like it, but if she's pushing you to the point of drinking—*

I wanted to rip my hair out.

In a snap decision, I envisioned the white realm breaking open and reappearing in our bedroom.

He was right there waiting when I did.

"You aren't listening," I ground out. "My choices are my own, for better or worse. She can't make me do anything any more than you can."

"Neither of us may be able to choose for you, but we can influence it. We affect you—and I don't expect you to be immune to it all. But if the only things she's bringing into your life are negative—if the only things she makes you feel are negative—why do you put yourself through this?"

He sat on our bed with his elbows on his knees, hands

together and head slightly bowed. Concern marred his features and tension rippled through him.

"Because she's my sister," I said weakly. Even I had to admit, I was beginning to sound like a broken record. This time she truly hadn't done anything, though. My reaction was on me. My temper tantrum—my problem. She truly wasn't at fault, even if she was mean at times. I was a grown-ass adult, and I handled it poorly.

"And Lucifer was my brother," he responded. "But I was prepared to kill him if he pushed the bond with you because of the risk it posed. He might have been blood, just as she is—but I valued us more."

I sighed. "Lucifer was half mad. Bree is a fully bonded demon—"

"She's not."

I paused. "What?"

"I can tell when a demon has completed the bond. Her power is still growing. Her rage, still growing. She's not bonded—even if she has found her atman."

My lips parted. Ronan wasn't a liar. Not at heart, and I knew that. I *knew* it. But Bree had said . . .

I blinked slowly.

"I might have assumed," I said quietly. "Given how adamant she was about returning."

"You want to see the best in her. I understand that. But your sister is not a good person. The rage in her has festered. Something ugly sits behind her eyes. And when I come home to the apartment as it was and find you in a bar —I am *concerned*." His hands clenched into fists and then unfurled. "You are so much more than Bree's sister—and just as you are hurt because her feelings haven't changed— I don't like to see what this is doing to you in the process."

I sighed and took a seat next to him. The bed dipped

under my considerably less weight. I reached over and took his hand, squeezing tight.

"As hard as it was to come to that, I know that. If anything, this afternoon helped because I see things clearer. She may not forgive me—now or ever—but I don't need her forgiveness. I never did. Just my own." I released his hand very suddenly and looked away. "It's why I didn't drink. I knew it would just make me feel worse. I'd be lying if I said I didn't want to—but I chose not to, for me. Not because of you. And the way I lashed out? That's also on me. Bree can be a bitch sometimes, but today my anger just got the best of me—and that's not on her. As much as you may want to excuse me from my own actions and blame them on her—she can't control me. Neither of you can."

"Look at me."

I half-turned my cheek, and he pulled it the rest of the way. Violet met steel as we stared at each other.

"I don't want to control you. You wouldn't be you if I did. But I struggle to see the influence she has on you and the way it sends you spiraling. One week. That's all I have to tolerate, and all you have with her. Am I happy about today? No. I'd send her back to Hell right now if you'd let me. But you need this week, and I can accept that—but I'm going to ask again, stay out of the bars. There's more than just liquor to worry about, and you're highly susceptible to spells and other magics. If you're going to go to one—at least bring Nat or me with you."

I riled against his request. The independence in me struggling to give at all.

"I can't promise I'll never go to one, but I will make a point to bring Nat with me."

The corner of his mouth curled upward in cruel amusement.

He noticed what I'd left out, just as I thought he might.

"Just Nat?" he prompted.

"That's what I said, isn't it?" My eyebrow inched up in a challenge, and his hold on me turned from stern to possessive as his calloused fingers slid over my jaw and down the column of my throat, positioning his grip at the nape of my neck.

"You're going to be the death of me," he uttered, before using his other arm to pull me on top of him.

"But such a sweet way to die," I purred, drawing a chuckle from him. I felt it in the brush of his lips all the way to the hard length between my legs.

"The sweetest," he agreed. Fangs pierced my skin, and everything dissolved into a lust-filled haze.

We stayed up, fucking till the early hours of dawn. I didn't realize I'd passed out until I awoke to an empty spot beside me.

The sheets were cold.

31
RONAN

When I arrived, she was sitting in her armchair, staring blankly out the window.

"I expected this sooner," Bree said quietly. She held a glass of wine in one hand, rolling the stem between two narrow fingers. Her nails were coated in iron and pointed in the shape of claws. "Piper never has been one that can tolerate her own negative feelings. She always has to *do* something. I'm curious what it was this time."

Darkness edged my vision. Instead of showing her the way her words affected me, I summoned a second chair with the flick of my wrist. Bree blinked slowly, the tell so similar to Piper that it irked me further. I took a seat without looking at her.

"She spent a decade looking for you. Not only that—she spent a decade keeping you safe. Do you know how your sister lost her virginity?"

I felt the cold of Bree's magic wrap around her. "Probably to some human boy. Maybe the officer that asked her to marry—"

"She gave it to an incubus in return for the necklace that kept your pathetic shell of a body alive."

Bree froze, recoiling so subtly I wouldn't have known if not for that vicious magic inside her.

"Not possible," she said after a moment too long. "She would never have let a supernatural touch her—"

"Under normal circumstances, no, she wouldn't. But she had nothing else to trade for that trinket that prevented you from wasting away. So she gave what she had. Just like your mother—"

"Don't," the rage demon hissed, the brands on her arms glowing a dark, dangerous green.

"It's the truth. Piper offered herself for a demon sacrifice to gain the power to protect you, and when that backfired, she sold her body. She starved for a year so that the apartment where you lay prone had heat. So that you were okay—so that *you* had a chance."

"She was the one that caused it," Bree snapped. "If not for her choices, I wouldn't have been unconscious. I could have helped. Our parents wouldn't have died. If you want guilt from me over what happened to her, you won't find it. I'm not her."

I chuckled coldly. "No, you most definitely are not."

The wine glass shook with her anger. She kept every ounce of magic in, locked tight in the flesh-and-bone body that confined her power. But I knew by the slight wobble of the red liquid . . . she wasn't all right.

And she shouldn't be.

"I tolerate your existence because despite all odds, Piper loves you." I sighed as if it were simply an inconvenience. "You don't deserve it," I added. "But she does. Which brings us to the point of this little visit."

"I'm not staying," she said quietly, a mere hiss that should have burned like acid, but it fell short somehow.

"I'm not asking you to," I replied. "In fact, I don't want you to. The sooner you're gone, the better off she will be."

Her face went stone-cold. Unreadable to most. Impressive for one so young. Only twenty-three to my ten thousand. But I'd seen stars born and planets die. I'd come face-to-face with the source of magic and been chosen instead of devoured. I'd ruled the very creatures her ancestors thought gods.

Bree Fallon could not fool me.

Neither was she capable of scaring me.

"My deal with Piper stands, and I haven't broken it."

"Your deal with Piper is meaningless to me."

The first crack of emotion made its way through her mask.

"What is that supposed to mean?" She might have whispered like death and tasted like poison, but there were worse monsters than this woman. Though part of me saw it, what she would be—could be—if she didn't bond. Not now. Not a thousand years from now. But one day—she might be strong enough to rival even chaos.

I hoped that day never came.

I hoped I never had to make the decision that might follow.

"Here's how it's going to be." I leaned forward and into my steepled hands, elbows flat around the armrests. "You'll continue teaching her how to control her rage magic. You will ask her about her life. Her hopes. Her dreams—and be the supportive sister you should have been." I let the black fire inside me shine through. It was the fire of chaos. The flames of real death. To her credit, she didn't shiver. It confirmed my suspicions about what she might be—if left to her own. "You will not upset her. You will not make comments about returning to Hell. You will not . . . be you."

Bree tilted her head. "Have you told her?"

I didn't respond other than to repeat, "Told her?"

A cunning smile spanned her lips. Salacious and malevolent. "You haven't." She threw her head back and laughed in exaggeration. "Of course not, but you sit here, scolding me as if you're some perfect mate. But you're not, are you? Just like I'm not the perfect sister." She snorted once, but it sounded . . . tired. And disappointed. Bree drained the rest of her wine in one gulp, then stood. "You're going to leave my apartment and not return—and hope I don't breathe a word of this *or anything else* to my sister before my departure—"

I only let her continue speaking because I was floored for a moment that somehow she knew. Somehow, she'd figured it out.

And I still hadn't told Piper.

Darkness leaked into my veins as my magic sought to crush her. But that wouldn't do. Not now . . .

"You really don't get it, do you?"

She paused mid-step to the kitchen.

"You. Are. Powerless." I stood then, and the chair vanished behind me as I closed the gap. "And if you want to return to Hell—it's in your best interest to not piss me off further by making threats. Because if you don't . . ." I leaned in close, unsmiling to let her see the truth in my words. "There will be no portal."

Bree blinked. "You can't do that. The bargain—"

"In case you haven't realized, *I am chaos*. Breaker of Bargains—especially those of magic. You need someone to ground the portal to make it a corridor. Only a demon can, and Piper *will not* be the one doing it. I will." I saw it then, that thing I was looking for.

Fear.

She feared not being able to return. Perhaps it would make her smarter.

I smiled, unkind, and showing fang.

"You've been to Hell. You accused me of not being active enough in ruling the demons. I won't make that mistake here—not with my atma . Which means you'll be on your best behavior until that portal opens. Because if I come home to something like I did today, *you* will pay the price."

Her lips parted. Equal parts anger and fear warred in her eyes, but she snapped her jaw shut and dipped her head.

"Yes, Harvester."

It seemed the girl did have some sense of the situation she'd put herself in.

Without so much as a nod, I stepped back into the void, satisfied my point had been made.

I could have sworn the echo of a wine glass shattering followed me.

32
PIPER

I SUMMONED STORMS OF FIRE AND ICE AND LIGHTNING. I MADE THE land turn dry and the plants shrivel to nothing before giving life back to it. I managed to lift a dozen boulders and have them circle around me.

And I did it all without saying more than two words.

"You're upset with me," Bree said when our four hours were nearly up.

"I was," I admitted, without losing concentration. While these lessons started as a way to spend time with her, they'd become more in the process. I wanted to excel at them, to conquer them—for myself. I'd always been adept at hunting and killing, but I wanted to do more with this power inside me than simply destroy. What 'more' was , I still wasn't sure. But I was starting to figure it out—to find my way.

I knew I wanted to make things better. My life. My city. I wanted to be a force for the right kind of change so that the rest of my immortal life wasn't steeped in war like the first twenty-six years. I wasn't Nat with her propensity for managing an entire network of people all over the city. But I knew there had to be other ways to change things. I just had to find mine.

Learning control of my magic was just a piece of the puzzle.

"Was?" Bree prompted when I didn't say more.

I shrugged. Ordinarily Bree would brush it off, but this time she didn't seem to want to. Her jaw clenched as she watched me.

"Why *were* you upset with me?"

I slowly turned to look at her, and the boulders continued around us, spinning in a circle, each one six-feet above ground and six-feet apart.

She stared impertinently. It reminded me of the thirteen-year-old that would pout about not being allowed to leave the apartment after dusk. While she knew the dangers, she never really took it seriously. It was as if all the bad shit we'd seen had desensitized her instead of giving her a healthy dose of respect and trepidation for what hid in the shadows. My parents always worried about that. Her boldness. Fearlessness.

"Does it matter why?" I asked, lifting a brow. "You'll be gone next week. Let's just focus on training, shall we?"

Understanding flitted over her. "This is about me leaving."

"Actually, it's not," I replied. "I don't want to get into it because you're leaving. There's no point. You won't be here for us to work it out, so it really doesn't matter."

My response seemed to only agitate her more.

She strode forward, her heels pressing into the soft earth, leaving indents behind.

"Training ended twenty minutes ago," Bree said sharply, grabbing my arm.

I blinked and dropped the rocks.

We vanished.

Today's training was back in Africa. A different spot than where we had been prior; a place known as Cape Town, near Johannesburg. Tall cliffs overlooked a blue sea. Their rocky edges made the terrain tricky when working with earth. The storms were more volatile when surrounded by the ocean. Fire could easily get out of control in the blistering heat of April. Meanwhile, ice was harder to hold on to, and any slip in concentration would lead to a monsoon of water raining down on the land. The wind was actually easiest here, roaming free and unrestrained over the glittering waters. It was an ideal place for me to practice.

It was as difficult in the challenges it posed in every element as it was for the devastating beauty that might have distracted me under different circumstances.

Not today.

Still, I made a note to come back here in the future. All my life, I'd only seen New Chicago. I never realized how much I was missing until Bree took me around the world. While I'd never leave the city, I wasn't going to let her return to Hell be the end of my travels.

Señora Rosara's storefront appeared. I pulled away before she dropped her grip. My body re-materialized in the physical plane right as Nat and the twins were exiting the shop.

"Oh good, I was wondering when you'd show. We're heading to the food bank on Second Street. You coming?" Nathalie's tone was light, her eyes dancing back and forth between me and something behind me. Bree must have made her presence known.

"Yup."

I fell in line beside her, expecting my sister to dip at the first chance she had.

"Mind if I tag along?" Her high-pitched voice came out haughty, but uncertain. I paused and Nat turned to me, lifting a brow.

I glanced back at Bree. She stood on the sidewalk in her high-heeled biker boots and ripped jeans, hands in her back pockets with her chin held high. "You want to come volunteer at a food bank?" I asked dubiously.

She lifted one shoulder in a slight shrug. "I have nothing else to do this afternoon."

I wanted to ask what she had to do every other afternoon—what made this one free—but I didn't.

"It's up to you," Nat said. "But I'm not paying her. Too many people in this city actually need the money." I could tell she'd pursed her lips a little with that jab before she slid past me, unlocking her car.

"You'll have to squeeze in the back with the twins," I said after a moment's debate.

Her face soured, but she cleared the expression quickly and started down the sidewalk.

I ignored Sasha's glare as I slipped past her to climb into the passenger seat.

"Thanks a lot," the succubus shifter hissed.

Sienna rolled her eyes. "I'll sit in the middle," she volunteered.

"Nope," Sasha said instantly. "She's the reason you almost died. I'll take the middle."

My sister's footsteps faltered by half a step as what they said sank in.

I hadn't forgotten about the bomb, but it didn't occur to me how uncomfortable the situation would make them.

"Do you want the front?" I begrudgingly offered.

"It's fine," Sasha said stiffly. She guided Sienna into the back with a hand to her elbow before sliding in after her. The engine purred to life right as Bree climbed in.

I wrinkled my nose at the metallic scent that filled the car. Sasha and Sienna's magic smelled more like cinnamon and Nat's like juniper, but their scents were faint by comparison.

"Are you using magic?" I asked suddenly.

"Me?" Nat questioned.

"No. Bree. " I turned in my seat to look at her.

My sister stared at me for a moment, something almost like pity crossing her features. "No," she said eventually. "I'm not."

I frowned, turning back around.

"I didn't know you could scent magic," Sienna said.

"Piper's full of hidden talents. Aren't ya, Pip?" Nat said, taking on my nickname Anders gave me.

I wrinkled my nose, side-eyeing her. "Am I?"

She snorted. "You're awfully good at serving bread to people. Bet you didn't know you could do that before. Should put it on your résumé ."

My chest shook with stifled laughter. From the backseat, the twins joined in.

"That's the dumbest joke you can make?"

Nat smiled, unperturbed. "I was being serious. I wasn't sure if you could do it without throttling anyone—let alone with a smile on your face. Someone should call the church because clearly Hell's frozen over."

The back seat erupted in sultry laughter. "You're something else," I huffed, crossing my arms, turning my cheek to the window so she wouldn't see my grin.

In the reflection of the passenger mirror, I didn't notice

it at first, but Bree was the only one not laughing. If anything, she looked pained.

For the life of me, I couldn't figure out why.

∞

CHANTS WERE the first thing I noticed. Around the corner from the bank, their voices reached me. Sasha let out a hiss in the back seat, tipping off Nat that we were driving toward trouble. She turned the corner right as I said, "Slow down. We've got protesters."

She hit the brakes, jerking the car to a stop.

A hundred yards ahead of us, the road was blocked by a mob of men and women. They waved signs that read, '*No Magic. No Problem.*', '*Equality for All*', and the one that made my blood run cold, '*Demon Days Are Over.*'

Nathalie threw the car in park, and several of the stragglers at the edge took notice. She reached for the handle and I grabbed her arm. "What are you doing?"

"That's my food bank they're closing in on. It's filled with innocent people. Those are my employees in there. Volunteers. I won't leave them."

"You can't go out there. Don't you remember what happened last time you were in an angry mob—"

She wheeled on me, wide brown eyes turning a hint of gold. "Then come with me."

A sinking feeling entered my gut. She wasn't going to yield, and she was right.

My lips twisted in a grimace. "Fine, but give the twins your keys. Bree—"

"I'll come too."

I reeled back like she'd slapped me. That probably would have shocked me less.

Even Nat said, "You will?"

My sister's eyes narrowed, not liking how we doubted her. Given it was earned, she could be butthurt. I didn't exactly care right then.

"You've progressed faster than I did," Bree said, ignoring Nathalie altogether. "Let's see how you do under pressure."

I narrowed my eyes. "Are you serious right now?"

Without hesitation she replied, "Completely."

I shook my head. Of course. I should have known she'd want to be here to see how I tested, and not for any other reason . . . fucking typical. I released Nat's arm and threw the door open. She tossed the keys to the twins and followed me out.

I waited just long enough for my sister to follow after and the twins to move to the front seat. Sasha locked eyes with me from behind the wheel. She didn't have to say it, but I might as well have read her mind when she tipped her chin to me.

Her way of telling me to make it out alive.

It might have been more touching if I didn't know the consequences to both of them if I didn't.

"Look what we got 'ere boys," one of the stragglers called, walking toward us, crowbar in hand. "The Witch Hunter." He said my title with a ferocious, yellow-toothed smile. "Fuckin' demon's whore."

Five of his closest buddies followed closely behind. Two held bats. One a shot gun.

My sister turned to look pointedly at me, as if asking whether I'd tolerate that.

Calmly, I stood my ground. "Go home."

Crowbar sneered, his fat nose scrunching like a pig. "Or what? Gonna call your demon—"

The ground dissolved beneath his feet.

"What the—" He dropped the weapon right as the ground melted and then hardened once more. His feet were stuck six inches in asphalt along with the end of the crowbar.

I stepped forward, leaning in as close as I dared despite his rancid scent.

"Listen closely. You'll want to tell all your friends, your family, your neighbors." My breath caressed his oily face. Eyes glowing violet and brands out for all to see, I summoned a small ball of white flame and let it weave between my fingers. "I'm not the demon's whore. I'm not even the Witch Hunter anymore." His buddies got too close, and I sank them too. Deeper. To the waist. The one with the shotgun lifted it, thinking he was out of my range.

I flicked the ball of fire and it shot down the street, entering the front end of his barrel right as he pulled the trigger. It backfired, and he exploded in white fire.

Crowbar tried to turn, the short-lived scream of his dead friend hammering home the very real danger he'd found himself in.

It hit me then. I might have laughed under different circumstances. But for weeks—months—Nat, and Ronan, and even Bree had been preparing me for this moment.

This realization of who and what I wanted to be.

"I'm the fucking Queen of New Chicago, and terrorists in *my* city will feel *my* wrath. Human. Supernatural. Demon. I don't give a flying fuck who or what you are—but when you threaten innocent people in my town—you'll find there's nowhere to hide."

The change in me wasn't instant, but it was subtle. I never wanted to rule. I never desired to own anyone or any place. All I wanted was some semblance of safety. Of peace.

But no matter what happened, someone was always there to threaten it.

In the absence of authority, there was power for the taking, and eager hands more than willing to grab on. The *idea* of power made people more dangerous than power itself, because for the idea of it—the sheer possibility—they'd do anything.

Whether me or Nat or some random human on the street deserved it.

For generations humans killed supes, supes killed humans, and the cycle never ended.

It was that thinking that started the Salem Witch Trials. That thinking that made Dorothea Abernathy kill the President of the United States on live television.

And it was that realization that made me take a mantle I'd never have chosen for myself under different circumstances.

Because I was fucking tired of people thieving and murdering in the open streets of this city. It was my home, and if no one else could fix it, then I would.

I stepped around him and his buddies, paying them no mind.

Nathalie walked on one side, Bree on the other.

Some of the crowd had taken notice when the shotgun backfired, and those people backed away. They knew what was coming if they stuck around, and they were smart enough to avoid it.

Good. I wanted them to. Messengers that could tell people what happened here were far more effective than dead bodies.

"Now's the time," I yelled. "If you don't want to get caught up in what's fixing to go down—then go home."

Unfortunately, not many heeded that warning.

Whether they thought they stood a chance or were willing to die for a cause—I wasn't sure. All I knew was that it couldn't continue. The riots. The fires. The death.

I wasn't Nat, running charities and managing half the city behind shadows. I never could be. I was too infamous for that. Nor was I like Ronan with a territorial nature and need for power that drove him to own things. I didn't want to own my city.

I just wanted to protect it.

"I'll clear a path. You get everyone out the back," I murmured to Nat, quiet enough I hoped no one else heard. She nodded twice.

"You be careful out here," she whispered. Her smaller hand grabbed mine and squeezed fiercely. She looked around my body, at Bree. The light brown in her eyes molted and changed, turning a brilliant, dangerous gold. A shiver ran through me at the lethality in her gaze. I wasn't the only one sick of losing people. "If anything happens while you're here—you won't be going back to Hell."

To my sister's credit, she didn't balk. Bree tipped her chin in acknowledgement. Nat held her attention a moment longer before the crowd started to close in.

"Do your worst, demon!"

"Kill us!"

"Burn us!"

Their voices rose. The scents of sweat, blood, and rage burned my nostrils. A gunshot went off.

The bullet stopped an inch from my face.

I turned to look at Bree, who had a hand lifted. She shrugged. "You'd survive it, but odds are you or the Harvester would level this part of the city for it."

As if Ronan heard her, I sensed a dark presence. There was chaos in the air.

Let me handle this, I projected across the bridge. The magic sizzled, not liking that command. I needed to act quickly before Ronan's self-control failed from whatever dark corner he was hiding in.

I took a light breath and let it out slowly. Forcing myself to calm.

Clearly some of the people here had no problem dying. If they died by my hands, it would just make them martyrs, and that wouldn't help. But I couldn't allow this to continue either.

I frowned. *Come on, Piper, think...*

Fire would burn them. Air would deprive them. Water would drown them. Earth would consume them. Lightning would fry them. Even if I could manage metal, that would simply poison or stab them.

I needed something else. Some other gift. Some other solution.

But the simple truth of it was, there wasn't one.

All the magic in the world, but I didn't possess the ability to change their minds and tell them to go home. For that, all I had was words.

But maybe... just maybe, words would do.

"I was one of you once," I told the crowd. "Human. Angry about my lot in life. Angry at the supernaturals for putting us on the bottom. All I wanted was to protect my family. That's how I got this power..." I lifted my hands and white flames shot from them, making the people closest jump back, falling into those behind them. "But I know what it's like not to have anything. To be cold. To be hungry. To look at your wallet and ask yourself what's more important, food or electricity. *I know.*" My fists closed, and the fire went out. "And I want to change that. I *want* to be different. I want New Chicago to be different—but that doesn't start with me. That starts with *you*." I spoke louder and louder, letting the wind carry my voice so that they could all hear it. Nat peeled away from my side, and I kept my eyes on her as she pushed through the crowd. Most of them stepped back like she was the plague, but no one made a move to hurt her. Not yet.

"New Chicago doesn't belong to me or the supes any more than it belongs to you. They were hit hard with Lucifer's death. That's true, and if you were going to strike back—now is the time."

"Piper," Bree started warily.

"No," I stopped her. "They're right that if there's ever a time, it's now. *But for the wrong reasons*. What happens right now decides if we will enter another magic war or find some kind of peace."

"Peace?" a lady near the front questioned loudly. "You talk of peace when you just slaughtered one of us—"

"He tried to shoot me first. And if anyone tries to hurt me or mine, I'll do it again," I replied. "I can kill easily. Death is in my veins. Fire *is* my blood. The difference is, I don't want to. I don't want to kill you. I don't even want to rule New Chicago."

"Then don't!" someone else shouted.

I smiled faintly. "Stop the riots, then. Stop burning businesses. Stop murdering supes for being different. It sucks for everyone right now. But here's the thing—supernaturals will always have an advantage. Nearly half the population has magic. You can't beat that. Not when one of them can kill dozens of you, more even."

"So you just want us to lay down and take it?" Another nameless voice from the crowd shouted. Several cries followed it, clearly agreeing.

"No. If someone attacks you, defend yourself. Strike

back. But this"—I motioned to the crowd around the food bank—"This isn't that. Your buddy back there tried to put a shotgun hole through me. I'm not apologizing for what I did."

Silence greeted me. Well, no one claimed public speaking was my forte.

"Look—you got issues with how things have been. I get that. This place is one of the few food banks that serves humans and supes. Attacking the people in there won't help any of you. In fact, some of your friends and family might go hungry because of it."

That got me a few ashamed looks and muttered agreements.

Which was more than I was getting five minutes ago.

"Like it matters to you!" another voice shouted. "If we go home, you save the day, and the people are placated for now. If you really gave a shit, you'd stop the supes from enslaving us and make it safe for us."

"Piper, I know you care about the humans, but I really don't think this is worth it—"

"Stop," I snapped at her. "It is. You may be so detached that you don't remember, but *we were them*. There was a time I would have given anything, done anything, for things to change. And they're right—if we really gave a damn, we would be better. I would be."

Nat had long since made it inside. I hadn't heard from her in that time, and I took that as a good thing. For now. The people gathered around me? They were a different story. Their plight was something I was all too familiar with.

And if I was going to have any bargaining power in the future, I was going to have to give. To actually *do* something to make a change.

"Stop attacking supes in the streets. Stop the riots—and I'll stop the slave trade. I'll do what Lucifer didn't, and I'll hold those people responsible. I'll stop others from joining them—but you gotta stop giving them ammunition too."

Murmurs broke out across the crowd. I let them whisper. Let them talk. Humans hadn't had a voice in two decades. Silencing them would only make them hate me and every other magic user more.

"What's to stop you from going back on us?"

"I can't," I said simply. "All magic has a price. The price of being a demon means promises are binding. If you hold up your end, I'll be forced to hold up mine."

"She could be lying," the woman in front said. Her brown hair hung in greasy clumps. She clutched a baseball bat in one hand and a sign in the other.

I shrugged. "I could be. I'll give you that. But ask yourself this: what reason would I have to lie? I could kill you all here. It happened in the Underworld. You've all heard the stories. Seen the barren patches of concrete and glass. I'm more than capable of it, but instead I'm offering the promise to try to fix things. The real question you should be asking is what do you have to lose in walking away?" I waited for them to answer. No one did, but I could tell by some faces they were coming to it.

"Nothing," I said. "You have nothing to lose because unlike me—you can go back on a promise. You can riot again. My fellow demons would probably call me weak for this—for not just squashing any resistance—but I'm giving you a choice. A chance. And in doing so, taking one myself, knowing that it may backfire."

A few people took a hard look around and lowered their weapons, turning to walk away. Many more stood uncertain, debating. I'd give them more time to think and decide.

Or I would have.

"No! You don't get to persuade us with sweet words."

I'd never forget the face of the speaker as long as I'd live.

A girl that couldn't have been more than sixteen or seventeen stepped forward.

Her cheek was smudged and her eyes hard. Cold. She unzipped a jacket, and my heart sank into my stomach.

She was a suicide bomber.

"You don't get to stop this. My sister was raped and murdered by an incubus because the last demon wouldn't keep his kind under control. I'm not leaving it to chance again."

People took notice and started to run. It was the wrong move.

She came here with one intent:

That nobody would walk away.

"The Illuminati are comin'," she said, keeping that edge of hardness despite the faint quiver of her bottom lip. "We will rise again."

Triggered by her words, there was a single beep. A switch flipped.

Then it was *green*.

33
RONAN

I'D SEEN MY ATMA HURT ONCE BECAUSE I WASN'T FAST ENOUGH.

It wasn't going to happen again.

The void closed in and this time I didn't go for Piper, but for the source of magic itself. The bomb.

I snatched the girl out of the crowd before anyone was hurt. There was no saving her. The explosives rigged in those metal canisters were inserted into her skin, pumping violent magic through her blood.

My arms wrapped around her as the humans in the road ran. She exploded without pre-empt. Dark, vicious, green magic taking her place.

I breathed it in, letting the power fill my pours, invade my system, fight against my own as a means to confine it. Only when it entered me to ravage did it writhe as my own chaos magic surrounded it.

Magic always did.

Like a cornered animal, it was more alive and sentient than most realized.

And I slaughtered it mercilessly in the span of seconds, then inhaled the remains that lingered in the air. My nostrils flared as the last of it winked out of existence and I took in the half-empty lot—growing more deserted by the second.

Apart from two.

Piper stood frozen in place, immobile from the realization I knew was finally hitting her. The magic in the bomb belonged to Bree.

She was the source. The cause of this.

I stalked toward her.

"This is your doing," I spat. "Your magic. Again."

Piper turned to look at her sister and shook her head. "I —" Her mouth opened and then closed. She clenched her fists. "We had a deal."

"And I've followed it," Bree insisted. Sweat coated her forehead and fear dilated her pupils. "I haven't given magic or talked to *anyone* once since—"

"Do you really hate it here that much? Are you so desperate that you'd"—Piper motioned to the spot where not even a single atom of the child remained. "I knew you were involved with some bad shit. But this? Suicide bombers?" She shook her head in disgust.

"I didn't know—"

"Didn't you?" Piper snapped. "The bomb that hurt the twins was your magic too. The gun. You even owned up to that one. Now this—fuck." Piper backed away.

"I gave some of my magic to *help people*. I didn't know it was going into weapons at the time, and I had already stopped before you approached me with the deal because of it. After the bomb that happened weeks ago . . ." She shook her head, real shame coloring her cheeks. "I haven't given since I found out about that—and they didn't have enough to make another. I saw to it. I don't know how this happened, but I'll find out—"

"Yeah," Piper said, sounding like she didn't believe a word of it. "Tell that to the dead teenager."

Bree reached for her and I stepped in between them. For once, my atma didn't stop me.

"Pipes," Bree pleaded "I'm telling you the truth—"

Behind me, Piper backed away—putting distance between her and Bree.

"That was rage magic," she shouted. "Green rage magic that smelled like metal. That's *you*. No one else could have put it there. So maybe you missed something—I don't know. All I can say is—we're done. You want to go home? Fine. We do it tonight."

Bree tried to step around me, but I blocked her path.

"Please," she whispered. "You can send me back, but I didn't do this."

"I wish I could believe you," Piper said. Through the bond I felt the hurt. The pain. This was killing her every bit as much as it was Bree. "But you'd do anything for Lorcan. Who's to say you wouldn't do this?"

"Pi—" Bree started. I could sense that Piper had left this realm and gone to her own before reappearing on the other side of the building where Nathalie was with the people she'd gotten out of the building.

Bree's eyes watered. For a moment she looked . . . lost. Hopeless.

It only lasted a second before the mask fell into place.

"Piper can't smell magic, but other demons can." She gave me a knowing lift of her eyebrow, as if taunting me. "Looks like I'm not the only one who's out of time."

Before I could respond, she vanished, leaving only her ominous words behind.

34
PIPER

I WAS SITTING IN FRONT OF THE FIREPLACE WHEN HE FOUND ME.

One leg was stretched out, the other bent at the knee so I could rest my elbow on it. I held the half a photograph in hand, but it was the flames I stared into.

For the hundredth time, I asked myself if it was a mistake bringing her back.

And for the hundredth time I knew the answer.

It was.

If only there were some way for me to have known that.

I felt his presence before the tendrils of chaos flooded the living room. After the confrontation with Bree, I helped Nat get her employees on their way home safely and locked up the food bank until further notice. I'd only been home for half an hour, but it felt like a lot longer as mental exhaustion weighed me down.

"You handled yourself well today," he said quietly.

"I was so close," I whispered. "I almost had them. Then that girl . . ." Her face came to mind, young and filled with hatred. I shook my head. "The only one who should have died was the jackass that tried to shoot me."

"She was going to detonate a bomb to destroy everything around her, including you," he reminded me, sitting down on the floor to my right and leaning back against the sofa.

"She was just a kid," I replied. "Just a stupid kid that was angry for the cards this world dealt her." Ronan was silent for a moment. The crackling fire the only thing keeping us from the deafening quiet.

"You saw yourself in her."

I nodded. "I was her. Just like I was the girl that died in the summoning that brought you here. I'm in all of them. These young, dumb people that think their hate will change things somehow." I shook my head again and sighed.

"Yours did."

"No, it didn't. My desire to help my family did." I glanced at the picture. At the hand that held mine, even if the rest of her was burned out. My love for her, for Bree, drove me to such extremes. "All the anger ever brought me was unhappiness and guilt. I'm still angry sometimes when I think about it. Angry I spent so long pissed off when I had the means to change things and make them better—even if I didn't want to admit it."

"You do better when you know better, Piper. That's part of living."

I snorted. "This coming from the ten-thousand-year-old demon."

"I spent five hundred years running from what I am," Ronan replied. I turned my cheek to look at him. "Being born to chaos isn't the blessing many would think. Not with my parents. From the moment of my conception, my mother claimed she knew I was destined to be the next Harvester . Maybe it would have been different if my father hadn't been the reigning Harvester, but they raised me with the knowledge I'd one day have to kill him—kill them. Not exactly a great bedtime story."

I balked. "Why would they do that?"

"Because they're demons." He shrugged. "In the Otherworld, being the Harvester is the highest honor. It never mattered to them that they'd have to die for me to take it."

"The Otherworld sounds like a shitty place to live," I deadpanned.

He chuckled. "It's different. Our customs are different. Our way of life is different. It's more beautiful than Earth could ever be, but also more dangerous. It exists at the precipice of the Source—and that's shaped it."

"If you didn't want to kill your parents, why did you? Couldn't you have chosen to never become the Harvester?"

A hint of old pain flashed through him, gone in a fraction of a second.

"It's not so simple. I tried, but the Source chooses the Harvester and forces them into the role whether they want it or not. In the same way the rage can force itself on you. I have to take in magic to survive—or I starve. It's the price I pay for being able to consume every kind of magic."

"That . . . sucks," I said lamely.

"Yeah," Ronan agreed. "It does. Things might have been different had my parents not presented me to the Source, but they did, and my future was locked and sealed. I tried to run—but my father hunted me down and issued a challenge to force my hand. He knew I was the stronger Harvester—that I would have no choice but to win."

I swallowed hard. "I gotta say, hearing about how things are done there—I don't get why Bree wants to go back so badly. Not even for love."

"I came here for less."

My lips twisted. "Thanks," I said sarcastically.

That dragged another chuckle out of him. He reached over and wrapped his large hands around my waist, dragging me to him. I could have fought it. Sometimes I did just for the hell of it. This time I let him, appreciating the comfort that physical touch could give.

"I smelled you and couldn't turn away. Had I known you or what we'd have" —his hand came around to curl possessively over my middle, pulling me closer— "I wouldn't have agreed to any deal. I would have ripped another hole through the dimensions, each and every one until I found you again."

He pressed a light kiss to my neck, running the tip of his fangs over the spot.

"You say you don't love me, but then you say the sweetest shit." I laughed a bit in amusement. "Well, sweet to me."

Ronan was quiet for a moment, then he leaned back, taking me with him.

"I've felt what humans call love. It's a form of attachment—but it's weak compared to what I feel. Love is an insult in comparison to the need I have for you."

I thought about that. In a way, he was right. Love was an attachment. To humans it was an extreme attachment, but maybe in the same way the Otherworld was *more*—more dangerous, more beautiful—maybe what they felt was more too.

"I know that Bree has done truly awful things, and she needs to be sent back—but I hope she finds that. Maybe she doesn't deserve it. It sounds like her response to me not sending her back would be considered acceptable to demons, but . . . whatever comes next for her, I want her to find happiness."

"She doesn't deserve your love," Ronan replied.

I snorted. How very . . . Ronan. "You just said love is an insult."

"Between us. You can love the rest of them, except Anders."

I busted out laughing, then twisted around on his lap so I was straddling him. "I've been with women, you know. They were usually better fuck buddies."

Ronan rolled his eyes. "You're not interested in the witch or the twins. Sasha pisses you off too much and Sienna is her doppelganger. Bree is your sister. But Anders—"

"Was a forty-something balding dude until recently. Not my type." I wrinkled my nose.

"He has affection toward you," Ronan replied, unmoving despite how absurd this particular jealousy was.

"No different from Nat. I shot him, remember?"

"You shot me too."

Well, I suppose he did have a point. "That was before. Anders and I weren't even friends. I'm still not sure if we are now. I'm still sore on the whole working with you and not telling me for over a month."

"Good." He looked far too happy about it and I narrowed my eyes.

"We need to start getting ready for the ritual soon," I said, eyes straying to the clock. "Assuming you're doing it with me like last time—"

"I'm not."

I blinked. It wasn't that I was hurt by his choice, more that I was confused by the tone he used. "All right. I've still gotta prep with Nat, though—"

Ronan sighed. "You're not doing the ritual tonight."

"Um . . ." I tilted my chin, narrowing my eyes. "In case you didn't hear me, I told Bree I'm sending her back—"

"No," he said. "You're not."

I put my hands on his shoulders to push away. Where was this even coming from? We brought her here together, and he wanted her gone for weeks, but now he was having hang-ups?

"Ronan, I made a deal. I need to send her home. A demon has to ground the portal—"

"I will."

I stilled.

He did not just go there.

All at once, I pushed hard against him, curling my toes under to stand up. His hands tightened on my hips though, refusing to budge.

"I don't know what the fuck has gotten into you, but that's not how this works—"

I was a hairsbreadth from pulling us into the light dimension, where I held all control when his words stopped me cold.

"You're pregnant."

Silence.

"You can't ground the portal, Piper. It's not safe."

A dull roar washed over me. It descended without warning and made my muscles lock—frozen in place.

Pregnant.

As in . . . a baby.

"No," I said slowly. "No. I can't be . . ."

"You can," Ronan said cautiously, trying to soothe me with his tone like I was a wounded animal. "Think about it, Piper. I can see magic. Feel it. There's magic right here" — he lowered his hand to a spot on my abdomen—"that isn't yours."

Slowly, my chin tipped down. I looked at my stomach.

It was flat as ever, not even the slightest bump, but—he wouldn't lie, would he?

My thoughts raced, searching through the past weeks for signs. Clues. Any grain of truth in what he'd said.

"The bar—" I started, then stopped. Too many questions sat at the forefront. I was torn between denying it—and asking how long he'd known.

Ronan may have withheld information, but he'd never outright lied to me.

I knew that.

But this...

A question finally worked its way to my lips, and it wasn't the one I would have expected. "When were you going to tell me?"

"After Bree left."

The sudden answer and lack of thought made me believe him, but damn did that hurt. "How far along?" I whispered.

"Two and a half weeks," he said quietly.

I reeled back. "That's hardly anything. How can you be sure—"

"That's hardly anything for human gestation, yes. Demons grow at a different rate. In the Otherworld, it's less than six months from conception to birth if the pregnancy takes. Magic forms as the fetus grows, and it doesn't take long for me to feel it. Smell it. I saw the first spark of new magic growing in you the afternoon I found you in the greenhouse. The day I brought you here." He didn't look around the apartment, but I knew that's what he meant.

"That's—you—ugh!" I pushed harder against him and still Ronan refused to yield. My nails grew claws that pierced his skin. Blood perfumed the air, making my fangs descend.

"I wanted to tell you immediately, but there's concerns. A demon born on Earth—it hasn't happened. Even in the Otherworld, how quickly you got pregnant isn't just uncommon, it's—"

"We never used protection."

"I didn't think I needed to," Ronan said. "Demons try for decades—centuries to have a baby. Because we live forever, it's hard to conceive."

"But it's possible," I hissed. "And now I am—would you have even done it differently if you knew the outcome?"

"No."

Fuck him.

My hands curled into fists that I pounded against him. Banging his chest with a force that rocked us both, but he wasn't letting go.

"God, I can't believe you right now," I said angrily. Stupid water started to fill my eyes, pissing me off even more. "I can't believe *me*. How did I not see it? The empty room. The bar. Fucking—fuck—" I growled, struggling even more. "Your reason for not telling me isn't good enough," I snapped at him.

"I'm telling you now," he replied, taking my fury without reproach. "And I was going to tell you after Bree was gone—but I do not trust her. Look at today, Piper. You may love her, but she isn't trustworthy. You know that. That's why you want her gone now."

"I—" Damn him. Damn him to Hell. He was right. But at the moment, I didn't give a flying fuck. "I had the right to know and decide for myself if she was told."

"The early weeks are tumultuous. One wrong step—whether that be too much stress or something more nefarious—can result in a miscarriage."

"Again, not a good enough fucking excuse, Ronan," I

growled out. "Did it even occur to you that I might not want kids?"

His face went stark. He hadn't considered that. Not once.

"Do you?" he asked quietly.

"I—it—" I opened and closed my mouth, letting out a furious breath. "I don't know. But it's a little late now, isn't it? A baby is—" I broke off and sighed. "It's a lot, Ronan. That's a step I never actually thought about. I mean I know people *can*, but it never occurred to me that *we* could. I wasn't born a fucking demon. My body is frozen in time. I don't know if I assumed it wasn't possible, but I just didn't think about, well, *this*."

"I know," he said softly, leaning to press his forehead against mine. "I hadn't thought it would happen this quickly. When you didn't enter heat—"

My mouth dropped open. He did not just . . . "I'm not a dog."

"I'm aware," he replied with a bit of bite. Not that he had any right to be anything except sorry, and he wasn't even that. "Female demons enter a state of insatiable lust called heat maybe once every year or two. During that time, the chance of conception is slightly higher. I didn't know if you could or not—but I think the weekend your rage took over you might have entered a lesser version. More in line with what the humans experience."

"You think?" I questioned, narrowing my gaze.

"There's no way to know for certain. Had you entered heat—I would have known instantly." His eyes darkened with hunger, but he kept it reined in, perhaps sensing I might castrate him if he tried anything. "You didn't. Not in any way I've seen or heard of."

I closed my eyes. "This is too much right now, Ronan.

Too sudden. Too unexpected. I've gotta send Bree home in a couple of hours—"

"You are *not* opening that portal. I will do it."

"Either way," I snapped back, "I told you to be honest with me about shit. To trust me. If you had, maybe I wouldn't be freaking out right now when a major ritual is taking place in a couple hours and my only sister is getting sent back to Hell—one way or another."

"You would have freaked out either way."

My lips thinned. "You're not helping."

"I'm pointing out the truths you would rather ignore. At the end of the day, it was going to be a shock whenever I told you. Whether it was two weeks ago, two days, tomorrow, or a month from now. You were always going to struggle in coming to grips with this and I wanted to give you a chance to 'clear your plate' so to speak. Send Bree back. Come to peace with that before dealing with this. It isn't how I wanted to tell you—not after a day like today—but I can't let you do that portal. The risk is too great that it would cause a strain. If you decide you don't want it . . ." His face turned stricken. Pale. Stiff. "We can figure that out after you've gotten over the initial shock."

I swallowed hard. "You make it hard to be with you sometimes."

"Only sometimes?" he asked, trying to make light of the situation. I didn't smile. Sadness tinged his expression, but he didn't let it out. "I know," Ronan said after a moment. "Being with me . . . it will never be easy. I'm from another world. Another culture. The way things were all my life are different than how things are done here. Different than how it is with you. If I were a better man, I'd have let you go after we bonded." He ran a finger down my cheek, the softest of grazes. "But I'm not a man at all, and I can't let you go. I won't."

"I don't want you to," I said after a moment. "But I'm upset right now. I need time to think about this. To figure out how I feel and convince myself not to shoot you again for the hell of it."

Ronan grinned. "I'd let you, if it meant you'd kiss it and make it better."

I glared at him. "You'd be lucky if I didn't unload the whole clip in you at this point. Maybe then you'd understand how hard it is for me when you pull this alphahole bullshit."

"Piper, in case you haven't noticed," he paused to put a finger under my chin and lift it, "I'm not the only alphahole in this relationship. You did declare yourself 'the fucking Queen of New Chicago' today."

I pressed my lips together. He might have had a point, but I wasn't letting him off easy for it. Nope.

Not this time.

35
PIPER

Five pee sticks taunted me with their glaring double red lines.

It wasn't exactly that I'd doubted Ronan, but I needed to see it for myself. In a way that I could understand.

I put my face in my hands and groaned. Two taps on the bathroom door jolted me.

"You good in there?" Nat asked uneasily.

"Yeah," I said, voice thick. I paused to clear my throat from the strange emotion bubbling up. "You can come in."

The doorknob twisted and Nat slipped inside, shutting it behind her.

Sad eyes focused on me, not even looking at the tiny sticks on the counter I had her procure for me at the last minute.

"I'm guessing you knew," I said hoarsely.

Nat pressed her lips together and nodded. She leaned back against the bathroom wall to slide down it and land on her butt with her legs sprawled in front of her. "I didn't realize you didn't, though. When I saw the little blip of magic... I assumed you were waiting to tell me."

My hands dropped in between my bent knees, lacing together.

"I hadn't put it together yet. Ronan told me this afternoon—after he said I wouldn't be the one to ground the portal for Bree's return home."

Nat sighed. "I'm so sorry. If I'd known—"

"It's not your fault," I said quickly. "This one's on Ronan for not saying, and both of us for not using protection."

Nat gave me a tight smile that said, *yeah, it kinda was*, but she wasn't going to be a dick about it.

"Is it too soon to ask how you feel about it?"

"Way too soon," I confirmed. "I'm pissed he didn't tell me. Even if he had decent reasons to wait."

She nodded. "That's understandable. What about past that? Anything other than being pissed off at your demon?"

It might have been laughable under different circumstances. Said demon was being overbearing about even letting me leave the apartment after I found out. Probably scared I'd run off. Until I pointed out that suffocating me wouldn't keep me around. I already knew I wasn't walking away. Not now. Probably not ever unless he did something truly unforgivable, but this . . . it would take me a while to get over it. His lack of groveling wasn't helping, but then, what did I expect from Ronan? He wasn't one to grovel. Ever.

"I'm scared to even think about bringing a child into this fucked-up world," I admitted.

"As much as no one likes to admit this, the world's always been fucked up," Nat said. "Since the dawn of time men have warred and raped. They've committed horrible crimes. Murdered millions in the name of gold, glory, and their god. Sure, now the humans know they're not alone—but relatively speaking, right now isn't that bad if we can avoid another magic war breaking out." She shrugged. "That's probably not what you want to hear, but I'm always going to give it to you straight."

I sighed. "Perhaps, but can you really see us as parents?"

I was hanging on to her answer more than I might have wanted to admit.

Nat smiled, a real, full-cheeked smile.

"Easily," she said. "You may be demons and assholes, but that doesn't mean you guys can't be parents. Sure, it'll be an unconventional childhood—but I can all too easily see you teaching your kid gun safety and how to throw a right hook. Ronan will probably handle more of the education side—because you lack the patience." I made a face that had her chuckling. "And I'll teach them the *useful* life skills," she added with a wink.

Oh god. Despite how stressful it was to even think about, I laughed. Because I could see it, the future she talked about. I could see it . . . and I wanted it.

"I'm going to need a doctor. Not sure how to find one that specializes in supes. Ronan said there's never been a demon born Earthside. Maybe Anders will know someone . . ."

Nat smiled mischievously. "You do know Señora Rosara was a doctor in her past life. Delivered all kinds of magical beasties. She was one of the best—part of the reason no one in the witch community messed with her."

I tried to imagine her delivering babies and couldn't.

"She's so crotchety for an OB."

Nat snorted. "But she gets the job done. If anyone can help you with your demon spawn, it's her."

I glared at her. "Thanks."

"Always." She grinned. "And if you ever need me, I'm here. Whether that's finding you ungodly expensive pregnancy tests because you cling to the human methods—or a doctor for your tiny overlord—I got you. Auntie Nat to the rescue."

"Thank you," I said more seriously. "Really. I—I appreciate it. Please don't say anything to the twins yet. I'm not ready to talk about it. Hell, I only half believe it myself."

Nat waved me off. "It's your business. I'm not saying a word. Just don't be surprised if they guess. Their succubus juju gives them a way with these things, and Sienna is bound to be overbearing in wanting to help you with baby stuff. Girl wants kittens like crazy but hasn't found the right stud." She shook her head, as if unable to understand it.

"I'm still early, so hopefully I have awhile yet."

"Hopefully," Nat repeated. "Now, if you don't want them to know something's up—we should probably go finish dinner before Ronan comes down. I figured we could eat, and Anders could do the dishes—add Ronan to dish duty now too—while I start preparing my athame for tonight. It needs to be cleansed from the residual magic of the last ritual, so it doesn't accidentally start pulling from you. Pretty sure Ronan would kill me if it did."

I nodded. "Yeah, I don't think even our blood bond would save you then."

"Forgive me for not wanting to find out."

I cast a wary glance at the tests on the bathroom counter. "What should I do with these?"

"Bag 'em. I'll put them in my bedroom trash and throw it out tomorrow morning." I did as she instructed, stashing them in a spare mini trash bag and tying it closed. "Now help me up," she griped, extending her hands. "My back is starting to hurt from sitting on the floor this long."

"You're twenty-two," I pointed out, even if I did offer her my help.

"Going on two hundred at this rate. Back pain does not have an age requirement. Anyone that tells you that is full of crap," she huffed.

I snorted, ignoring the odd looks from Sasha when we exited the bathroom. She didn't need to know what went down in there. All that mattered was that I was feeling okay again.

Or at least not freaking out.

Given no one was shot, burned, or bleeding—it was a win, all things considered.

We all knew I'd done worse for less . . . my eyes dropped to my stomach for a second.

I couldn't help but think that I'd do worse yet for the spark of life growing inside me.

36
PIPER

I was still picking at my mashed potatoes when Ronan and Anders were finishing up the dishes. We, by which I mean mostly Nat, made Chicken Marseille with potatoes and green beans. It was delicious. One of the best meals I'd ever had . . . but every tick of the clock was like the countdown to a bomb. Despite being the one to make the call about tonight, I wasn't ready.

But I knew I never would be.

Sienna was chatting up Anders while he dried the pots and pans when the couch dipped, her sister taking a seat beside me.

"Do you need something?" I asked. My voice didn't hold the same bite it once did, but the words themselves did the job.

"You made the right choice today," Sasha said quietly.

"I know you're trying to be nice, but I really don't want to talk about Bree right now—"

"I'm not referring to your sister," she said. I glanced up from my plate to see her staring at me with an unnerving intensity. I stared right back. "I'm talking about the mob.

The humans. You told them this is your city—and you're right. It is. Lucifer knew it. Ronan knows it. Every demon within a hundred miles—a thousand—knows who walks these streets, and we're safer for it."

I blinked, not expecting what she'd said. "Thanks for the support . . . I think."

Sasha snorted. "I'm not coming to you completely out of praise. You're still young. New to this. You don't know what it takes to rule a city—and Ronan will help, but you're going to need someone that knows the ins and outs. Someone that you can trust."

My lips parted. *Ah, now I see.*

"You think that someone is you."

Sasha shrugged almost flippantly. "I think it can be. I was one of the first you did a blood oath with. I'm powerful in my own right. I served Lucifer faithfully, and I know my way around this city's supernatural circles better than Anders does."

I made a face. "Anders is Ronan's guy."

She smiled faintly. "My point. I could be yours."

I set my plate aside and crossed my arms, leaning back. "Why you? Why not Nat? Sienna? Hell, I could pick a random off the street that would listen better—"

"Because your second shouldn't be someone that just listens. They should challenge you to think through your choices. Support you always, but not blindly. They should also bring stuff to the table—and you're not going to find someone better than me for that." Her confidence bordered arrogance, but she wore it well.

"I have Nat," I pointed out. "And she'd probably take offense to that."

Sasha nodded. "You do. She is your second *right now,* for all intents and purposes, but I don't think that's her long-term place. If I'm wrong, I'll step aside with apologies. But Nat is running her own businesses, trying to make this shithole a better place. She can't do it all. She can't run all these businesses—and devote herself to being your second. It's going to be a full time job when you make that transition, and I don't think she'll want to give up what she's got. I don't blame her. It's a good gig—but it's not forever for people like you and me. We all want to make a difference, and we can do that. Sienna is content to run numbers and be Nat's errand girl—but I'm not. I want more."

"Making a power grab from me would be a dangerous move," I said. "Ronan would tear you limb from limb."

"Good thing I don't want to be the face of New Chicago. I want to be the Queenmaker—and I want to be it for you."

I studied her through narrowed eyes.

"Why?" I repeated. "Why me?"

She ran the tip of her claw down the slope of her jaw and under her full bottom lip. Emerald-green cat eyes zeroed in on me the whole time. "I was sold to Lucifer at thirteen. He was good to us. It worked out better than most, but I know so many it hasn't for. Little boys and girls that end up with sick fucks. When the dead ones are the lucky ones . . ." she tilted her head. "You would change that. I can see it, and I don't have to like you to use my eyes. You would be fair to my kind, and to the humans."

"Ronan would be fair," I pointed out.

"He might," she acquiesced. "But he doesn't have the same fire for transgressors as you. When Lucifer stumbled upon it, he put a stop to it. Ronan would do the same. But you'll smoke them out. Hunt them like you hunted the witches. You won't wait—you'll track those fuckers down and make sure it never happens again."

I considered her words. She couldn't lie to me. That

wasn't even a question. But still, the choice of taking a second . . . that took forethought.

"I need to talk to Nat first, but I'll get back with you."

She tipped her chin and then stood up, walking away like we hadn't talked at all.

One bright side of taking her up on her offer was I wouldn't have to bullshit, not that I could. But she wouldn't expect me to be anything but straightforward, and that's all she'd be with me.

I thought back to how she handled us trying to put up a ruse for the gun that stole magic. She kept up well and didn't shy from a fight.

She could do it.

But still, I needed to see what Nat wanted. Then I'd think on it. No need to rush into anything.

"I'm surprised," Ronan said. I blinked, and he was standing before me. "You never have food left on your plate."

Guilt flashed through me for not finishing, but every bite was ash. Every swallow felt like lead in my gut. "Not hungry tonight."

"Hmm." He picked up my plate and dealt with it before returning to the couch. It squeaked under his weight as he settled in beside me and placed his arm over the back. "It's going to be fine, Piper. I'm more than strong enough to anchor the portal on my own."

"It's not that," I said quietly. "It's Bree. I just . . . I don't like this being how we leave things knowing she'll never be back."

"You don't know that for certain," he said, twisting a strand of my hair between two of his fingers. "It's easier to make a portal from Hell to here because the Source can help power it. She may decide to come back eventually."

"You don't sound thrilled by that idea," I pointed out.

"I'm not," he agreed. "But there is a possibility. Even if it is unlikely given the difficulty getting back proposes—and she doesn't exactly trust us to just open a portal at any time. Not that she should. Portals are dangerous business. For us, for her, for Nat. Not to mention both worlds."

I sighed. "I just wish things were different."

"In that, I think she does too."

A quiet knock at the door made me freeze. All talking came to a halt.

The clock ticked, showing it was just after nine.

"Should I—" Sienna started.

"I got it," I answered, jumping to my feet like I'd been electrocuted. My movements were jerky. Jarring. I walked with heavy feet toward the front door.

Every lock I unlatched echoed through the apartment. The last one, leaving an ominous note ringing in the air.

I reached for the handle, not letting myself have time to catch my breath before I opened it.

She looked the same as she did when I left her, minus the betrayed expression. She didn't wear makeup because she didn't need it. Not with flawless skin and jewel-toned eyes. There wasn't a trace of redness or puffy eyes that might have hinted at her being sad to leave. No, if anything my sister looked utterly perfect.

"Am I interrupting something?" she asked, arching an eyebrow.

"Not at all," Sasha said from the kitchen. "We were just leaving. Right, Anders?"

His answer was a second too slow, and I glanced back to see him staring at Bree with something like . . . hunger. Maybe, longing?

His piercing blue eyes stared past me like I was a window and Bree was all there was to see.

"Right," he drawled after a second, blinking slowly. An easy-going smile placed itself on his face, every ounce of intensity dissipated like I'd imagined it.

He came to the door, and the twins took up their spots on either side of him, each claiming an arm. I stepped to the side, opening the door wide to let them pass.

Bree assessed all three of them, head held high and proud. Infallible. Untouchable. She stepped out of the way to let them by, but I didn't miss the quick flick of her eyes over her shoulder as they disappeared down the hall. I motioned for her to come inside.

Without another word, she did.

Bree didn't greet Ronan, and he certainly didn't say hello to her.

We waited in tense silence for almost fifteen minutes before Bree finally lost the battle with her patience, and said, "What are we waiting for?"

Nat's bedroom door opened.

She walked quietly, at ease with herself in her own home.

When she got to the end of the hall, she presented the athame and then pointed it toward the tarp on her living room floor.

Ronan shifted, going to sit in the middle. I moved beside him, not able to partake but still needing to be there.

Nat cast my sister a dismissive glance, and said, "Take a seat. It's going to be a little while."

37
PIPER

The first cut was the worst, and it wasn't even my skin.

Being bonded to Ronan let me feel his pain as my own —even if he stomached it without a sound.

Nathalie chanted, softly at first. Surer this time than she had been when we summoned Bree. It was easier in a sense because we weren't trying to find a person, just a world. A dimension.

I held Ronan's hand in mine as Nathalie cut away, tracing his brands with the wicked edge of her knife. Blood pooled around us, running freely. While we healed fast, the spell itself seemed to slow his magic. Dragging out the pain.

I didn't look at Bree as the ritual started, but I sensed her looking at me. Maybe she was wondering why I wasn't the one being cut up. Why I hadn't said anything before now. Why I hadn't gone back on my words or even said goodbye.

The truth was . . . it was all I could think about, and yet not.

I couldn't bear it. So I closed it off. Cut that emotion

away like the sweep of the athame that split Ronan's skin. Nat started at his free wrist and worked her way around his forearm and bicep before starting on his chest.

Thick red blood smeared the tarp. The scent of chaos magic steadily thickened in the air. Growing heavy. Powerful.

A bite of rage nipped at my flesh as it recognized me.

Desire came next, soothing that bite with its sensuous touch.

Spirit had a more ethereal feel. It was the steadiness that wrapped around me—like his own ability to stand by me through it all.

Next was the essence of death, but it wasn't a cold unfeeling thing. It was like an old friend. One I'd been well acquainted with many times over the years.

These things were separate, but still similar all the same. They twined together, fusing tighter than any bond. Twisting. Writhing. Together with that strand of power, they were Ronan. His magic. His being released from his flesh body—if only for the ritual.

The candles went out as a wind that didn't belong snuffed them. Nat continued, chanting and cutting like a possessed woman. Somehow knowing where to put the blade despite hardly having any light.

Ronan released me for a brief moment to roll over and give her his other arm. Our fingers interlaced again, and I grit my teeth against the urge to stop the ritual. To stop the cutting. Stop the pain.

It made no logical sense, but feeling it firsthand, something came over me. To keep myself from moving, I had to grip him just as hard as he did me.

"Look at me, Piper," he said.

It wasn't a big ask since I hadn't looked away.

"It's almost over."

I nodded, keeping my attention focused on him as his magic swirled around us like the makings of a storm.

Nat chanted louder. Faster. Her movements growing feverish. That same trance had fallen over her and pulled her deep into a vision I couldn't see.

But I felt it. That coming storm.

She was one, but her voice echoed with the power of dozens. The power of a demon.

Just like last time, thunder boomed despite a previously clear night. Lightning flashed through the thinly veiled windows, casting us in shadows.

I felt those final moments before the black hole opened, slow—but fast. Silent, but loud. Nathalie's spell wove around us, all-consuming.

And then it happened.

A portal opened—a corridor straight to Hell.

Ronan clenched my hand tighter as once again that call to enter it sang in my blood. I knew it to be the Source trying to pull me home. But unlike last time, the things I'd heard of that place kept me firmly grounded.

My magic might come from there, but it was no home of mine.

All eyes turned to Bree as she stood slowly.

Awe and something like pain crossed her features as she took in the portal.

I closed my eyes, not wanting to watch. Not wanting to—

Arms wrapped around my shoulders. I gasped. Pulling back a fraction, just for her to hug me tighter. The scent of metal filled my nostrils.

"I love you, Piper," she whispered. "I love you so damn much—and I forgive you. I want you to know that. No matter what, no matter how many worlds are between us—I am your sister, and I always will be."

Emotion thickened, forming a hard knot in my throat that I couldn't swallow. Water filled my eyes. I released Ronan, and he let go so I could wrap my arms around her in return.

"I love you too, Bree," I said hoarsely. Silent tears streamed down my cheeks and I wasn't ashamed.

I pulled back to cup her face and give her a watery smile, as much as it hurt.

"Thank you for these last weeks. For teaching me how to use my magic—and helping me let go this time . . . it means more than you'll ever know."

She nodded, water glassing over her own eyes.

The portal loomed at her back, darkness and stars and galaxies that I'd never see —ready to carry her home to Hell.

"Keep learning. Practicing. You never know when the day will come that you'll need all your might. Make sure you know how to use it before then—and never grow lax. Ever. There are people out there—human and demon alike—that would end you both if they could."

I nodded. It's not like she was telling me something I didn't know, but the way she said it made me think there was more. That she was trying to tell me something but couldn't say it.

"It's time," Ronan rasped. "We can't keep the portal open longer without risking it destabilizing."

Bree took a heavy breath and kissed my cheek.

She leaned in close, her lips brushing my ear. "I know

you'll probably never understand, but I did this for you. It was the only way."

I wanted to ask her what she meant.

But we were out of time and we knew it.

I let Bree go, and it felt like she was taking part of me with her. She stood on stronger legs than I could have and faced the portal unflinching.

One step.

Two.

She lifted her foot, prepared to cross the threshold of no return when a slow clap started.

From the shadowed corner of the apartment, a figure appeared.

A man.

Bree froze, mid-step, eyes wide with . . . horror.

I squinted, seeing past the darkness. The storm outside carried on and lightning flashed, illuminating a face I'd seen once before.

The stranger from the bar. The man with platinum hair and red eyes who chilled me to my core.

All at once, the portal collapsed. Nathalie let out a pained grunt as she doubled over, breathing heavily. Beside me, Ronan was tense. More than that. Violence rang through the bond.

"I didn't know if you had it in you. I must confess, I doubted you there at the end. I should have known my bitch would always return home."

I didn't understand, but a tiny whisper in my mind told me I did. Some part of me had completely shut off, and the rest had gone into overdrive, reacting on instinct. I jumped to my feet and shifted in front of my sister. She placed a firm hand on my shoulder, forcing me to the side.

"Bree, who is this?" I asked. I had to know. I needed the

confirmation to put the pieces together. To wrap my brain around this one impossibility that reframed everything I knew about Bree and the last few weeks.

"Lorcan."

To be continued...

Milton Keynes UK
Ingram Content Group UK Ltd.
UKHW020652211124
3018UKWH00038B/237

9 781960 167200